IT'S A CRIME

IT'S A CRIME

a novel

JACQUELINE CAREY

BALLANTINE BOOKS

NEW YORK

Published in the United States by Ballantine Books,
an imprint of The Random House Publishing Group,
a division of Random House, Inc., New York.

BALLANTINE and colophon are registered trademarks of Random House, Inc.

LIBRARY OF CONGRESS CATALOGING-IN-PUBLICATION DATA
Carey, Jacqueline.
It's a crime : a novel / Jacqueline Carey.—1st ed.
p.   cm.
ISBN 978-0-345-45992-3 (hardcover : alk. paper)
1. Accounting fraud—Fiction.   2. Corporations—Corrupt practices—Fiction.
3. Victims of crimes—Fiction.   I. Title.
PS3553.A668555I77   2008 ·
813'.54—dc22   2008005494

Printed in the United States of America on acid-free paper

www.ballantinebooks.com

2 4 6 8 9 7 5 3 1

First Edition

Book design by Mary A. Wirth

For Maureen

ON
DOUGLAS
POINT

Pat didn't understand right away what Yolande Culp wanted to talk to her about. She didn't even realize that Yolande wanted to talk. She never had before.

"We can talk at the flower show," Yolande had said with a significant roll of her eyes toward the front seat of the LinkAge company car, where the capped driver sat muffled in silent deference.

Talk?

Yolande never did talk much. Sometimes she caught her breath as if she'd thought of something to say, but then decided to save it for a more deserving audience. It did not occur to Pat that Yolande might want to discuss anything in particular. She assumed that Yolande meant Pat could ease up on the flow of chatter for the moment. Yolande, whose husband had sponsored Pat's in his rapid rise through the company, had always expected to be entertained. Pat didn't mind. Although she preferred to speak to a person who would tell anecdotes, who would be indiscreet, who would interrupt, and who would top her own confessions with more damning ones, she never minded having to speak for two.

Besides, she was designing a garden for Yolande, so the trip made a certain amount of sense. If Yolande had an ulterior motive, it seemed obvious and mild; she wanted a free docent for the Philadelphia Flower Show. Pat was going full throttle by the time the women made their way through the first of the garden rooms illustrating the theme "English Ingenuity." At the Cottage Garden exhibit she cried, "Look at that peony! The white one! My God, those blossoms are the size of babies' heads! All those folds are going to make me weep! Do you know how many flowers they must have gone through to make this one beautiful specimen? How many flowers they cooled and heated and wrapped and lit up all through the night? How many flowers they nearly asphyxiated with great plumes of carbon dioxide? How many flowers they pumped full of fertilizer, flushed out with water, then pumped up again! It's staggering! The mind boggles!" Her voice swooped like an excited starling through the upper ranges of her register.

It was March, and the LinkAge driver had had to navigate through a light snow on the two-hour trip from northern New Jersey, but this peony was already as big as a plant in a science fiction movie. Forty-four-year-old Pat cantilevered herself over the side of the exhibit for a better view. "Wires," she said. "I should have known. Those huge blossoms are being held up by wires. See? They look like nooses!" For a moment she let her tongue loll and her head droop as if just she'd just been hanged, then she snapped back to her usual effervescent self. "Staking would never have been enough!"

By design, a cottage garden's plantings are overabundant and disorganized, checked only by nature, so here nothing reined in its excess. The clematis vines sagged precipitously under their heavy blooms. The delphiniums were as big as baseball bats. The roses were the size of boxing gloves. Even more bizarrely, these summer flowers were intermingled with earlier spring blossoms—narcissus, creeping phlox, grape hyacinth.

"I wanted to be sure we could talk in private," said Yolande. "You can't be too careful."

The literal meaning of this was so improbable that Pat blinked, waiting for Yolande to explain herself. When she did not, Pat said, "It can be exhilarating to try to do something so contrary to nature. Don't you see? Spring and summer flowers together—it's like seeing Lillie Langtry on the same stage as Elizabeth Taylor!"

The only trouble was, forced plants were weak, and their flowers, short-lived. Few would survive the show.

"This is a particularly important time for all of us," said Yolande.

For the first time Pat took a good look at her companion. Yolande gleamed and glinted as a trophy wife should—skin, hair, and teeth all comparable to white gold catching the sun. Her only flaw, if you could call it that, was to appear a bit preserved. She may have been twenty years younger than her husband, Neil, but that made her Pat's age. In fact Yolande didn't look all that different from Pat, who was also a bottle blonde (going on ten years now), who also wore sleek black microfiber pants, and who was also still this side of overripe. Yolande was so fully convinced of her own worth, however, that it was hard to forget her price tag when you were with her.

"Important?" said Pat. "Really?"

"How is Frank bearing up?" said Yolande.

"He's fine," said Pat, her interest waning. Frank was Pat's husband. Everybody loved Frank Foy. He might be an accountant, but he did know how to enjoy himself. He loved to drink expensive wine, as the Foys often did with the Culps, loved to haul a wine bottle around by its neck, loved to hound Pat about the produce, loved to joke about the finest china, the best glassware, the thickest linen, loved to boast and flirt, loved to talk big and make impractical plans, loved to put on a good display.

But Yolande evidently wanted to talk company politics, which bored Pat to death. It was hard to get too terrifically excited about a CFO's retirement (even if it had been Neil Culp's) or the ensuing SEC investigation (which Frank swore would be just pro forma).

"I have an idea," said Pat. "We will build height into your garden. Just here and there. If everything's tall, it won't work. We'll put in a few giant alliums, and the eye will be forced to travel up at each one. 'Things are looking up,' right? Isn't that what people say when things are improving? You don't want a faint-hearted so-so garden. You want a garden that goes up, that says yes. That says it over and over: yes, yes, yes."

"Yes plants" instead of "yes men." Pat loved the notion; she hadn't got so carried away in ages. But her words died as she found herself backing into a ten-foot, four-layer birthday cake made of moss. The edges were packed with thick lines of yellow chrysanthemums designed to look like flower chains squeezed from an icing tube. Bright red gladiola candles sprouted from each layer. A cheesy nightmare, in other words, but great fun.

Startled by the cake, she was at a temporary loss for words and so could hear footsteps on the other side. The general public hadn't been allowed in yet, but exhibitors were everywhere, scrambling to finish before opening day. These footsteps sounded more linear than that, though, and they were heading straight for Yolande and Pat. Yolande had been let in early because she was rich; maybe a fund-raiser from the horticultural society was checking up on them.

"Do you know what Frank said to the SEC?" asked Yolande.

The SEC? Pat probably would have answered this as best she could—and with her full attention at last—but a voice came floating out: "Pat," it said, oddly familiar, smooth, and husky, the sort of contralto used to sell perfume. And emerging from behind the cake was no scantily clad young lady. It was . . . Oliver Gregoire.

"I can't believe it!" cried Pat. Talk about "yes men." Oliver, who worked for her husband, was king of them. But you couldn't dislike him for it. You couldn't dislike him at all. How delightful to see a friend in this place.

"Pat, dear," said Oliver, leaning over her protectively. He was over six feet tall and as wide as a door, but his was a gentle bulk. He had an endearing lisp, and his eyes melted with interest at whatever you were saying. He was also openly gay, making him such a wild card in corporate life that anything was acceptable from him.

Pat already felt lighter about the shoulders and through the back. Given Oliver's highly cultivated courtier role, he was bound to take over some of Pat's responsibility for entertaining Yolande, who said, "What are you doing here?" It was clearly a warning. Maybe she was guarding against requests for favors. Since Oliver had gone to a lot of trouble to run into her, he must want something pretty special.

"I was seeing a client in Philadelphia," said Oliver blandly. "And I know a couple of the judges here at the flower show."

Of course he did. Oliver knew everyone.

"Pat and I were having a talk," said Yolande.

"Yes?" said Oliver.

"A tête-à-tête."

"Lovely," said Oliver. "And how's your family?" he asked Pat.

Pat was not unhappy to be spared the "talk" with Yolande, but it struck her as odd that Oliver would ignore the wife of Neil Culp. "Ruby spends her time trolling for killers on the Internet," said Pat gaily. She probably should have started off with her older daughter, Rose, who was off at Princeton, but sometimes it was hard for Pat to believe that she was related to such a straight arrow.

"And Frank? How is your wonderful husband getting along?" asked Oliver.

"Ruby had a dream that Frank showed up at her school wearing a coconut bra," said Pat, whose voice had a great range. For her earlier stream of horticultural chatter her voice had been high and musical. Now it was deep, with plenty of vibrato, almost guttural.

Oliver seemed to have forgotten all about asking after Yolande's family (and Neil had been on the cover of *CFO Magazine*). "I want to get a leather jacket like Frank's," he said.

"Don't forget the Austrian accent," said Pat. Frank often adopted one for humorous effect.

"I think Pat has the perfect life," said Oliver.

Yolande frowned.

"She's paid to plant *flowers*," he said. That was one way to look at it, Pat supposed. "She has a *daredevil* for a husband." Naturally Pat was very fond of Frank, but, really, daredevil? He was an accountant. "She has a daughter *who's premed at Princeton*." No mention of young Ruby this time, but at least Rose could always patch her back up, no matter what happened. "She has enough money that she can tell everybody *to go to hell.*"

"Not yet," said Pat, looking at Yolande speculatively. "I wonder how much that would be."

But this was certainly not when Yolande would rejoin the conversation. The richest person in any group is always the deafest when the subject of money comes up.

Oliver was delighted. "I've tried to figure it out," he said, shaking his head. "The number keeps getting bigger."

They had wandered over to the Black and White Garden, highlight of the show. Enclosed in a severe square of boxwood were eddies of black and white blossoms. Violet-black irises. Purple-black hollyhocks. White foxglove spikes barnacled with little pink-tongued bells. Huge white pompom hydrangeas. The dark plum–colored 'Black Jewel' tulip, with its shark-toothed petals.

"How fabulous!" cried Pat. "Weeping forms are so out, they're back in again, if you know what I mean." She indicated a small umbrella-shaped tree cascading feathery white flowers and talked even faster. "But grafts usually go wrong. And it's hard to get a tree to bud this early. If it doesn't, it's roasted on a spit, turned to keep it an even green."

Oliver did not even pretend to look at the tree. All of his attention was on Pat. "I find the company is rife with rumors," he said. "Don't you?"

"What rumors?" said Pat. He couldn't be referring to the rumors about the resignation of Yolande's husband, no matter how topsy-turvy the day had become. "Are they interesting rumors? It seems to me that rumors used to be a lot better, back when people believed in sin. Just like mystery novels were. I want to hear about love and lust *and crimes in high places!*"

"Crimes?" said Yolande reprovingly. "What could you mean?"

But Oliver's laugh was pleasant. "Actually, I heard that Frank had room for someone new in High Risk."

So that was what Oliver was after. High Risk had always been the sexiest of the departments Frank oversaw. Originally it was responsible for accounts at the greatest risk of default, thus its name. But soon the name took on a new color: At Frank's company accountants were not just number crunchers. Yolande's husband, Neil, was a wizard, and under his leadership accountancy became an arcane, secret, and living art. Frank's young men in High Risk had the flashiest smiles and the biggest bonuses. They ribbed one another about their "extreme accounting." They were all such boys.

It must have been Pat, not Yolande, that Oliver had arranged to run into. Wow. This was court intrigue at the Philadelphia Flower Show. It was incredible that Pat Foy, free spirit, could even recognize it. Now that Neil had retired, Yolande Culp, whether she knew it or not, was over, out, gone, kaput. How extraordinary to be the more important wife.

"Oliver!" said Pat, genuinely curious. "I thought the SEC was wandering all over the building. Isn't everything at sixes and sevens?"

"The job has been open for a while," said Oliver. "I've just been wondering if there was any . . . reason that a decision might or might not be made."

The last time he'd come to dinner he and Frank had gone into faux gay riffs about seasoning and the freshness of fish flesh. Ah, the freshness of fish flesh. It had been funny at the time. But the memory of it must embarrass him.

"Frank thinks the world of you," said Pat. "I don't always pay a whole lot of attention to what's going on in the company, be-

cause my God, don't you think the telecommunications industry can be just a *teeny weeny bit dull*?"

Oh, well, a person who talks as much as Pat can't be expected
to pay attention to every single word she says.

"No," said Oliver with a slight chuckle. Then his voice sank
to a whisper. "One rumor is that everyone in High Risk will get
a retention bonus."

"Retention bonus?" said Pat, trying to catch up. Actually
Frank had intended to give the job to Oliver a while ago. He
really was fond of him. Pat had no idea why he hadn't simply
gone ahead with the promotion. But retention bonus? What did
that mean?

"When the company goes bankrupt," said Oliver.

This did not seem to be news to Yolande, but Pat was still
flummoxed when two tinny bars of "When the Saints Go
Marching In" fizzed out of Oliver's gray suit. How sensitively
dressed he was: the fine suit in deference to the importance and
loveliness of the women, but no tie, because of the intimacy of
the occasion.

"You don't mean that LinkAge might go bankrupt, do you?"
said Pat.

"I'm so sorry," said Oliver, flipping open his phone. "These are
a pain, aren't they? I liked the old days when you could truly escape." His happy patter died as he read the text message. "Just
a minute."

While he pressed buttons, Yolande whispered fiercely, "No
one did anything wrong, and we'll all be fine if everyone remem-
bers that."

Confused, Pat gazed down at the blossomless black-leaf
dahlias, the black pincushion flowers (*Scabiosa* 'Ace of Spades'),
and the black-veined, fabric-like leaves of a "Looking Glass" be-

gonia. But something—a slight gasp, maybe—made her turn. Oliver's mouth was open. A "no" escaped.

He gave Pat a quick, piercing look and moved his bulk softly, gracefully away from her. A chill ran up her spine, and her eyes continued the trajectory upward to far above the exhibit, where the intense lighting of the Black and White Garden did not reach and darkness collected.

"The police just showed up at the LinkAge offices." Oliver no longer seemed to be speaking to Pat. He was talking for the first time directly to Yolande, holding his cellphone up as if to explain the machine itself.

"The police?" said Pat, eyeing the phone.

"There have been . . . arrests," said Oliver, still addressing Yolande.

"Arrests?" echoed Pat.

Finally Oliver's attention reverted to her. "Everyone from High Risk has been arrested."

"What?" said Pat. "Come on."

"That was the message."

"Are you sure?" said Pat. "I mean, I like a rumor as much as the next person, but it should be somewhat credible. I have visions of a southern chain gang with a lot of men in shackles breaking up rock. Good God, it's beyond ridiculous . . . I've got to talk to Frank. He's worked very closely with them."

She opened her quilted silk purse and looked under a vintage "mapback" mystery novel for her own cellphone.

"Actually," said Oliver, "Frank was arrested, too."

"Frank?" cried Pat. "Oh, no, this is terrible. He's going to be really mad. He is not going to see the humor in this at all."

"Tell him not to say anything until he gets a good lawyer" was Yolande's contribution.

The Culps were sure to have one all lined up, considering the way Neil exploited the company loan program.

"Did you know about this?" said Pat softly.

"No one has the right to proprietary business information," said Yolande. "Neil wants you to tell Frank that." To Oliver she said, "They haven't bothered Neil, have they?"

"Not as far as I know," said Oliver.

Yolande nodded. "They wouldn't dare." Once that was taken care of, the two of them edged farther away from Pat, as tight as ticks.

"What did they arrest Frank for?" said Pat.

Yolande and Oliver *could not* be exchanging a veiled look; Pat refused to believe it. "Just remember," said Yolande. "No one did anything wrong."

"I'm sure it's a mistake," said Pat. "The High Risk boys are so . . . simple."

The town of Hart Ridge was set against a large hill, with the four main streets running in tiers. The lowest street was commercial, and the immediate area was shabby: two-family houses, old brick apartment buildings, several rows of Cape Cods. As the elevation increased, so did the size of the houses and lots. The next strip was of beautiful old four-bedroom Colonials surrounded by rhododendrons and dogwoods and magnolias. This was a middle-class buffer zone, looking as if it had been elbowed in, although its roots were deep. Another notch up was a mix of grand old Victorians and real mansions of many odd styles—Federalist, Italianate, château, hacienda. Once you had money, you could let your taste run riot.

The town had consisted of these three levels for over a hundred years. As late as the 1950s the fourth and highest road did not exist. There were just a few houses scattered among the bluffs of Douglas Point, dwellings known for their eccentricity and inconvenience. That all changed with the construction of

Douglas Road in the sixties. A soap opera diva moved there. Then a retired football star. Suddenly, in the eighties, everyone, it seemed, hankered after a secluded new house on virgin land with a splendid view of the Manhattan skyline. (Create your own fantasy! With a city backdrop!) Douglas Point came to stand for extravagance and excess.

The Foys weren't living in Hart Ridge at that time, although both had grown up there, Frank near the Record & Radio on the first tier and Pat more snugly in one of the solid Colonials the next level up. In the late eighties Rose was still a preschooler, and they lived in a little brick house in a valley to the north, separated from their next-door neighbors by banks of forsythia, which Pat never, ever complained about, because it was such a useful early bloomer, but she did sometimes wish it would be useful somewhere else, so she'd have an excuse to try a more unusual hedge.

"I'm beginning to realize that the phone company is not the place to be if you want to make money," said Frank after a day spent back in Hart Ridge visiting his parents. Pat could not help but receive this statement with mild contempt. How could he possibly have thought it was? Ma Bell was the most tedious company in the world to work for. Everyone knew that. Certainly that was the point of those jobs: You could ignore them and get on with your life.

But new phone companies had begun sprouting up everywhere, and AT&T was forced by law to provide them with deeply discounted long-distance minutes for resale. Frank jumped from AT&T's broad back to one of these upstarts, LGT Communications, whose initials stood for nothing but were intended to imply that calls placed through the company were completed at the speed of light. "Guess where the CFO lives?" said Frank his first day. "Douglas Point." And when this talented CFO, Neil Culp, took an interest in Frank, even Pat was stirred.

LGT Communications was located in an industrial park near Basking Ridge, not a bad commute from the little brick house, but when telecommunications giant LinkAge bought out the company in the mid-nineties and made all the employees a hefty paper profit, Frank began to find excuses to swing back through the tier of roads in Hart Ridge. Symbolism required a move up to the third rung, higher than either he or Pat had started. (Frank was big on symbolism. He wouldn't let the girls leave the house in their pajamas, for instance, although they were far less revealing than their clothes.)

Rose was dubious about the third-tier mansions, most of which were fabulously out-of-date. "Is that house haunted?" she would ask. Or, "Why do you always like houses that look as if witches lived in them?" Sometimes Frank would drive higher, to Douglas Point, where he'd slow to a crawl for a glimpse of Neil Culp's cedar deck Most of the houses on Douglas Point were equally hidden, so his excursions were usually confined to the third tier. There the mansions were all forthright and stately, easily visible perched high atop huge swelling lawns that were underlined rather than concealed by the formal front hedges.

Although LGT Communications was still run pretty much as a stand-alone company, Neil soon became the CFO of *Link-Age*—of the whole shebang, in other words. His genius had been recognized. He worked closely with CEO Riley Gibbs, and everyone had heard of Riley Gibbs, whose management skills and keen foresight had transformed a local enterprise into a Fortune 500 company. Frank couldn't believe his luck. He followed

Neil to LinkAge headquarters in Meadowlands Center, which had been fashioned out of a swamp near New York City that used to hold nothing more than a few dozen Mafia victims. No one admired Neil more than Frank did. When Pat turned forty-one, he took her to the Manor for dinner on Neil's recommendation and told her how Neil had recently engineered LinkAge's acquisition of the fifth-largest long-distance company in the country. "A goldfish swallowed a whale!" he repeated happily. "Now we're really going to be rich!" "Money" for Frank did not mean just a bigger check; it meant luster and excitement.

On the way home, he drove through the usual mix of mansions in upper Hart Ridge, saying maniacally, "How about that one, dear? What do you think?" and "Forget it! Where would we put your collection of winter-blooming cacti?" (such plants probably being the sole type she did not own) and "No way could I learn to live with only one swimming pool!" (when there wasn't a single one in sight). Finally he said, "No, none of those are good enough for us," and made the right up toward Douglas Point. Pat was still laughing when he turned up again, this time into a driveway that went straight through the trees and looped by the front door of one of the more conventional houses on the Point, a huge new white neo-Georgian. The two and a half stories of the place towered like four, a couple of mansard roofs rippled back from three equally elevated front gables, and a Palladian arch above the door was intended to aggrandize it as if it were a throne. Between roofs and front walk, on the other hand, wasn't much: white paint, ten-foot unshuttered windows. The house itself could have been a barren expanse of cliff; the only visual interest was in its acme.

"We're here! We're here!" he said as he always did when he had to turn around in a strange driveway—although of course

never before on Douglas Point. Then he *got out of the car,* a bit
of a surprise to say the least, and spread his arms in front of a
smudge of pink mums, crying, "It's all yours! Happy birthday,
honey!"

"My goodness," said Pat, playing for time, looking around.
Frank was so pleased and proud. Evidently symbolism required
a leap to the very top of the ladder. Which of course she should
have known.

"That's all you can say? I bought you a whole house!" he said.

"Wow," said Pat. She'd have preferred it if he'd consulted
with her, of course. But what the hell.

"No old boyfriend of yours could buy you a house on Douglas
Point!" crowed Frank. "Now matter how famous he is!"

They were in the middle of moving to this pinnacle of existence when Frank learned that Neil Culp was moving, too—
down to the even grander town of Rumson, where an
eighty-year-old estate and a new wife half that age (Yolande)
awaited him. Frank was uncharacteristically silent after he told
Pat the news. He looked quizzically around the nearly empty living room. Then he jumped up and said, "We need a sofa that
can sleep a football team!"

Four years later, most of the largest rooms in the Foy house
were still nearly empty. The foyer was as big as a two-car garage
but contained only an abstract tapestry that Frank had pur-
chased from the previous owners. The lone occupants of the
dining room were a huge, vaguely Gothic trestle table, which sat
twelve, and a sideboard the size of a Dumpster. In the cavernous
living room was a similarly oversize coffee table flanked by a
couple of olive green couches that could sleep at least part of a
football team. Even so, they were dwarfed by the curtainless
floor-to-ceiling windows and their view of Manhattan. Frank

liked the spaciousness and thought that the whole house was clean if there was no clutter in these few rooms.

The kitchen was Pat's. Topiary magnets affixed innumerable school papers to the refrigerator. On the wall were three botanical illustrations of hollies, one so tenaciously crooked that it didn't matter how many times she straightened it. On the marble countertop was an Edgar Allan Poe action figure, a collection of bobbleheads (Jack the Ripper, Pope John Paul II, etc.), a huge spill of CDs with morbid covers, and the handset of a phone. The room was L-shaped; at its foot was Pat's home office, where nursery catalogs and garden magazines were stacked.

A red light blinked on the answering machine when Pat returned from the flower show: Frank's secretary, Ellen Kloda, had left a message saying not to worry, Frank would call soon. She did not mention the arrest, and the panic in her voice was such that if Pat hadn't got the news from Oliver already, she'd have assumed that Frank was dead at the very least.

She called Ellen and got her voice mail. Then she tried the Culps in Rumson, and she got the housekeeper. Pat hesitated, then called two wives of the High Risk boys and got machines. This sense of stasis was reassuring; nothing really could have happened.

Then she realized she'd better try Rose at Princeton. Although Pat was sure that nothing would come of all this, she didn't want Rose to hear about it from anyone else. Rose's reaction, however, was a bit unexpected. Pat had barely started before Rose cut her off: "I knew it. *I knew it.*"

"What do you mean?" asked Pat, alarm sending her high voice even higher. She had called Rose's cellphone, so Rose could have been anywhere, sitting in a lecture hall waiting for the teacher, walking to the library with her serious-minded friends—or dissecting some animal with a blade that could cut off her finger as if it were Jell-O. Frank used to say he was going to will his body to science as long as medical school students were required to play pranks with it. Pat began to pace across the kitchen with the handset of her phone.

"Jesus, Mom, what do you think the point of all those stories of his was?" said Rose.

"What stories?"

"The gum ashtray and all those."

"Oh," said Pat. "Those were just funny stories." Or not funny exactly, but Frank had told them in a funny way. When Frank first started at LGT, it sold a lot of its telephone time to small companies that made phone cards. LGT gave them generous terms, and there wasn't much overhead, but these operations were always welshing on their debts, anyway. In fact, they tended to disappear before paying anything at all beyond the startup fees. When Rose was in elementary school, she was particularly taken with the tale of an office in Paterson, where one guy read the comics on a chair tipped against the wall and the other pushed a piece of gum back and forth in his mouth and contemplated the ashtray in front of him. It was lined with chewed-up gum. "If you lifted it carefully out of the glass, you'd have another, smaller ashtray made entirely of old gum," Frank explained with delight. "You wouldn't believe this place. Garbage everywhere. Papers, boxes, burlap bags piled in the corner. The guy with the gum ashtray kept swearing he had no money, but you know what, *every single one of those burlap bags was filled with cash.*"

Frank's early run-ins had all been like that, involving men with tics, men with "cousins," men with short blond hair and long black roots.

"I told him they were criminals," said Rose.

"Oh, honey," said Pat. "You know what your daddy is like. He just thought they were interesting. And he had to collect the money. That was his job. But he was the good guy."

Rose wasn't listening. "What does he say?"

"I haven't been able to get hold of him yet. Neil, either."

"Big surprise there."

"I'm sure the place is a madhouse. All the High Risk boys were arrested."

It was hard to imagine the High Risk boys restrained at all. They were wild. They came to the house as a group for parties, and they moved as a group, jumping up to shout an opinion or racing to the ice bucket or fighting over a spurting garden hose at a barbecue. Their hair fell over their eyes in carbon copies of Frank's; their guffaws echoed his. Fads swept through them. After Frank moved to LinkAge headquarters, the High Risk boys formed a Swat Team that reported back to him from all over the country. In the field they would push the numbers. Then they would get together and compare their finds: a fish-shaped beer mug from a bass tournament off the Carolinas, a bullet-riddled plaque for "perfect attendance," a restored Indian motorcycle.

"Those guys were always obnoxious," said Rose.

After getting off the phone Pat looked out the back bank of windows at the border lining the stockade fence. The dusting of snow had melted. It was time to prune the red bark dogwood and the thigh-high fountains of perennial grasses. As she picked up the clippers in the mudroom, however, she heard someone upstairs. Ruby was home from school awfully early.

When she knocked on Ruby's door, she couldn't quite tell if Ruby said "Come in," but she decided to take it on faith. So much in Ruby's room was mysterious. Take the riot of fabric amid the other litter on the floor, for instance. The dark red velour could be hat, sweatshirt—or theatrical curtain. The off-white cotton canvas could be chair back, spring jacket—or sail. And what could that chrome rod be, with the rubber tip? Baton? Crutch? It was hard to believe that as a first-grader Ruby had once cleaned out the cellar to make a bomb shelter, thanks to some anachronistic children's literature. Pat picked her way across the floor, saying, "I'm so glad you're home. I want to talk to you."

Ruby was listening to music, IM'ing her friends, and talking on the phone at the same time. She looked up from her laptop to say, briefly, "Pep rally."

Pep rallies in middle school! Kids grew up so fast these days.

"Honey, I don't want you to worry about this, because I'm sure it's all a mistake," Pat began. "God knows governments make millions of them, everyone agrees, no matter who you are or what your political beliefs, so much so that I can't believe anyone supports the death penalty. Entrust life and death to the same people who figure out your property tax? Or at least the same sort of people—"

Ruby watched her mother with an impatient expression, eyeing the clippers. "What are you doing with those?"

Pat looked down at the unwieldy item in her hand as if not sure how it got there. "Nothing," she said, trying to fit her thoughts back into their proper order. "There's been a problem at LinkAge. A whole bunch of people have been arrested, and I think your father was one of them."

Ruby froze for a moment as she looked wildly into her mother's eyes; then she jumped up, shot into the hall, and raced down the back stairs, calling, "Did you lock the door?"

"Oh, honey, you're not in any danger," Pat shouted, following her.

"How do you know?" cried Ruby. The dogs began to bark. "At least Foster is here to protect us. He's pretty fierce."

Foster, the Lab, was bigger than the other two. But as he yelped away he looked more like he was going to have a nervous breakdown than go for the jugular.

"It's okay, it's okay," said Pat, she wasn't sure to whom.

Frank Foy's wife and daughter had just finished locking the door against him when he climbed the last of the forced-stone back steps. Already there was something foreign about him. He looked leaner, harder, crazier. The dogs did not stop barking when they realized who it was. "I think we're going to need this," he said, handing Pat a bottle of champagne with a spill of blue curling ribbon at the neck.

"What a wonderful idea!" said Pat. Frank was a *nice* man. Last summer he wouldn't let anyone turn on the back flood-lights for fear of frying the nest of mourning dove eggs perched on top of one.

"So let me sit down already," said Frank. "It's not every day I get arrested."

"Were you really arrested?" asked Pat.

"Unless I'm dreaming," he said. "Let's have some glasses out here. Get the new crystal." As she left, she heard him say to Ruby, "Aren't you going to give your old man a hug?"

At first Pat picked out three matching wineglasses, one apparently for twelve-year-old Ruby, clearly a sign of hysteria. Or maybe an arrest was like transubstantiation; everybody got to taste the result. Pat looked at the third glass dumbly, then returned it to its glass-fronted cabinet. If necessary, Ruby could have a sip of hers. As usual with kids, however, Pat's decision was totally irrelevant. Ruby had left the room by the time she returned.

"So where did they take you?" Pat asked Frank. "To . . . jail?"

"No, no, we were just put in an office down at the courthouse," said Frank, popping the cork. "They even gave us coffee. Worst I ever had. It tasted like stomach acid. I thank the Lord for inventing champagne." In one smooth motion he poured with his right hand and drank with his left.

"I'm out on bail," he said. "Two million dollars' worth. Can you believe it? This is one expensive arm." He lifted the elbow, the custom-made shirt masking the very male disjunction of forearm and upper arm.

"Don't worry," he said. "It will all blow over. Everyone massages their earnings. Neil just did it smarter and better than anyone else. We went to some new places that most people just don't get. No one expects an accountant to have any imagination."

"And they should!" cried Pat loyally. "They should!"

"You think LinkAge would have got where it is today without Neil's ideas?" said Frank. "In the old days Gibbs acquired companies to try to *save money*! It's laughable!"

"It's all so confusing," said Pat.

"That's because you're not drinking." He topped off her glass. "It's not like any of this was a secret. Everyone knew."

"I didn't know."

"Yes you did."

"I did?"

"You knew how important the stock price was to the company. You knew the gyrations everyone went through every quarter to hit our targets. And you knew that we always did it, no

matter what." It was true that he'd told her far more than she
was interested in.

"I remember you telling me about Gibbs and Culp lending
themselves a lot of company money," said Pat.

"I didn't have anything to do with that!"

"Rose thinks it's about the gum ashtray guys in Paterson."

"That was rompers," said Frank. "That was diapers. That was
baby formula. Oh, we proved ourselves that way. But no one
cares about uncollectible receivables. Not even the SEC. This
is the big leagues." He was refilling his glass every time he took
a sip.

"I'll tell you exactly what happened," he said. "The company
needed to keep expanding. Our financial strategies depended
on it. And to expand at the rate we required we had to keep buying other businesses. Remember when we bought this house?
That was because the stock soared when LinkAge took over
such a big competitor. Everybody made out like a bandit. But
then the SEC nixed the Orbex acquisition. And for no good reason, either. You know Neil's motto—"

Actually Pat couldn't quite place it.

"If you don't like reality, make a new one," said Frank impatiently. "The Swat Team would tell us where the numbers were
soft, and then we'd go to work. Maybe Neil went too far too fast;
it's possible. But you have to be able to control your financials,
otherwise you can't control your company. Oh, the risks we took!
And it was all for the good of LinkAge." He shrugged. "Everything would have been fine if the economy hadn't gone south."

On the vast glass-topped coffee table between them was a
stylized suggestion of domestic life: pink coasters, a tray of pa-
perwhites forced in gin and water.

"But why did they arrest you? Why not Neil?"

Frank held up the bottle to gauge the level of the spirits: still one quarter left. He said, "You know that Ellen circulated a document she wasn't supposed to."

Pat did remember something like that. "What document, exactly?"

"It was a memo with the real numbers. When I found out what she'd done, I e-mailed some of the High Risk boys, saying, 'Where do I go to sign my confession?' "

Pat must have winced because Frank was practically shouting when he said, "It was a joke!"

He gulped down the rest of his champagne. "The trouble is, the SEC got hold of the memo, too. And then they went sniffing around and found my e-mail. I could have quit. But I was too loyal to Neil."

"Really? You were thinking of quitting your job?" said Pat.

Frank shrugged again. He never used to shrug. "It's not like what we did was a crime," he said. "It was more like a gamble. I may be just a guy who works for a phone company, but I tell you, sometimes I felt like Jimmy the Greek. Sometimes I felt like I was playing in the highest-stakes poker game in the world." Frank had a vaguely animal smell, as he did after running.

"Well," said Pat, recovering some of her buoyancy. "I'm sure you have nothing to worry about."

He patted her hand. "I know you always thought accountants were boring. I don't blame you for it. You didn't think the company that fed and clothed you all those years was worth the time of day, did you? *And* that bought you this huge house on Douglas Point as a birthday present."

"It's funny," said Pat. "Oliver was telling me today what a great life I had."

"Oliver?" said Frank, perking up as if sniffing the air. "Did he call?"

Pat shook her head and decided not to tell him that she hadn't been able to reach anyone.

A piercing scream from above: Ruby. Pat leapt up as if this were what she'd been waiting for all along. The scream trailed off before she reached Ruby's room. And there she was, staring at her computer screen. In the center of the blue window for the Internet portal, above the news from Afghanistan, was the Link-Age corporate logo. "More arrests in the telecom industry" read the caption. The logo blinked into a photo of Frank, evidently taken earlier. His hands were cuffed behind his back. His face was in shadow. Then he was transformed back into the LinkAge logo. Photo, logo, photo, logo. Pat watched, mesmerized.

Frank spoke from behind her: "Just a guy who works for the phone company."

Pat felt sorry for anyone without a real past. She was proud of having had a youth she wouldn't want to describe to her children. It could make her smile in the unlikeliest settings—the dullest fund-raiser or sit-down company dinner: "This is not me, I have a wild core, *I am in disguise.*"

Pat had been so spirited and friendly as a teenager that no one noticed how eccentric she was. She barely noticed her parents' divorce. She had money to spend because her mother paid her to iron her own clothes, and she could have a cheerful conversation with anyone. She was the only person who could make Ginny Howley giggle. Most kids were afraid of Ginny, because her mother had killed herself years before, and because she could spend a whole evening sitting in a corner and frowning, a feat Pat wished she could pull off but had never been able to. What the other kids didn't seem to realize was that Ginny's severity meant she mattered. Sometimes when classmates said idiotic stuff, it was easier for Pat to nod and agree. Ginny's face would darken, and she would tell Pat later what was wrong with the stupid comment she had agreed with or been amused by. Pat didn't mind. Ginny never thought that what Pat said was stupid, although a lot of it was.

The two girls read mysteries all the time. Their tastes were surprisingly similar, given how finicky Ginny was in the rest of her life. She didn't like anything regular—"nice" boys, for example, or girl singers or trips to the beach. Pat didn't expect her to like the books of Scott Fein, creator of the first counterculture detective; he seemed a bit too pop for her taste. But Ginny liked them so much she put a newspaper photo of the author up on her wall. He was young and curly-haired.

It was Ginny's idea to go to Fein's book signing at The Black Cat in the city. In fact, she insisted. Then they decided to tell their parents they were going to be at each other's houses that night. They figured out that between them they had enough money for a room at the Chelsea Hotel, a place they'd read about in *Rolling Stone*. Ginny was going to contribute the most. Although her allowance was minimal and she'd never been paid for ironing clothes, she always seemed to be able to find an extra twenty. Pat gave her what she had to make up the difference.

Pat tried to straighten her hair with an iron, and Ginny curled her hair by weaving dozens of little wet braids all over her head. Ginny's attempt was the more successful. She was undoing the braids when she bought one-way tickets from the conductor on the train, and by the time they reached Penn Station, she had a puff of zigzagged hair. It shivered a little as they walked uptown.

Pat and Ginny had spent endless hours at Hart Ridge Books, where the mysteries had their own metal racks. But The Black Cat was different, a hybrid of bookstore and club. Two writers sat at a long cafeteria-style folding table at one end of the store. Customers lined up in front of each to get their books signed. Scott Fein, Ginny's baby-faced poster boy, was even cuter in person than he was on her wall. His eyes sparkled; his smile lit up the ordinary words that Pat managed to overhear as she slid by. "Aren't you going to go up there?" she asked Ginny covertly, opening a mystery by the other author—a red herring. When Ginny shook her off, Pat couldn't help a quick glance around to see if anyone had noticed.

The other writer was Lemuel Samuel, a name with vague but intellectually exotic associations for Pat. Maybe she'd read about him in *Rolling Stone,* too. All she could see of him was a knee, a calf, and a boot sticking out from the end of the table. The knee was bent, the calf was covered in dirty black denim, and the boot had a strap at the ankle that was fixed in place with a steel triangle. She passed on his new book, which was still in hardback, but bought his first, a paperback called *Follow Me.*

"Great title!" she enthused when she got to the head of his line. He was a big man, tall, with large hands and heavy features.

"Follow me," he said. It was a practiced joke, or Pat might have been tempted to say, "Okay." Instead she said, "What I like is when I delve so deep into a story that I'm surprised when I'm interrupted and then I look back at the page and see just type. Just words, I mean. When a minute before, I was seeing these wonderful colors in my head. You have to have real suspense in a story to produce a spell like that. Don't you think?"

Lemuel's face was wide, shadowy, enigmatic. His lips were pulled back in a half smile or maybe a grimace. Pat continued at a higher pitch. "Not that that's the only thing," she said. "You need a really wild setting. You need to stretch right into a different mind. You need a truly *black* night or a truly *green* jungle or a really *red* pool of blood."

"Sure," said Lemuel. He left it at that, so Pat rejoined Ginny, who hadn't moved from her spot at the end of one aisle, her newly crinkly hair obscuring her averted face. Pat pretended to leaf through a sequence of books, but she glanced up often enough so that Lemuel could catch her looking at him.

The lines in front of the authors were gradually disappearing. "You're going to miss Scott Fein if you don't hurry," Pat whispered to Ginny. Pat's next glance caught both authors with mouths agape, laughing mirthlessly. "No one's with him," she said. Her last glance unexpectedly ricocheted off Lemuel Samuel, who was sauntering in her direction.

"You like to read about serial killers?" he asked.

Pat backed up against a bookcase. "What?" she said. Then she realized they were standing under a sign saying just that.

Ginny threw them a brief, hard look and turned back down to the book she was holding.

"You old enough to go get a drink?"

"Of course I am," said Pat, insulted despite the fact that she was lying.

"Well?"

Pat's heart leapt. This must be an invitation. "Ginny?" said Pat. "Shall we go?"

"Which book are you looking at, Ginny?" asked Lemuel, his tone almost sickish-sweet.

Ginny was furious at the use of her name, Pat could tell. "I'm not looking at anything," said Ginny to her book. It came out almost as a hiss.

"Oh," said Pat. "Okay."

"You want to come, then?" asked Lemuel.

"No," said Ginny.

"I'll meet you back at the hotel room," said Pat, so proud to be uttering this phrase in front of Lemuel that she felt as if she were lying once again.

"No," said Ginny. Another of her abrupt, all-dismissive, closed-faced nos.

"Oh," said Pat, now uncertain.

After a pause, Lemuel wandered back toward the folding table, and Ginny spat out, "I'm going to go back."

Scott Fein had disappeared. Lemuel was picking up a small army pack. This quotidian burden made him more familiar to Pat and made his imminent departure more real. When he returned and said "Well?" once more, he was clearly just pausing, already half gone. Pat said to Ginny, "Okay, I guess I'll see you later." She could feel Ginny's eyes on her back as she left.

"You're up for anything, aren't you?" he said. "Unlike your friend."

"She has something to do," said Pat.

"Yeah, she looked like the sort who would have something to do."

What did that mean? Pat was the one who was always busy. She looked behind them but couldn't see Ginny.

They walked in silence to a bar called Jimmy's. Lemuel let her go first, so she got the full brunt of the patrons' skeptical glances. When she hesitated at the first stool, Lemuel parked right there. He placed a couple of bills on the bar and tapped them with his index finger. It occurred to Pat that Ginny had all their money, but it didn't seem to matter.

"Where are you from?" he asked, as if trying to determine what drink to order from the information she provided.

"New Jersey," said Pat promptly and then wished she'd offered up "Los Angeles," home of the hard-boiled detective, instead. But Lemuel accepted the state with his imperturbable half smile. Because his lips were usually pulled back in this smile, you didn't realize at first how full they were. They looked swollen, maybe bruised. His hair was thick and dark.

"You need a beer," said Lemuel, fingering the inside of his empty breast pocket. "You don't have a light, do you?"

Of course she had matches. At high school, even people who didn't smoke carried them. Plus they were from the Watering Hole, which was a pretty tough bar for suburban New Jersey. She hadn't believed it when she'd spotted them on a shelf in the local drugstore. Not that that meant a whole lot here, she realized. Still, it was a shock to see the matchbook, which suddenly seemed so little, in his hands, which were so large. Hair sprouted from the fingers, the skin was pitted, the knuckles raw and red. Oh, to feel that rough grip.

"You're full of surprises, aren't you?" he said with his half smile.

She was still looking at him expectantly as the bartender put a beer down in front of her.

"That's yours," said Lemuel.

"I know," she said, blushing. She made no attempt to lift the mug. "So . . . you live around here?"

"I have a place I stay when I'm in town," he said, downing his shot. "In the Village."

"The Village," she sighed. "That's great."

"So you like mysteries," he said.

"Of course I do!" Pat enthused. She was slightly handicapped in that she hadn't read any of his books yet, but she forged ahead anyway. "It must be great to be a writer. I mean, to think up all these people and watch them track each other down. No one, absolutely no one, is cooler than a private eye. 'Down these sun-blinded streets,' right?"

"How about a private eye writer?" said Lemuel. "How cool would he be?"

"Even cooler than a private eye!" said Pat. "Really!"

"You wouldn't believe the shit I get sometimes," he said. "One old bag actually called me up to nag at me."

This seemed to be the extent of their conversation—Lemuel was already turning away—and the beer really was awful. "You know what I hate," Pat said quickly. "Clues."

"Oh?"

When he shook another couple of cigarettes loose from his pack, he offered her one, which she accepted. She was lucky Ginny wasn't here, as this opinion had originally been hers. "I hate alibis, train schedules, floor plans." Pat frowned, trying to remember. "Slips of the tongue!" That had been Pat's addition. "Riddles in verse."

"You're a funny girl," said Lemuel. "What's your name, again?" And when she gave it to him, he said, "Well, Pat, it's time to go. How about I drink your beer if you're not going to?"

"Oh," she said, a little crestfallen, fearing the night was about to end. But out on the street he seemed to expect her company. The air was cool, and the buildings were deep in shadow. Curlicues of neon letters were beginning to emerge from the gloom. At the next intersection the sky was thick, dark, and radiant, as if the smog were reflecting the city's light back upon itself.

Lemuel stopped in front of a bank of revolving doors, indicating with even more showy gallantry than last time that she should precede him. As he waited for her to comply, he looked her up and down and said, "You're so . . . untouched."

Pat found herself in a hotel lobby. Clerks sat behind flaking gilt cages. A monkey-faced bellboy in a red cap stood beside a luggage cart heaped with mismatched suitcases. The marble walls were grainy, dull, important. Pat could feel her breath come shorter as Lemuel Samuel, mystery novelist, author of *Follow Me* and many other books that you could buy in real bookstores, lit another cigarette with *her* matches and pushed the button for the elevator.

She had not expected an elevator man. He turned his wheel with a wide, air-filled clunk, as if steering a boat. When he glanced around for floor numbers, Pat saw that he was ruddy-faced and black-eyed, like her runaway father. But Lemuel was standing between them with his shoulder hunched and his hands in his pockets, which made him look especially large. There was no way to avoid her awful, delicious fate.

The elevator doors opened on a huge arch, where a flock of women with clipboards hovered. "Mr. Samuel, we're so pleased that you could come," said one.

"This is Lydia Bunting," said Lemuel, indicating Pat roughly with a thumb.

Oh, God. Lydia Bunting's amateur sleuth was an old lady who rode a bicycle. Pat feared some lurking cruelty. She blushed red.

"Miss Bunting?" said the woman with confusion. She looked as if *she* could have been Lydia Bunting, actually.

Pat coughed, dry-throated. "How nice to meet you," she said.

Behind them a man snickered.

"I don't see what's so funny," said Pat, letting her real annoyance show through her faked annoyance.

This was too much for the woman with the clipboard, who mechanically handed out name tags.

"I don't see what's so funny!" repeated Lemuel, striding through the arch. "God, you are priceless!" He was heading straight for the bar set up at the far end of the room. Pat heard his name called a couple of times as they wove through the crowd. Most of the men were in black tie; the women were in evening gowns. Lemuel's dirty black jeans and oversize scuffed boots made him look like a gate crasher.

He stopped only when people actually got in his way. Usually they ignored Pat, but one woman did say, "Lydia Bunting? I pictured you so much older," and her companion said, "That's not Lydia Bunting. That's just Lemuel up to his usual tricks." At which point they didn't seem to expect Pat to be able to talk, so she didn't.

Someone brought Lemuel a drink. Soon someone else brought him two, one of which he passed on to Pat. She didn't know what it was, but she sipped at it gamely, anyway. It tasted as if the setting sun had been caught and put in a glass. The men gathered around him were the guests not wearing tuxes, or even suits. An arm snaked around Lemuel's chest, from behind. Lemuel crouched and turned roughly, elbow out. "Hey, man, hey, man," the owner of the arm gasped, either in propitiation or because he could get nothing more out.

When the swift, ugly moment had passed, the woman with the clipboard approached Lemuel. "We've set a place for your friend at table seven next to you."

"Did you hear that, Lydia?" Lemuel boomed.

Pat nodded, wondering if he'd forgotten her real name.

In the next, much larger, better-lit room were dozens of round tables covered with white linen. At the far end was a podium flanked by tall, crane-like orange and purple flowers.

"Who's the girl?" asked a skinny blond woman with lots of silver rings on her fingers, even her thumbs.

"Lydia Bunting," said Lemuel before Pat realized they were talking about her. She started to say something, but it came out wrong, so she decided to shut up.

"You should be ashamed of yourself," said the blonde. Pat wasn't sure whom she was speaking to—Lemuel or Pat herself.

Later she pecked at a round of steak with brown sauce. People kept getting up and speaking into the microphone at the podium, and it was a while before she realized that prizes called Edgars were being given out in different categories, just like at the Academy Awards. Feeling a bit more balanced, she sipped her wine and looked around. How extraordinary, to be sitting here with all these mystery writers! A surge of joy suffused her heart and even splashed into her head. She realized she recognized the name on the blonde's name tag from the shelves back at Hart Ridge Books.

Then Lemuel won. The new book, *Road Kill,* was named Best Mystery of the Year. Various cries could be heard over the applause: "Samuel! Samuel!"

His acceptance speech was short. "Who's ready for a road trip!" he roared, lifting the little statue. "What a great hood ornament this'd make!" An explosion of applause.

Later they were in the elevator with a fleshy, pumice-cheeked, closed-off man Lemuel Samuel said was a famous Hollywood director.

"Is that true?" asked Pat.

"Yes," said the man. He was wearing an open-collar shirt

under a safari jacket. Something unpleasant rested just below his genial tone.

"Call him Mister Hollywood," said Lemuel. "That's what I do." He rolled around a bit as if unaccustomed to standing on his hind legs. "This is Lydia Bunting."

Mr. Hollywood's insincerely affable smile remained unchanged. The name obviously meant nothing to him.

"We have to humor him," said Lemuel. "He's going to give me a lot of money."

"That's the plan," said Mr. Hollywood. At a dark bar on the West Side, he spoke in a kind of singsong: "*Follow me* . . . channel the violence . . . *Follow me* . . . capture the power . . . *Follow me* . . . feel the glee . . . *Follow Me* is the best book about freedom ever written."

"Damn right," mumbled Lemuel, shaking his wrist.

"People think it's about crime, but it's not," said Mr. Hollywood. "There are lots of different freedoms, and you have captured the sweetest of all, which is the freedom to act without consequences. Not without *fear* of consequences—without any consequences at all. Think about it. What would you do if you could do one thing without consequences?"

"Drive across country without stopping once," said Lemuel, "not even for gas."

Sleep with Lemuel, thought Pat, although maybe it was the consequences that she wanted.

"Not even for gas," repeated Mr. Hollywood. "What a detail. That's what makes you a genius."

"Geniuses come to this bar," said Lemuel, with an odd swift sweep of his forearm flat across the table. "And jazz musicians. Stuntmen. It's so dark in here you can pass counterfeit money. No one's going to question *them*."

"Stuntmen?" said Mr. Hollywood.

"You can pass counterfeit money here," said Lemuel. Suddenly the words seemed to be sloshing out of his mouth. "Counterfeit. Money. And race car drivers."

"What are you going to do now?" asked Mr. Hollywood.

"We're gonna go to California tomorrow," said Lemuel. "Right, Lydia?"

The heat was awful the summer after Frank was arrested. Pat periodically checked the large outdoor thermometer, which was as big as a wall clock and decorated with painted cardinals. She watched in dismay while the hand approached and then rose past a cardinal's beak, where the nineties began. The house on Douglas Point had central air, of course, but Frank spent Memorial Day weekend in his shirt sleeves at a Days Inn in Queens, combing through LinkAge financial documents and separating out numbers that he described to the FBI as "wild," "risky," or "really out there."

He had not intended to cooperate with the authorities. The night of his arrest, he tried the Rumson number and left a message. He figured Neil would soon set the government straight. Neil could explain the difference between stretching the limits and something downright wrong, like embezzling. Whatever he and Neil had done was only temporary, after all, designed to guide the company over a few rough spots. Neil would know exactly how to phrase it. As soon as Frank hung up, the phone rang in his hands, but it was a reporter, and so was the next caller, and the next. Pat ordered caller ID, as she should have ages ago, given her husband's field of employment.

LinkAge's stock price, which had been falling all spring from a high of sixty-two dollars, stopped trading at sixty cents. Frank's meeting with the Justice Department was scheduled soon after the company declared bankruptcy. His attempts to reach his old boss became frantic. Finally he called Ellen, who said, "Tell me what to do. There are FBI agents everywhere. They're rummaging through all your papers, and they put your computer in a box."

"I guess there's not a whole lot you can do," said Frank.

"No?" said Ellen.

He learned that on the advice of counsel Neil wasn't talking, but did that mean he wasn't talking to *Frank,* who had always done anything for him?

Then Frank's case was switched from New Jersey to New York—not a good sign, according to his lawyer, a local man named Lou Lugano. Political pressure was demanding a hard course. Too many accounting irregularities had been revealed at major companies recently; too many bankruptcies had been declared; too many top executives had sailed off in yachts bought with the impoverished shareholders' money.

When Pat got home from Whole Foods the next day, she found Frank standing in the middle of the kitchen, sipping cabernet.

"Where have you been?" he asked, although it was obvious, because of the name on the bags, and he didn't wait for her to answer. "There's a message for you."

"Oh, really?" said Pat, afraid from his manner of what it might be. But she went ahead and hit the button.

It was Yolande Culp, who said that given the circumstances, she was going to put off their landscaping project for now. The only unusual thing about the message was how late Yolande had left it. Other LinkAge-related clients had already canceled. But Yolande had probably been reluctant because Pat had given her such a big discount on the job. Frank had suggested that Pat undercharge her for the design of a garden because it would pay off at bonus time, which it already had—to the tune of half a million dollars last Christmas. And since it was the company that paid Frank the bonus, no one was out of pocket.

Yolande's message went on: "Neil's attorney says it's better right now if there's no communication between him and Frank. I'm sure you both understand." Yolande's self-absorbed tone was so usual that at first Pat had trouble taking in the meaning of the words, but then Frank said, "Am I crazy? Or is that the kick in the pants I think it is?"

"Oh dear," said Pat, as he followed her into the pantry.

"I have to decide what to do here," he said. "Dominic tells me he's going to cooperate." Dominic Cerise was Frank's lieutenant and the most senior of the High Risk boys. "And he's a stand-up guy, if you know what I mean."

Frank obviously meant to invoke Mafia terminology, but his inner turbulence was such that he was beyond irony. Pat hoped she wasn't supposed to laugh.

At five o'clock Frank switched to single malt, saying, "Wherever Neil is, he's playing it smart. You can count on that. He's always got something up his sleeve. Clearly he expects me to talk to the feds. So all right. I will. I just have to figure out what to say. I can't go too far wrong if I simply recite the facts. I will put my own construct on it if I can, but mainly I will confine myself to what happened when. Neil is the one who's good at interpretations. I'll leave that up to him. He'll eventually cast the right light on all of this."

"There's certainly nothing wrong in describing what you did," said Pat. "No one can expect any more or less of you. Tell them exactly the way you told me! It doesn't matter what Neil does."

She and Frank used to interrupt each other all the time—it could be a problem at dinner parties—but now their conversation started as abruptly as a windup toy and tapered off the same way, jingly.

Frank ended up cooperating with the government as a condition of his plea bargain. In June he spent his weekends at the Days Inn. Because he was home during the week, and he wasn't paid for any of his tasks, it was as if he had the opposite of a job. Later in the summer, he was moved to a government office in downtown Manhattan. That was worse, because he had to come in during the week, just as if he were commuting to a job, and he still wasn't being paid. He continued to pore over documents looking for fixes. Now he described numbers as "questionable." It was a less boastful characterization than his earlier ones, and it signaled a new air of resignation. Neil never did call.

Pat spent the early mornings watering. If she left the house later, the hard heat of the day would hit her in the face. Many of the plants, particularly the rhododendrons, had swooned; there was no starch left in them. At cocktail hour she fed ice cubes to those that were suffering the most. Even the leaves on the few pathetic weeds fell straight down the sides of the stems, minimizing the surface area exposed to the direct sunlight. She'd never expected to feel sorry for weeds.

Rose was in Dublin working at a private clinic Gibbs and Culp had contributed heavily to, so she must have been okay. But Ruby called from her camp in the Catskills to say that a bunkmate had collapsed from dehydration. "I tried to put a Pop-sicle in her mouth, but she was so out of it she didn't know what it was," said Ruby with unsavory excitement.

It was in August that the feds finally okayed Frank's trip to the Foy's country house in Lenox, Massachusetts. Even Pat had grown somewhat impatient. She loved the house, which they'd bought shortly before Ruby was born. It had been struck by lightning the year before. A ball of sparks flew out of the TV at the children. The floor lamp in the living room fried, as did the answering machine, which was in the hall. The electric burner that had been on high to boil water for pasta remained so per-manently; the only way to turn it off was to unplug the whole stove. Pat looked back at this tame adventure with great fond-ness. All the tumult was suffused with the blessed cool damp dimness that she associated with every summer house.

The first evening in Lenox, Frank walked to the end of the communal driveway to put out the garbage from dinner, mainly corn husks. Although the walk was a half mile over uneven ground, and many of their neighbors routinely drove it, Frank had always liked the leisure of the slower stroll. But this time, as soon as he returned, Pat knew that something had happened. She could not think what it might be, however. "Frank?" she said. Instead of answering he snuck to the closest window and peered around the edge of the café curtains, careful not to dis-turb them. Then he started to scratch his back and chest and shudder dramatically. He told her that he was sure he'd been watched the whole time he was taking out the trash. The Foys returned to New Jersey the next morning.

Back in Hart Ridge, Frank stopped running; he was crossing paths with too many people, some of whom he knew, which was bad, and some of whom he did not know, which was worse. "If they're not at work, why aren't they out in the country?" he asked irritably. "They *must* be FBI. They can't all be housewives and househusbands." This last was accompanied by an irritable look at Pat, who, it was true, had not consulted with a client since the arrest. She didn't even know where to find her tote bag with its tattered clippings and thumbed-through plant books and discarded blueprints. But why should he care, since he swore up and down that his lack of employment would make no real dent in their financial status.

Frank stopped leaving the house, and when one of those talking heads on TV said that everyone at LinkAge should go to jail, he stopped watching television as well, except for baseball. Even Pat started scrutinizing the people she ran into. Didn't they realize who her husband was? But the gas station attendant, who was from Trinidad, smiled as much as ever. The cleaning ladies were as cowed as ever. And the nurseryman, crusty old Whit Beck, never had noticed anything that wasn't stuck in the soil.

It was almost a relief when the summer was over and it was time for Frank to go to court. Pat would never have said this, because you didn't know how he was going to take things these days, but she thought it would be good for Frank to put the plea behind him, even if it did mean paying a fine, a possibility he spent a lot of time parsing out. There were few clues as to how much it would be. Sometimes he would write various numbers on pads of paper, cross a few out, then add more in, and figure out the range, the mean, and the average. It could be nothing, of course, but the more likely low estimate was, say, a few thousand dollars. On the other hand, it could be as much as . . . well, it couldn't be infinite. Maybe a half a million. Or a whole one, at the very, very outside. "No exotic plants until we know how much it's going to be," warned Frank. He was less worried about the length of the suspended sentence he was going to receive. He'd have to stay out of trouble, but that shouldn't be difficult for a man who'd have no opportunity to get into it. "I'll stay away from offices and confine myself to pool halls, where there won't be as many temptations," he said, shaking the ice in his glass.

Pat and Brenda Cerise, Dominic's wife, were not friends. Brenda rarely talked about anything but the darling clothes and furnishings she bought. But Frank and Dominic shared a court date, so Pat called up Brenda beforehand to find out what she was going to wear and to figure out how long it would take to get into the city. "It's not like we can be late," said Pat. "Maybe we should spend the night in one of those new SoHo hotels."

She wasn't serious, of course, but Brenda said, "Dominic is living on chocolate-covered doughnuts."

The non sequitur was disquieting.

"I think she's upset about her kids," Pat told Frank as he fought traffic in the Lincoln Tunnel the next day. "Brenda told me they were going to take them out of Catholic school. I don't know why. Lots of Catholics are criminals."

"That's a comforting thought," said Frank sarcastically. He had a suit on for the first time in months, and already there was something indefinably wrong with the way it hung, more than could be explained by the few pounds he had gained recently. Pat, too, was wearing a suit but it was short and red.

"It's not?" said Pat.

"Dominic probably can't afford the tuition," said Frank. "He didn't cash in his stock the way I did. He sold some a while

back, maybe thirty thousand dollars' worth, but he owned millions on paper at the time. It all disappeared during the bankruptcy. Why he kept it in one stock, even LinkAge, I will never
know."

"That's so sad!" said Pat. For some reason her heart was stut-
tering like a jackhammer.

They parked at a lot near the South Street Seaport and
started walking toward Foley Square with plenty of time to
spare. The day was hazy and cool. As they turned the corner
onto Centre Street, Pat could see in front of the shallow steps of
the federal courthouse a half dozen men with cameras slung
over their shoulders. The cameras were black, with long lenses.
Although both Frank and Lou had talked about how to deal with
the newspeople, Pat didn't realize right away that they were
waiting for Frank. In the few moments before they spotted him,
she kept walking in vigilant ignorance. Then they were on
him—and Pat—sidestepping and pivoting, the cameras in front
of their eyes clicking and clattering. The cloud of nervous energy they kicked up was frightening. Pat managed to match
Frank's slow and steady pace although she thought she was
going to walk right into them. Somehow she never did.

A security guard stopped the more persistent of the photog-
raphers at the bottom of the steps, and Pat said, as she and
Frank continued their numbed ascent, "Wow. We're okay, right?
I think we're okay."

Lou Lugano, a round-faced man perpetually short of breath,
was in the courtroom already, near the door. Although he had
never touched Frank before, now he couldn't stop. He shook
Frank's hand, brushed his arm, and clapped his shoulder, saying
all the while that there was more media interest than he had an-

ticipated. This touching must have been a show for the audience, which consisted of about twenty people, but Pat couldn't
imagine why Lou thought it would help.

When he and Frank moved to the other side of the railing,
Pat dropped into the front row beside a middle-aged buxom
woman with waist-length blond hair, who immediately began to
sketch on a board propped up in front of her. She was drawing
Frank.

The background (brown bench, blue wall) was already filled
in. Now she was working on Frank's hair. His face did not yet
exist. "Hi," said Pat.

"Hi," said the woman, switching pastels. She was swathed
from head to toe in black leather.

"How are you?" asked Pat.

The clocklike swing of the artist's attention between Frank
and drawing board was momentarily interrupted. She let loose a
wide and bashful smile. "I'm fine," she said.

Brenda Cerise, in a beige suit, took the seat on the other side
of Pat, who said, "What a nice blouse." It was printed with de-
mure little daisies, or maybe they were supposed to be asters.

"Neiman Marcus, fifty percent off."

Brenda always talked like that; it wasn't just because the
Cerises had lost their money. As a kid she'd probably been more
interested in ferreting out a deal on a bike than in riding one.

Pat wondered what in her own past could have spawned this
bewildering present. She and Frank had often teased each other
about their youthful recklessness. Pat would say, "Tell me again.
What percentage of your time was spent on the slopes?" Skiing,
of all things—a rich boy's sport. But Frank, who had received a
scholarship to Syracuse, not too far from Song Mountain and
Greek Peak, was simply good at it. And he got along well with

the thoughtless, cocksure boys who drove from the campus to the resorts. They were the precursors of the High Risk boys.

In the courtroom Pat imagined a young Dominic venturing forth eagerly into the world, saying, "And someday if I'm lucky, I'll *get to turn state's evidence.*"

Maybe Brenda, years ago, gazed out from under her wedding veil, beyond the full skirts of her new wedding gown, and over at her newly betrothed and thought, "What a tall, handsome, twinkle-eyed, rough-lipped, strong-armed, fine-browed, straight-backed *future defendant* I have united my life with."

Everyone rose for the judge, who sauntered to the bench, staring straight ahead. Instead of looking at the lawyers or the defendants or the audience, he gazed at his papers or off at the wall, hooding his eyes. All you could really see was his mouth, which was stiff but not unkind, Pat was sure.

Dominic's case was first. He began by pleading guilty to two counts of filing false financial statements. Then he tried a short allocution: "Senior management directed me to apportion—"

"I took a look at some of the LinkAge statements," the judge interrupted, his eyes fixed on the doors to the hall. "I read the footnotes over three times and couldn't find a lick of sense in them."

Dominic stood there, still straight and tall in his gray suit, but now evidently uncertain what to say. Finally he tried, "No, Your Honor." He turned briefly to his lawyer and then began again, "Senior management directed me to—"

"Are you using them as some sort of excuse?" said the judge.

"No, Your Honor."

Next time Dominic started, he got through his entire statement. The judge said, "Did you know what you were doing was wrong?"

"Yes, Your Honor."

Looking at the papers in front of him, the judge spoke at length about his "search for balance." On the one side was the gravity of the crime and the need for deterrence. On the other was Dominic's cooperation and the necessity of sending the right signal to other cooperators. "Because of these considerations, I feel a much shorter period of incarceration than the guidelines recommend is called for. I hereby sentence you to a period of five months. A fine will be waived, pending the outcome of the civil suit. I will not demand restitution because the identity and monetary loss of the victims is impossible to determine."

Brenda was rigid. Pat touched her desert-colored sleeve.

Five months? What did that mean? How could Dominic be going to jail? Did he say the wrong thing? Didn't he help track down figures the way Frank had?

There was a general stir in the courtroom. Pat decided that this must be some formality that the judge was then going to set aside.

After Frank pled guilty to the same counts Dominic did, he stood and read, automaton-like, from a piece of computer paper. He'd let down his family, he'd exposed them to risk, and he would never forgive himself. Pat had read the statement at home several days earlier and had been moved by it. Now it was hard to figure out exactly what he was apologizing for.

His sentence was twelve months and a day. Pat was stunned. How could Frank be sentenced to jail after he had done everything requested of him in return for probation?

The judge asked if there was any legal reason that he should not pass this sentence.

Lou Lugano stood. "Not really," he said, gasping. Frank sat down suddenly, as if someone had hit him on the head.

Outside the courtroom, at the elevator bank, Lou told the print reporters that he was disappointed in the outcome and that he was going to consider an appeal. Pat said with a single, surprising sob, "Frank is not a bad man. He never meant to hurt anybody."

Then the convicted felons, their lawyers, and their wives crowded into an elevator hung with pads to prevent damage to the fine wood interior. It was dark and claustrophobic. The lawyers decided that the group should split up in order to minimize contact with the TV cameras and newspaper photographers. The wives would leave first and retrieve the cars. In five or ten minutes Frank would go out the front entrance, and Dominic, out the side.

Pat and Brenda wove their way through the meandering white corridor of the basement to the side door. They did not falter because each assumed that the other knew where she was going, and in fact they ended up within sight of a pair of heavy double doors and an idle security guard who, while he did not have to monitor the metal detector, was leafing through a real estate guide to Sullivan County.

How curious that Pat and Brenda should share the same awful fate. Maybe exulting over a new Chinese redbud wasn't all that different from exulting over a new red couch.

They paused before the doors. "Do they really have to go to . . . jail?" said Pat.

Brenda looked at her suspiciously. Then she opened the right door and let in the blinding sunlight. There were a few over-eager flashes, but the dozens of pairs of eyes were straining to see behind them. The two women were watched, not photo-graphed, as they strode self-consciously down Pearl.

"We'd better hurry," said Brenda. She and Dominic had found the better lot. Pat's was farther away. Once she was in the car, she had to circle around to get to Worth, a side street up-town from the courthouse, where she got stuck behind a deliv-ery truck. She could see Frank walking up Centre Street in her direction, trailing photographers. He half hoped to shake them, but he also expected her to drive up behind him and so kept looking back for her. At first the cameramen clicked feverishly, but one by one, they gradually left. The departures were worse than the assault, implying an embarrassed pity. The lone re-maining photographer started to take his camera from his face periodically and direct his gaze back in the direction Frank was looking, uncertain whether to continue. The energy had dissi-pated, and at last he put his equipment away. By the time Pat reached Frank, he was alone on the sidewalk.

CHAPTER

5

Youth is full of fits and starts. You can be jerked this way and that way and then six more ways you'd never even heard of.

When Pat staggered out of the bar on the night of the Edgar Awards, leaving Lemuel Samuel with Mr. Hollywood, she returned to Penn Station via a flashing, streetlamp-lit sequence of empty sidewalks, scattered couples, man with dog, man in a sweatshirt. Possible threat? Doesn't matter. Walk, walk, walk through the dark, and never stop. At last a huge harshly bright three-dimensionally confined space opened up around her: Penn Station. All the newsstands and shops were shuttered. The floor was dingy with abandonment. Pat's footsteps echoed eerily. And sprawled on a banquette near the departure board dozed a familiar figure under an alien puff of hair.

"Ginny," said Pat stupidly.

Ginny was instantly alert. "You don't have the money for the train, do you? I have it all, remember?"

Pat looked down vaguely at the tiny camouflage shoulder bag

flung crosswise from her shoulder to the opposite hip. "Oh, right," she said.

"I realized when I got to Hart Ridge, so I took the next train back," said Ginny, jumping to her feet.

"We didn't get to go to the Chelsea Hotel," said Pat.

"Oh, well, all I wasted was the two fares, out and back," said Ginny.

"You've been waiting?" said Pat.

"I bought *Follow Me*," said Ginny, waving her copy. "It's great." She looked at Pat with uncharacteristic curiosity. "What happened to you?"

Pat just shook her head. "You have saved me, Ginny," she said.

Ginny examined her sideways for a moment. But all she said was "Let's go. Otherwise we'll have to pay a surcharge for buying tickets on the train."

On board Pat said, "If you could do one thing without consequences, what would it be?"

"Die," said Ginny.

The next morning, when Pat read in *Follow Me* that private eye Bud Caddy ordered a drink in a bar, she promptly threw up. Then she returned to the extravagant, gaudy, exhilarating loop-de-loops of Lemuel Samuel's prose. What bliss, to be one of these rubber-skinned characters who bounced right back up after a sock in the jaw. They all drove around madly, from bar to bar and suspect to suspect and beating to beating. Everyone, win or lose, enjoyed the fisticuffs. The complaints about bruises and wounds sounded like boasts; the dead were strewn about like actors.

Next Pat bought *Road Kill*. It was the first hardback she'd spent her own money on. She and Ginny agreed that it was almost as good as *Follow Me*. Pat liked to study the jacket photo. One of Lemuel's cheeks was deeply creased, the other less so, which gave him his smirk. That half smile of his must not have been a reaction to her, but an old scar. Still, lots of teenage girls wandered through his mysteries, and Pat imagined herself first as one, then as another.

Every little twist and crisscross of the plot reminded her of her joyous dread in the hotel, a feeling that had already started to dwindle in her mind. She wanted to keep hold of it, palpate it. What had she been so excited about? So scared of? Why hadn't she stayed at the bar? Her mother hadn't expected her home. Would she have ended up in California with famous author *Lemuel Samuel*?

As Pat was leafing through *Life* magazine the next month, she came across a photo feature on Lemuel and his movie deal for *Follow Me*. One of the captions read: "What clinched it was the story I told him about passing counterfeit money," says Samuel dryly. "You know how crazy Hollywood is about money."

After her heart leapt in recognition, she felt a wave of fear. *What if nothing ever happened to her again?*

But toward the end of her senior year in high school, she went to another of Lemuel's signings at The Black Cat, and this time Ginny came drinking, too. The three of them ran through the White Horse, the Corner Bistro, Chumley's, the 55. The next night Lemuel asked Pat to come to the apartment in the Village. Just before he made love to her, he bumped his head on the frame of the borrowed loft bed. He kept groaning, whether from pain or pleasure it was hard to tell. After that he called her every few months. She never knew where he was in the interim.

She moved around, too, but he could always find her through her mother, who seemed willing to give out her number to any lowlife who called, not that Lemuel was one of them.

Pat had graduated from Maryland and moved to Manhattan by the time Lemuel published another Bud Caddy mystery, *The Fleabag Massacre,* which sold more copies than either *Follow Me* or *Road Kill,* but wasn't nominated for an Edgar. Lemuel said he'd pissed off the wrong people. He brought her to Fire Island for a long weekend, where they stayed in a white clapboard house that belonged to his editor at Black Cat Books. The property was riddled with poison ivy, so Pat was careful walking around while Lemuel did phone interviews. She didn't mind that Lemuel never mentioned her. He had to appear footloose. Which God knows he was. That Tuesday he left for the Beverly Hills Hotel, where Mr. Hollywood was putting him up so they could work together on the script of *Follow Me,* half a decade after the project had begun.

Detective novels were changing. The hard-boiled "everyman" was making way for detectives who ran against type: female or old or deaf or homosexual. Bud Caddy was a bridge between the two. He was yet another half-romantic, half-cynical PI, but he was such an exaggerated, outsize version in *The Fleabag Massacre* that he'd become puffy and nearly incoherent with drink and drugs. It was hard to tell why he did anything. No detective devoted more time to intoxicants. No detective got into more fights for fewer discernible reasons. And no detective tore across a page the way he did.

Ginny Howley started writing short mystery stories, as Pat had always told her she should, given her name. Well, they were sort of like mystery stories. In her first, "The Red Door," a detective tries to sneak past a variety of doormen and receptionists and security guards only to find that beyond them are more doors waiting to be opened. The story was bought by mainstream *Argosy*—not bad considering it had been repeatedly rejected by mystery magazines. Pat found a postcard of a church with a fancy red door, which she circled. "Cool!" she scrawled on the back. She sent it off to Providence, where Ginny had gone to college, and where she'd simply stayed, despite Pat's perfectly reasonable argument that she could find crime for her stories anywhere, even in New York City. Pat sent a copy of the *Argosy* with Ginny's story to Lemuel at the Beverly Hills Hotel, but received no reply.

Over the years Ginny's tone had become more dispassionate and her conversation more lurid. Of Lizzie Borden she said, "She was forty, and she was tired of waiting to have a good time. Everyone knew she'd killed her parents, but the crime was too big and too awful to acknowledge. So she got off. Then she started to throw parties. Can you imagine getting an invitation?"

When Ginny left a message on Pat's machine, Pat should have called her back right away. But she went to a solve-it-yourself theatrical event that night and didn't try her until the next evening. By then it was Saturday, and Pat was in Hart Ridge, where her mother turned out to be reading "a book by that mystery writer you know with the funny rhyming name." Pat didn't reach Ginny until Monday morning.

It was hot, so hot for a September morning shortly after Labor Day that even at this early hour Pat could see the air shimmy off the train tracks at the Hart Ridge station. She was surprised at how bad it was possible to feel when you weren't hungover. Her head pounded in the rising heat. At the end of the platform were two glass phone booths, each with a retractable door, a hard brown plastic shelf to sit on, and a Hart

Ridge phone book dangling from a wire. Pat was sitting in the farther booth when she got Ginny. The door was open, and her forehead was pressed against the cool metal of the pay phone.

"I'm going to Maine," said Ginny.

"Oh, I wish I were," said Pat. "It's so awful here." Beside the steps to the platform were some shrubby roses that reminded her of the beach.

"I mean I'm moving there," said Ginny.

"Really?"

"I'm not sure if I told you I got married."

"Married!" exclaimed Pat.

"It's not what you think. But I can't talk about it right now."

"Why not?"

"I'm afraid," Ginny whispered.

"Of who? Your husband?"

"No, no," she said with sibilant impatience. "Nothing like that. Maybe myself."

The face of the black engine appeared around the bend just then, its clanks and hisses suggesting a drizzlier, cooler, cozier climate, maybe in black and white.

"Give me your phone number, and I'll call you back when I get into Penn Station," said Pat.

"I don't have one. I have this idea of . . . of the dark woods," said Ginny.

"Wait," said Pat with the sense that the conversation had gotten away from her. "The train's here," she said. "But we've had such good times. Why go so far away? We have to stay friends, right? Right?"

Pat sat on the left and more scenic side of the train and tried to picture Ginny married. She had always been alone in a way that Pat knew she never would or even could be. Not that Pat's odd glancing association with Lemuel would have suited most people. Out of laziness or maybe lower standards, she put up with all sorts of nonsense. But it had sputtered along as other, more intense romances evaporated.

"Pat!" This warm greeting was from Frank Foy, a Hart Ridge classmate she hadn't seen in years.

Pat looked up and said, "I warn you. I was shot at once on this train. Here." She pointed to the bottom right-hand corner of the window near the seat in front of her.

"Really," said Frank, sitting down easily beside her and leaning over for a better look.

"I don't mean the shooter knew it was me," said Pat. "I was just a person. He probably couldn't see more than a silhouette. A head, maybe? Hair?"

"What did you do?"

"Oh, screamed. Not much. Just a little scream. It was more interesting than scary. There wasn't time for my life to flash before my eyes or anything like that. Suddenly there was a crack, there was a bullet hole in the window, and there were slivers of glass on my lap. The conductor must have told me a dozen times that I was all right and that it was only a BB gun. I think he was afraid I was going to sue. The same thing happened to me once when I saw a caterpillar in my salad at a fancy restaurant."

"You were shot at in a restaurant, too?" Frank was wearing a red and blue rugby shirt, his hair was tousled, and he was leaning in so close that Pat could see the sheen on his fresh, taut skin and the tension in the muscles underneath. Muscles are supposed to work two ways, one against the other, and for the first time in her life, Pat could believe it.

"Of course not," she said. "I've only been shot at once. Isn't that enough?"

"I'm so glad that I ran into you today," said Frank. He was celebrating the successful pursuit of some sort of job. Pat wasn't exactly paying attention, but there was such eager joy in his face, she happily agreed to meet him for dinner that night. She'd been aware of him all her life. He was a good Catholic boy like any other; she remembered him from the church basement, where nuns taught catechism to small groups of elementary school kids sitting on folding chairs. She knew the sort of home he'd grown up in: small and neat, with a print of the Annunciation in the hall—one step up from a crucifix. She knew the sort of parents he had: increasingly angry as the years went by, and bitter about liberals, but generous-hearted in their own way. She knew the sorts of friends and beer and sports and television programs he liked.

It was months before he mentioned catching her "on the rebound" from Lemuel Samuel. "I couldn't believe my luck!" he crowed.

They were at a drive-in movie theater, waiting to see a spy movie. Frank was still living with his parents in Hart Ridge, but he had his own car, a red Firebird with taped-up seats, and they spent a lot of time in it. "What are you talking about?" asked Pat.

"I overheard you on the phone with him that day. The door to the pay phone was open." Frank was spilling popcorn all over himself in his excitement. "I never would have had the courage otherwise."

Maybe. Pat had never met a cockier fellow, actually. But she tried to piece together which conversation he could mean. "That was Ginny!" she said at last. "We were talking about her moving to Maine!"

"Oh, no, he mentioned marriage and you said you wanted to be friends. Friends! Ha! What a kiss-off!"

"Lemuel Samuel would never do anything like get married," said Pat. But Frank got such a kick out of dating Lemuel Samuel's old girlfriend that it was impossible to get him to understand that she and Lemuel could not have "broken up" because they had never been "together."

"But we're together, right?" said Frank.

"Of course," she said.

Frank was so young. He hardly drank at all, except in sporadic bursts. He was always ready to make love, and he actually paid attention as he did it. He liked to have fun. He was just . . . regular. Pat started to wonder when she'd hear from Lemuel again. It had been several months, so it was about time. But he didn't call. Then the leaves started to turn, even the oaks, and still he didn't call.

Very early on another Monday morning, shortly after New Year's, Pat's phone rang. She woke in her dream, and it was Lemuel. Then she woke again. The room was black, but her mind was clear. It was Frank's mother. Frank had wrecked his car driving back from Hunter Mountain. He and his friends were in a hospital in Kingston. At least one of them was supposed to be critical. But she had spoken to Frank. He sounded okay. He'd mentioned Pat.

During the drive north, Frank's parents sat in the front seat, and Pat sat in the back. Eerie portents appeared: an untended fire in a metal barrel, dark twisted tree branches obscuring a green sign; bright, brittle light in the hospital lobby. Frank's hair was deeply black against the white pillowcase, shadows had formed hollows under his cheekbones, his eyes glittered.

He and three friends had been skiing until dark on Sunday. Then they'd drunk a few beers. It had been snowing, but it had stopped by the time they set out. They were in the fast lane. A

Buick going the other way spun out, jumped the divide, and ended up in their path. Frank wrenched the steering wheel toward the fog line, but it was too late. He hit the other car at an angle. Once it became clear to Frank's mother that everyone was going to live, she pressed for details and kept repeating what she heard. Pat couldn't keep all the injuries straight. Frank had gotten off lightly; he'd broken his right leg. He asked his parents to leave the room and then asked Pat to marry him. She said, "Wow, what an idea." Suddenly she could make sense of the past few years: This must have been the direction they were heading in.

Recovering at his parents' house, Frank declared his intention of reading the Bud Caddy novels. Pat bought him a new copy of *Road Kill.* She didn't want him reading hers. "It's really good," he said later, scratching under his cast with a straightened coat hanger. "Great sex."

"Sex?" Could he be joking? At this point all she could remember was a lot of shooting and drinking. "Like between a man and a woman?"

"I'm not saying it was with you."

"Heaven forbid," said Pat happily.

Shortly before the wedding Lemuel Samuel published *Mallow,* in which all the murder and mayhem, the guns and the gore, revolved around one central female character.

Mallow is the street name of a teenage runaway whose case still haunts Bud Caddy years later. Her father hired him to find her, claiming that the cops wouldn't take him seriously because he smoked some marijuana now and then. Naturally Bud suggests smoking more. As they go on to other drugs, though, Bud begins to notice peculiarities about the man, who acts as if he's in a time warp. Mallow turns out to be wary, screwed up, wild.

She says her father sexually molested her. After many pharmaceuticals and much tight-lipped agony, Bud does not hand her over. Then he finds out that her story could not be true. The father, who was never the custodial parent, has been living in Mexico and hasn't even seen her since she was a baby. Fifteen years later, he is dead, and Mallow shows up on Bud Caddy's doorstep to ask him to solve his murder. This time as events unfold he refuses to be tricked, so he loses her again.

Mallow has eyes "as green as go lights." She has "fringe" toes. She has a bottom like "jungle fruit." Once she gets the chance, she talks a blue streak in her "untamed soprano voice."

"My God, this is me!" Pat exclaimed to Frank as they lay on the beach at Ocean Grove. She recognized these descriptions. Lemuel had used every one while talking to her—more often in bars than in bed. It was as if he'd come up with his own version of her life while she was trying to figure out the real thing.

When Pat married Frank in a very traditional white dress (floor-length satin, lace bodice, oversize bow in back), she walked down the aisle as Mallow. Everyone knew. The book had made the *Times* bestseller list the month before, the first of Lemuel Samuel's mysteries to do so. Frank told all his friends and family, although none of them had any particular interest in fiction. "Hey, she's got fringe toes," he would say. "I've seen them."

Naturally most people had not read the book. But they knew its reputation. They assumed that Pat was as wild as this Mallow. After all, she had rolled around with the ruffian author for years. No one who knew her associated her with the more pathetic aspects of the character, of course; she was too young and fresh and warm. And enthusiastic. She still bubbled over. When a friend of Frank's asked if she'd really run away, all she did was laugh. She laughed, too, when her mother said she thought the book captured her ex-husband's sinister qualities. She laughed even when Frank said, jokingly, on their wedding night, "And I'm supposed to trust you?"

Pat had called Ginny's stepmother to get her address so that she could send her an invitation. That's when she learned that Ginny had sold a story called "First Funeral" to *Clock* magazine, which was named after the publication in the Nero Wolfe books. So Ginny couldn't have buried herself too far in the dark woods. She never did send in her response card, but she showed up, anyway. She was all in black, with purple lipstick, black fingernails, and a Celtic cross—not exactly a look that Pat associated with the state of Maine. There were plenty of people in black at the wedding; no one worried about that stuff anymore, but Ginny looked scrawny, pasty-faced, and unhealthy in her black garments. At the reception at the local Marlboro Inn, Pat hugged her, which Ginny never used to let her do, and said, "You must tell me everything that has happened."

"Sometime," said Ginny with a slow, brow-furrowing smile. She handed her a wedding present—a teakettle for "Lydia Bunting"—and a card with notes on *Mallow.*

SHOOTINGS:

three drug dealers
porn peddler
Mallow's father
street minister with sinister motives
cocaine-sniffing widow of Senator
Bud Caddy (flesh wound only)
an unspecified but large number of dogs at an animal
    rescue shelter

BEATINGS:

massage parlor owner
mailman
person drinking in bar who refused to give Bud Caddy
    information in an unpleasant way
bartender
bartender's brother, filling in for him
Bud Caddy
Vietnam vet friend of Bud Caddy
different bartender

Pat put this away with her paper wedding bells and her
(mailed) telegrams and her white satin shoes with their three
bows apiece.

Frank's voluntary surrender date was in two months. The ensuing time was a bit like one of those exercises: What would you do if you knew the world were going to end tomorrow? You'd act the same, Pat concluded, only much, much more so.

Frank tried to call many people, not just Neil. The morning after the sentencing, as Pat passed by his study, she heard him say, "When did you give him the message?" There were dozens of people he could have been referring to.

Then he started ordering packages from all over the world. Pat had never known before what was available. Premium meats from Colorado, live lobsters from Ogunquit, jams from Devonshire, England, spices from New Orleans. Once a heart locket arrived for her from Tiffany. Soon unopened boxes littered the kitchen (though still not the cavernous living and dining rooms) because Frank rarely had the patience to cook or to wait for Pat. And there were so many restaurants to visit before his incarceration. How could he bear to last a year without having another warm spinach and shrimp salad from Blue Heaven?

They drank a lot. Frank ordered a mixed carton of single malt whiskey and three cases of wine, nearly all red. He and Pat drank wine at lunch and then had another glass with every little snack (even, redundantly, with a handful of grapes once). When Frank was disappointed in a vintage of wine, he simply opened another bottle. Pat lined up all the opened ones on the deep shelf under the row of windows in the kitchen. The sunlight shone through the colored glass, corks sticking up from the necks like sprouted seeds.

Frank never seemed particularly drunk—or sober. One night he said, "There's no reason not to drink all the time. At least that way you get to be happy for a little while." His tone indicated that he considered this a devastating indictment of the situation, but Pat could see only its truth; she nodded cheerfully.

The only person Pat went out of her way to call was Brenda, who said, "Instead of going to jail, these guys should have been sentenced to community service. They could go to an Indian reservation where they might do some good." Though what help a couple of crooked accountants would be on an Indian reservation, Pat wasn't sure. Maybe one of the casinos could use them.

Pat's problem was that she was tired a lot of the time. It's hard to keep drinking in the afternoon. She was hyperalert, however. She felt she had to match Frank's windup appetites with a semblance of vivaciousness. If she weren't there to help buoy the moment, who knew what horror would ensue? And if a hangover was particularly acute, it was all the better an excuse to block out any thought at all.

Neither she nor Frank slept much. Pat spent a good deal of the night in her "library," which was on the third floor and featured two walls of mysteries and one of plant books. (She'd been collecting mysteries longer.) There she would sit in a large leather armchair under a full-spectrum light and either read novels or memorize plant lists. Before his arrest Frank had left for work before six in the morning. Now she would find him in the early hours gazing through his study window at the untidy sweep of Manhattan skyline. Or holding his closet door open and looking at his suits. Or stroking the ears of the Boston terrier, who was the only one of the dogs he really got along with.

Curiously, when Ruby went back to Hart Ridge–Tooner Academy in the fall, her schedule seemed to become more erratic as well. In the morning Pat dropped her off at the park across the street from the school, where the bad kids had always hung out. Then Ruby would show up at odd hours, saying that there weren't enough computers to go around, or that there had been a fire drill and she'd gotten cold. Once after Pat returned her to school for her last-period class, Frank asked irritably, "How much do we pay for her to go there? I want you to keep an eye on her." Without waiting for a reply, he said, "I'm going to prison. I still can't believe it, but I'm really going to prison."

Absently he asked Pat to take off her clothes, which she did. Then he brought up his "last supper" as a free man. Frank wanted to make love at all hours of the day, but he often got sidetracked and started to talk instead. "I don't know what to do," he said. He had to be at Allenwood on the following Tuesday, and Monday evening was not the best time to eat out. "I don't care how expensive the restaurant is; they're liable to serve food they couldn't get rid of over the weekend."

"How true," said Pat, lying naked in the same place she would be a week later, alone. Her pillow was unaccountably familiar; it was her head that held the strange future in it.

She offered to cook Julia Child's chicken in cream and port wine, Marcella Hazen's pasta with Bolognese sauce, or Eula

Mae Dore's yellow cake, each of which he had declared to be his favorite dish at one time or another. Better not to mention that she would miss the sex: its frequency, yes, its regularity, yes, yes, but also its continuing capacity to surprise. He would not see such a remark as a compliment. He would take it as a criticism of his present inaction or he'd remember it later and worry about her fidelity.

Still startlingly present and palpable, Frank made a face and shook his head so slightly the movement could have been involuntary. Whether this meant "No" or "Don't bother me, I'm thinking," Pat couldn't tell.

It occurred to her that Frank was behaving as he thought a "man" should under the circumstances. This struck her as funny, because she never thought of him as a "man," just as Frank. She idly wondered if she ever tried to behave like a "woman." No, she decided, definitely not.

The last weekend was an intense version of the days preceding it. Frank couldn't have slept at all, except for an occasional hour or two of wine-induced napping. He had always been single-minded, and now his focus seemed to be on consuming as much as possible before the deadline. After a midmorning shower on Saturday, he wandered into their bedroom, slapping the white flesh at his waist and saying, "I think I've put on twenty pounds in the last two weeks."

He was a tallish man, skinny and gangly most of his life, but he'd finally started to thicken through both the shoulders and the stomach. The tension in his voice did not express dissatisfaction over his weight, however. It reflected the intensity of his unconscious goal: to incorporate as much of this life into the only thing he would be allowed to take with him on Tuesday— his body.

He picked up the Chilean wine he'd left on Pat's dresser. "Veal, maybe," he said. "They keep veal calves in little cages, so I may not have the stomach for it later."

Pat wondered if he was serious.

"We could make it all," she suggested. "Julia, Eula Mae, the works."

"Yes," he said. "Yes, that's exactly what we'll do. And there's no reason to stop. Paella! I want Yorkshire pudding, too, so we'll have to have a roast. And fresh vegetables, lots of them. They will be scarce inside, I'm sure."

"Do you want to invite anyone else?" asked Pat.

Frank lay down, full length, on the bed. "The only person who will talk to me is the person who got me into this in the first place," he said.

"Who's that?" asked Pat, puzzled. He couldn't mean Neil, not after Neil had told him to leave him alone.

"Ellen Kloda," said Frank.

"Oh," said Pat. "That's right, the memo."

Frank closed his eyes. "You know she cried when I called her."

"Look," said Pat. "Why don't we give Oliver a try?" She could not really believe he was avoiding them. The three used to so-cialize a lot, considering they were grown-ups. They'd had din-ner every month or so. Oliver exuded charm. "Why don't we just see what he says?"

"I have left a dozen messages for that man," said Frank with-out opening his eyes. "Do you think maybe his dialing finger is broken?"

"Well," said Pat. "Stranger things have happened."

"Right," said Frank.

"What matters is that your family is going to be gathered around you," said Pat, deciding on the spot that she'd better get

Rose to come back from college. They were the ones who'd bought her that lime green VW Bug. Let her put it to good use.

By Monday evening the dogs had been banished to the basement, and every surface of the kitchen was covered with Cuisinarts, nesting bowls, cutting boards, colanders, and food of every texture and color. On the island alone were veal chops dredged in flour, strips of red, yellow, and green peppers, oysters in their brine, tomato halves inverted on a rack, a small bowl of freshly baked and processed bread crumbs, bunches of watercress, arugula, and parsley—and more, always more.

Pat tried to write down the various cooking times on a pad of paper by the phone, but when she asked Frank how long the paella would take, he said, "Who knows?" So she abandoned the idea of coordinating the dishes and simply carted them whenever they were finished to the huge trestle table in the dining room.

Ruby, who'd been shaking up her brain on the rides at Six Flags (she really was fearless), eventually showed up, saying, "Where's Rose?"

She was late, but Pat didn't care. "She'll be here soon."

Ruby's black eyes slid silently over the heaps of food.

Frank carried a crock of soup from the kitchen. "You've got to taste this," he said, his voice overloud for the room.

Pat dipped her spoon and made exaggerated slurping noises. (She didn't know when he'd added soup to the mix.)

"Tasty, isn't it," he bellowed. "A mob boss couldn't have a better send-off."

"Oh, Frank," said Pat, feeling the dishes to see which were still warm.

Rose at last showed up with a backseat full of impatiens that her class had just finished experimenting on.

"Isn't that nice," said Pat, although what she was going to do with a load of supermarket flowers like impatiens, she did not know. Maybe she could think of some experiments of her own.

The four of them sat as they always had, at the center of the very long dining room table. Frank and Pat were on one side, and Rose and Ruby on the other.

"How's school?" Pat asked Rose.

"Fine," said Rose, who used to be as chatty in her own way as Pat.

"You like your classes this semester?"

"Yes."

"The teachers are nice?"

"Yes."

"What's wrong with her?" demanded Frank. The words were somewhat loose, because of his drinking.

"Are you still getting along with your roommate?" asked Pat.

"Mom."

"For some reason my roommates kept freaking out on me," said Pat. "One tried to kill herself, and another left school and became a topless dancer."

"*What?*" said Frank.

"It wasn't my suggestion," said Pat.

There was a silence.

"Ruby seems to have a lot of assemblies this year," said Pat.

"Really," said Rose, with a long look at Ruby.

"Yup," said Ruby.

"I'm really going to miss you guys," said Frank, putting his head in his hands.

"I've got to tell you," said Pat. "I've been reading this suspense novel, and you wouldn't believe what happens. It's about this guy who manipulates the stock market out of revenge but ends up making a lot of money for himself. And he's a good guy. He's not a good bad guy among bad bad guys, who are all tricking each other. He's a *plain old* good guy, up against a *plain old* bad guy." She spoke faster and faster, and details started to fly: newspaper leaks, a change of clothes, a masked courier. "Don't you see!" she cried, her voice soaring. "This guy is a hero! You did something not so different, and they're sending you to prison for it!"

"People don't mind if the fix is in—as long as they're in on it," said Frank gloomily.

"It's not like you really hurt anyone," said Pat.

Ruby was staring at them with her silent and unblinking button eyes.

"You're going to be fine financially," said Frank. "Unless we're socked with a big civil judgment. Just don't go wild when I'm gone."

"I have to have my cellphone," said Ruby in a self-righteous, aggrieved tone.

"That's fine, just no castles in Spain." He popped the cork on another bottle of Montrachet. "Do you know that one out of every eleven American men will be imprisoned at some point in their lives? It's unbelievable. It's emasculating. What kind of society puts that many of its men in jail? The government may end up indicting everyone in the telecommunications industry. We may not have made the best business decisions at LinkAge, but we didn't do anything that unusual. I'm wondering how the American people will communicate once we're all in prison. The *post office*?" He laughed.

"I have to get back," said Rose, standing up.

"Don't you want some dessert?" asked Pat.

"No."

"No dessert?" said Frank.

Rose was adamant. "I've got a lab due tomorrow," she said, as if nothing they did could compare. On her way out, she said to Ruby, "Watch yourself, kid."

"I will," Ruby replied with uncharacteristic anxiety, leaning forward to stress her seriousness. Then she ran upstairs, the sound as quick and regular as the shuffling of cards.

When they were alone, Frank said to Pat, "I have to talk to you."

She tried to think of excuses for the girls. "About what?" she said, starting to clear the table.

"Whatever you do," said Frank, grabbing her arm, "don't sleep with that detective writer when I'm gone."

7

Pat was on guard against the obvious problems that could result from not having another adult around to talk to or have sex with. Because Frank had traveled frequently on business, consulting with his Swat Team, she was used to having dinners with a girl who said "I hate you" so often that you could almost believe it was true. Nor did Pat miss Frank when it was time to change a lightbulb out of her reach or grapple with a heavy bare-root oak leaf hydrangea; she had never gone to him for help with these things. She had always made most of the household decisions simply because he wasn't interested. And sleeping alone in a king-size bed was really no problem. You could always lie sideways. Plus there were mysteries piled up around her now—including Lemuel Samuel's.

Still, she detected subtle quandaries. It was hard to keep the house as it used to be. Frank had a few quirky but unyielding tastes—a stainless-steel kitchen, peeled shrimp at every cocktail party, a remote control for each electronic device. She used to give in without thinking. She didn't much care either way, and for Frank, these were signifiers of the good life. There was no point in arguing that sometimes people liked a change. Frank didn't. He'd got it in his head that stainless steel, shellfish, and remote control devices were classy. Just try to take such notions away.

She was not about to redo the kitchen, but losing the remote for the entertainment center did make her heart do a small backflip—"What will Frank think?"—before she realized a minute later that he wasn't going to be saying much about it in the near future. She also knew that Frank would have freaked out if he could see how she was letting his living room slowly fill with epiphytes and thrillers and *MAD* magazines from the sixties that she'd found on eBay. She even added a couple of occasional tables from a consignment store. Was she insulting him, letting him down, taking advantage of him, betraying him? Or was this efflorescence an unconscious attempt to muffle her loneliness? Maybe it didn't matter, either way. Pat wasn't obliged to follow his preferences while he was in jail; this was the twentieth century, after all. Well, actually, the twenty-first.

When she'd first dropped Frank off at Allenwood, she'd come away with an awful feeling of emptiness. But that was not surprising. So much of their life together had been defined by Frank and his job. Pat had met some other mothers through Rose and Ruby, but she'd never had the time to see a whole lot of them. Frank entertained frequently; that was part of the fun of working for him. The High Risk boys, of course, were particularly coddled. When members of the Swat Team were in town, Frank would take them out for elaborate dinners at LinkAge's expense. His favorites he would invite to the house.

It was time for Pat to get back to landscaping. She'd started to design other people's property not long after Ruby was born because she got tired of perpetually rearranging her own. What she needed now was to consider some bright, orderly colors, but she didn't exactly have any ongoing jobs, so she decided to check out some of her old work, i.e., the artificial wetland at the LinkAge building in Meadowlands Center that she'd had installed a year and a half ago. The project was a particularly important one for her. Too many of her previous jobs had been for friends or friends of friends—the sort of people who might end up coming to one of the Foys' parties. For these clients she was forced to lug around that missing canvas bag and waste endless extra hours negotiating plant lists. The profit margin was slim. Commercial projects, on the other hand, could be unsatisfactory in other ways. Landscaping ordinarily lies at the tail end of a development, when deadlines are near, budgets are tight, and tempers are short.

How wonderful, then, to be handed commercial landscaping work unrelated to any building construction. The construction in this case was long completed. In fact, it was the problem. As LinkAge expanded, management decided that they needed more parking, and they created it by simply filling in a good piece of the tidal swamp adjacent to the existing lot. Unfortunately this was legally defined as wetland and thus protected. If anyone had warned LinkAge about the problem—and several LGT people claimed to have done so—the company hadn't been listening. At first they ignored warnings from the EPA, unable to believe that anyone would want more of the reed-filled wasteland that already dominated the view from the turnpike. When the EPA persisted, LinkAge refused to re-create any of the trashy old terrain, but did promise to fashion at great expense an entirely new "bog" garden (to use the most modish term). Pat was charged with designing a half an acre of wetland with a panache that would symbolize LinkAge's vision, growth, and imagination.

Her employment was Frank's idea, of course; she hadn't even had to submit a proposal. He told Neil Culp and the rest of senior management that she "loved swamps." Pat laughed at first; Frank could be such a salesman. But the more she thought about his statement, the more she realized how true it was.

There is nothing clean or crisp about a swamp. Its slow breath can be fetid and rank. Prehistoric plants slither from the muck. Insects thicken the air. Gothic vines glower from damp trees. All is doom, gloom, miasma, scum, froth, decay, and death. Also life. Gooey ooze is where life starts to percolate; sputters become animate; breeding begins. Fertility is spongy, viscous, spermy. A swamp may be waste. It has a hundred ideas when only one is needed. But that one will crawl out and start to walk.

Not that LinkAge was ready for such a raw presentation. Pat tried, however, to move beyond the old-fashioned lily pond and hint at these paradoxes. To do so she opted for sheer lavishness. When the asphalt was broken up and carted away, she made sure a levee was left between the weedy, invasive reeds and the dear little pond dug with a backhoe. (What a madhouse that had been! Only the overseer spoke English, and he usually wasn't there. She might as well have been playing charades.) Then she supervised construction of a cedar boardwalk and the planting of a grove of black willow, black cherry, and black tupelo. Dozens of summer sweet, swamp rose, and serviceberry bushes followed, their fragrance strong and spicy; there were no stagnant vapors here. The flowers, too, were abundant—seven-foot Turk's-cap lilies, startlingly spherical globeflowers, and giant swamp mallows (of course).

The boardwalk began at the outer limits of the original parking lot, where a stone bench sat amid thick stands of cardinal flowers and royal ferns. From this decorative spot, you could gaze on the star of the garden, Pat's environmental coup, a plant so persnickety it was in danger of disappearing: the swamp pink. It needed ground that was saturated but not flooded, sunlight that was plentiful but not too hot, and soil that was rich but not overly so, since then other, stronger plants would crowd it out. Sometimes—only in years when conditions were right—it would produce a single flower, lasting for no longer than a week. This flower would sit at a slight tilt, ingratiatingly, but in truth it wasn't much. It looked like a bottlebrush and was the creepily intimate pink of a cat's tongue. It turned Pat's bog garden into a living museum, though. She spent thousands of dollars on seedlings at a specialty nursery near New Hope, Pennsylvania, and the garden and its living treasure were featured prominently in the year's (otherwise misleading) report to the stockholders.

Although Pat shrank from returning to LinkAge property, she was eager to learn how her bog garden was faring. She still knew where she could find the pass she'd been issued during the landscaping. But when she arrived at Meadowlands Center, the guard at the gate told her the pass had expired.

"Really," said Pat, taking it back through the car window and then turning it over a couple of times. There was a photo of her looking like a psycho, also her name and title, Special Projects Director. "I don't see any expiration date."

"That's the old-style pass. We don't use those anymore. Not since the bankruptcy."

"But you know me," she said.

"Well," said the guard, an old man she'd greeted pleasantly one hundred and fifty times, "I might, and I might not. But I can't let you in."

Pat thought of Ginny's story "The Red Door." She could have come up with innumerable ways to get past this guard if she hadn't already tipped her hand. She glanced in the direction of her wetland. All you could see in any direction was reeds. Evidently her plantings were still too young to be visible from the road. It wasn't possible to take a car around, but if necessary she might be able to sneak around the perimeter on foot.

Pat's bright smile did not waver through this ticker tape of thoughts. "I think you'd better call then," she said. Who did she still know at LinkAge? "I'm here to see Ellen Kloda."

"She has to come and get you," he said.

"Okay," said Pat, unfazed.

"You're going to have to move."

Pat awkwardly maneuvered the Touareg to the side to wait. Soon another car pulled up, a green Land Rover like Oliver Gregoire's. Yes! There he was behind the wheel! He'd always had a gentle silhouette. How perfect that there should be at last a real accidental meeting, as opposed to the one he'd orchestrated at the flower show.

Pat suddenly remembered all the little gifts Oliver had brought her when he came to dinner. A glass bottle in the shape of a tulip blossom. A recording of the Duke Ellington music from *Anatomy of a Murder*. And on the very first evening he came to visit, a small photography book that he said was so grisly he had to apologize for it. Pictured were the poisonous parts of plants: a glistening wink from some purplish black belladonna berries, a flesh-crawlingly hairy henbane leaf, a cluster of spiky red fruit from the castor bean, each harboring enough ricin to kill all the High Risk boys at once.

But he couldn't resist the book, he said; it was so beautiful. "Yes," said Pat quietly. It was one of the best presents she'd ever got, and she'd never met this man before. Funny, how she'd taken his generosity for granted. All the wining and dining the Foys had done in return was just throwing around LinkAge money.

Oliver had barely started working at LGT when Frank made it clear that he preferred him to the High Risk boys he'd been palling around with. Maybe Frank was tired of clones. Maybe he was tired of the increasingly panicked agitation in the Link-Age accounting department. His relationship with Oliver had had no depth, clearly. Yet even if this had been pointed out to the Foys at one of their dinners, they wouldn't have cared. Why should they disapprove of corporate maneuvering? So what if they hadn't known him long—if he might not stick with them through thick and thin? Frank believed in instantaneous sympathies, the sanctity of ambition, and the unending rise of the stock market.

Pat lowered the window, calling out excitedly, "Oliver! Over here! Oliver!" She waved briskly, then started to open the car door. Before she could get out, he was through the gate. Had he seen her? Judging by the fast pace at which he bolted to the building, he must have. Pat could not believe her eyes.

Once Ellen okayed her entry, Pat met her at the far end of the parking lot, which was less than half full thanks to layoffs. (LinkAge had not needed the additional space, after all.) At first when Pat got out of the car she thought she'd mistaken the place because all she could see was reeds. Then she realized that these cunning, indestructible plants had hopped the levee and taken over the pond, the garden, the boardwalk, everything.

"It's too bad, isn't it?" said Ellen. "All your beautiful flowers. I guess there was no money for upkeep."

Ellen was small and slim with chipmunk cheeks and a page-boy so restrained it was hard to tell whether it was intentional. Her voice was as smooth as lukewarm tea.

"Where are the *tupelos*?" said Pat, still trying to compare what she was seeing with what she had planted. There seemed to be a couple of swamp pinks left. Maybe they weren't as fragile as they were reputed to be.

Ellen shook her head. "How's Frank?" she asked.

"Fine," said Pat. When this rang sourly in her ears, she added, "His roommate is from Pittsburgh, Pennsylvania." Oh, God. She sounded as if she were pretending he was away at college, like Rose. So what should she have said—*cell mate*?

"Everyone was surprised when Frank had to go to jail," said Ellen, still gazing into the reeds.

"Oh, dear," said Pat.

"Lots of people complain about stuff," said Ellen. "But it's nothing compared to going to jail."

"What do they complain about?"

"Oh, you know. The pension plan."

"What do you mean?"

"I guess it was wiped out."

"But that doesn't make any sense," said Pat. "The company is still here." She gestured at the very solid steel and glass building behind them.

"We might get a few cents on the dollar when the reorganization is through," said Ellen.

"I never thought," said Pat. "I'm so sorry."

"Actually," said Ellen quickly, "I lost a deposit I'd put down on a summer cabin."

"How much?" asked Pat.

Ellen shook her head.

"How much?" asked Pat again.

"Ten thousand."

It was sad to realize that neither she nor Frank had liked this decent woman as much as they'd liked Oliver. Pat was still looking at Ellen when she had a terrible thought. She tottered, grabbed out for Ellen's arm, and failed to reach it.

"Are you all right?" asked Ellen.

"My goodness, yes," said Pat, righting herself. "Well, it's time to go, isn't it?" She smiled gamely at the one LinkAge employee who would speak to her, then escaped to her car, where she showily arranged herself with a lift of the shoulders and a perky wave.

What a fool she had been to mistake the smooth dexterity of Oliver's ambition for any kind of emotional connection. Not that it mattered. The thought that had just struck her, that had struck her so hard that she actually lost her balance, was far worse than any brush-off Oliver could have come up with.

Frank had liked Oliver. He'd wanted him to succeed. Pat had always known that. No matter what Frank said—or what he couldn't bear to admit to himself—he'd refrained from giving Oliver the job in High Risk because he was protecting him. Frank really was a kind man. If Frank had been shielding Oliver, then Frank knew that what he was doing was liable to get Oliver into trouble. It didn't matter what Frank said later. He knew that he'd gone too far.

at was planting bulbs on the side slope of the lawn. She loved the fall. She loved all the seasons, really, but she especially enjoyed whatever was at hand, and right now it was October. The still-green grass was papered with freshly fallen, sweet-smelling yellow leaves. Hart Ridge turned gold in the autumn. By mid-October the sugar maples, lindens, tulip trees, chestnut oaks, pignut hickories, cherries, sassafras, witch hazels, and black birches were an intense amalgam of honey and saffron and topaz, in color combinations that you couldn't quite name. Even the light was yellow and thick—and slanted, producing a glut of tinted shadow.

How different this was from the spring, such a simple season, with its clear colors and clear shapes. Hart Ridge was full of azalea bushes that in April sprouted crimson and magenta blossoms as if ripped from the jugular. Hard reds splashed loudly in front of the car wash, behind the bus shelter, beside the Dumpster in the CVS parking lot as if crying "We're alive, we're alive!" until the innocuous green smudge of foliage closed up around them. Today's few autumnal reds, which peeked out from a limited number of ornamental bushes and dwarf trees, were mottled, muted, slightly frayed. Later the last of the oaks would burst briefly into scarlet, but they would be so quickly overtaken by brown that they would seem to gasp, "Oh, sweet death, sweet death . . ."

Yesterday she had finally emptied and thrown away the dozens of wine bottles in the kitchen. At first she'd kept them out of respect for Frank—to show herself that she was as distraught as he was. But the bottles created an atmosphere that might have been a bit too disturbed for a middle schooler, even Ruby. It would probably have been better if Pat drank more. Then she would have finished off a bottle or two already.

Last night she hadn't been able to sleep (as usual), so she'd wrapped two hundred purple crocus bulbs in cut-up chicken wire, several at a time, to protect them from squirrels. Then she wrapped four hundred creamy-white-striped crocus bulbs. Eventually they filled two galvanized steel tubs on the kitchen counter. When she popped downstairs this morning, as animated as if she no longer had any need for sleep at all, Ruby asked tensely, "What are those things in cages?"

Cages! As Pat pierced the turf with her bulbing trowel, and scraped at clay, and pried at rocks, she could not stop thinking about Frank and their past together.

Rose celebrated her twelfth birthday right before LinkAge bought LGT. It was Frank's job to clean up the books in preparation for the sale. Already, he'd started to make real money. So they gave in to Rose's request for a party at a hotel out on Route 17: plush red carpet, fountain in the lobby, fake stone in the large dim catacomb of lobby, restaurant, and bar. Because Frank probably wouldn't get off work in time to drive a second car, Pat hired a white limo to accommodate all the young guests.

"Cellular" phones were rare back then, and although Frank scoffed at the cancer risk, they had a dangerous aura, like the cigarettes Pat still occasionally snuck. She tended to hold her new pocket-size cellphone a few inches away from her head, so as not to encourage the growth of brain tumors. When Frank called the first time, it was hard for either of them to hear. Pat was more interested in keeping the girls in their seats, anyway; they were whirling and squealing and poking and yelling to passersby, "I know where you were last night!" She didn't want anyone to smack the driver in the head, causing him to veer sharply, hit a bread truck, and set off a series of accidents up and down the highway. Besides, all Frank had to say at that point was that he was going to be later than expected.

What great fun it had been: Pat Foy, aka Mallow, trot-trotting up and down the red wall-to-wall carpeting of a tacky New Jersey hotel (and let's face it, it was really tacky) in gold ankle-strap sandals with four-inch heels, the sort of sandals that a danger-ous noir heroine might have worn at one time but were now rou-tine attire for New Jersey matrons who were indistinguishable from their overpriced and overlandscaped suburban homes. (Overlandscaped, definitely, although Pat benefited from this trend.)

She had reserved two hotel suites, one across from the other. Rose and her nine guests disappeared into one to drop off their bags. Pat and Ruby waited in the other, Pat alert for unexpected loud noises, Ruby peeking out occasionally to hiss, "What are they *doing*?"

Pat heard a thump, which might have just been a duffel bag thrown down, but as she stood up to investigate, her phone rang.

"The trouble is that we can't show all these uncollected receivables," said Frank without preamble.

"Really," said Pat, carefully holding the phone away from her head.

Frank could tell she wasn't listening. "The gum ashtray companies," he said impatiently. "And the astrologers. And the pornographers." Those that LGT resold their telephone time to, in other words. "All those bad debts will give LinkAge the wrong impression. They won't want to go through with the purchase, and that would be a mistake for everyone."

Another thump.

"I'm sure you'll figure it out," said Pat.

"I won't be too much longer. I'm going to use my LGT time machine." He was referring to postdating invoices or something equally dull, but it did sound a bit as if he were going to get into a time machine and meet her as she entered the hotel.

"Well, we're fine here." She could hear the girls running up and down the hall outside the room.

"You should see Dominic," said Frank, lowering his voice. "He's really into this. One of the High Risk boys asked him how he should describe the promissory notes, and Dominic told him if he repeated any numbers to LinkAge, he'd throw him out the fucking window." Frank laughed. "He'd do it, too. He told me he thought he was having a heart attack, and I said he had to have it later."

This time Pat joined in the laughter, picturing Dominic straightening up in mid-attack. *He'd do it, too.*

The girls fit into the elevator only after a lot of pushing and squealing and general percolating. Little Ruby stood with exaggerated compactness, back and head against the wall, palms flat out beside her. The rest of them were like a shook-up soda can, ready to blow. They swarmed through the lobby to the restaurant, which was everything you'd expect: chandeliers like pirates' treasure, a dessert cart in one corner, a grand piano in another. The girls sat at two large semicircular red leather banquettes. One kid or other was always kneeling up on the seat in order to speak to the adjacent table. Pat ordered a martini and took out a lipstick mirror, which was immediately shanghaied.

Her phone rang. "I swear, it won't be much longer," said Frank. "We're close, we're real close. Neil said that uncollectible debt can't be recorded as thirty-three million. He said it's got to get down to three. We're at about six now."

"Six million dollars?" said Pat. "That's a lot of . . ." She glanced around at the girls squabbling over her mirror. She could hardly finish up with ". . . phone sex for hire," so instead she said, ". . . phone cards. And horoscope readings!"

Rose's voice piped up above the others: "Watch it. You can get *addicted* to lip balm."

"Woodstock was pretty tame at first, too," said Pat, "so I've got my eye on them. I think we're safe as long as the medical supplies hold out."

"Love you," said Frank.

"Love you," said Pat—to the phone, to her daughters, to the table at large, to the shuttered piano, to the tiered desserts, to the glittering chandeliers. And later, after all the corridors were explored and all the beds were jumped on and all the pillows were rearranged and all the pay-per-view movies were quarreled over, Pat was still riding high across the hall in her suite, her body deliciously spent, her mind soaring. Ruby was asleep in the bedroom, and Pat was spread out on the red velvet couch looking at her gold film noir sandals propped up on the matching red velvet hassock, when in walked Frank with a bottle of champagne. "Room service is over," he said, sounding giddy with fatigue. "But the bar was still open. Let me sit for a moment."

She stretched and crooked her arms behind her head.

"I had some of the High Risk boys call all the scumbags we could find phone numbers for, whether they'd gone through Chapter Seven or not. We told them if they didn't send out a FedEx letter today we were going to block all their calls at the switching point. That's not actually possible: We'd have to shut down a whole section of the operation, but they don't know that. They don't know a thing about the industry, the leeches." By now Frank had the cork out, and he took a long drink directly from the bottle.

"How funny, that that would work," said Pat, twisting a little in place. The warmth that she'd been feeling earlier had shot all through her. Soon they would be making love. Frank never could resist a hotel room.

"It worked well enough," said Frank, taking another long gulp. "I'd drop dead on the spot if any of those letters had valid checks in them. But all we needed were FedEx tracking numbers. Then we could record the bills as paid."

Pat drank, too. All these years later, as she planted the crocus bulbs, she could still recall the cool glassy lip of the champagne bottle in her mouth.

Her work on the side slope was mechanical: pierce turf, wriggle trowel, embed wire ball, smooth earth. But her progress was slow. The clay was cold and hard. Despite her black canvas

Mary Janes, she was intensely aware of her feet folded back toward the house and her heels pressed up against her bottom. She could feel an odd chilly texture of pebble, acorn, and twig through her jeans. And although she was wearing her goatskin gardening gloves, ghostly impressions of struggling with the trowel, or twisting and pressing the wire, remained in her palms.

LinkAge had barely glanced at the LGT books, either before or after the purchase. Oversight of their individual acquisitions was minimal. The stock price was not affected by such trivialities, and LinkAge was not interested in the tedious process of coordinating the back office systems. When Frank followed Neil to LinkAge headquarters in the Meadowlands, they applied their talents to a larger scale, but the crazy deadlines continued. The LinkAge financial year ended with the calendar year, so for the next four years the Foys did not celebrate New Year's Eve. Such festivities were for ordinary folk, who did not expect sacrifices—or greatness—of themselves. The Foys would schedule a suitably sumptuous trip during the first week in January.

Frank expected nothing different for the millennium. Neil Culp ended up quitting a month later, but no one had any inkling of it at the time. The debt, however, was particularly recalcitrant that year. (LinkAge was more concerned about the debt they owed than the debts they couldn't collect on, as LGT had been.) Frank could not leave for West Palm Beach on January 4 as scheduled. He told Pat that she and the kids should go without him and he'd join them later, but she nixed that idea; she would miss him too much. Besides, the extra fees the postponement entailed were part of the cost of earning all the money that he did. They decided to go in mid-January, when the financials were sure to be resolved. Pat bought Frank new snorkeling gear and three Hawaiian shirts, one with a bird of paradise pattern. She hid them in his suitcase as she packed.

The mid-month deadline came and went. "There's only so much the High Risk boys can do with revenue," said Frank, tying his blue-and-gold-striped tie the next morning. "They've put their fingers on every soft spot they can find. But don't worry. Neil will figure it out, and then we'll just hop on a plane at the last minute."

Pat kept the suitcases packed and turned the uncertainty of their departure into a guessing game for the girls. "Whoever comes the closest gets a chocolate orange," she said, wielding a glue gun. (They were way behind on their Christmas crafts.)

It was Pat herself who won when Frank called Friday of that week and said, "Neil's devised contracts that transfer the debt from the corporate books to the books of individual acquisitions like LGT. He's such a genius. The idea is simple, but the execution is exquisite. Get us some tickets for tonight. We can meet at the airport."

"You think this is really it?"

"Yes," said Frank. "We've finally got it."

When he called again, Pat was in the first-class lounge with a martini, and the girls were each sipping a Shirley Temple, which they'd ordered without batting an eye, although Pat had no idea where they'd heard of one. At their feet were three matching leather shoulder bags that looked as if they could be diplomatic pouches.

"Is there a later flight?" said Frank. "We've run into a . . . bit of a . . . snag with the auditors."

"Maybe you could run onto the plane at the last moment," suggested Pat. "That's always fun."

"Okay," said Frank. "You go ahead and board. If I don't make that flight, I'll be on the next one."

It shouldn't have worked, but it did. Frank took a different airline and joined them at the West Palm airport half an hour after they arrived. The car that Frank had called from the plane was waiting for them. As always, Florida was like a postcard come to life: hard, glossy, lukewarm, the night sky decorated with interesting coconut palm silhouettes.

"Oh, it was wild," said Frank in the car. "No one can read the books but Neil at this point. Some of it has to be taken on faith. Believe it or not, we ended up locking the door. Neil told a couple of the High Risk boys to bar the door until the auditors signed off."

"You're kidding."

"They were going to sign off, anyway. They had no choice. They couldn't risk losing our business. If they were comfortable making waves, they wouldn't have become auditors. But they appreciated the theater."

Pat had not wanted to jinx Frank's arrival by making a hotel reservation, so, in a rush of exhausted exultation, they simply stopped at the first motel they saw. It was a squat series of boxes next to the highway. The girls waited with the driver while Pat followed Frank inside carrying his wallet, which he'd left on the seat. A ceiling fan sliced the air, a wire rack promised cheesy delights. The clerk was apologetic. The only room available was a double for a thousand dollars—clearly a rip-off of monumental proportions. Frank leaned across the counter, looked the clerk in the eye, and said, "I was looking for something much, much more expensive." It was hilarious. It was also, come to think of it, true.

Two weeks later, LinkAge was forced to issue a major financial restatement.

If Pat had counted right, she was on her two hundred and ninety-eighth, two hundred and ninety-ninth, and three hundredth bulb. She went inside, washed her hands thoroughly in the mudroom sink with her Gardener's Friend, and sat down and wrote a note to Ellen Kloda on one of her sunflower cards. Before sealing it, she added a check for ten thousand dollars.

To get to Allenwood Federal Correctional Complex you drive west from Hart Ridge through the heavily screened and decorated suburbs of the New York metropolitan area, past rows and rows of trees being strangled slowly by Asiatic bittersweet vines, and into a rural corridor of towns like Lake Hopatcong, once a little resort where Frank's family had been proud to go for two weeks every summer and now a mix of expensive summer houses and ramshackle starter homes for people who commute to Morristown. New Jersey turns into Pennsylvania at the raffish Poconos, where fraudulent development left a scrim of pink champagne and pink bathtubs. Keep going and dairy farms give way to the Appalachian Mountains. Amid a rolling feast of forest that was gorgeous even on this black and white day were several prisons, a clutter of small but valiantly kept-up houses, a few trailers and shacks, and a scattering of motels more dismal than the one in Florida. "TV" bragged one sign, and more meanly, "American owned."

Ruby kept her eyes fixed out the window the whole trip,

headphones from her CD player stopping up her ears. She was looking rather tarty, if truth be told, in her magenta lipstick, tight bright pink top, rolled up painter pants, and three-inch heels. Until recently she had been a tomboy, and she had always thought she could do anything, maybe because she was able to climb trees and swim lakes and make caterpillars do her bidding while other girls hung back and watched.

Her mind was as unfathomably twisty as the inside of a shell. Rose, who was very smart, much smarter than Pat, had never gone through a "code" phase. But after Pat took Frank to Allenwood, Ruby started using a code that was as obvious—and confusing—as pig Latin. She doubled up her responses, first saying the socially acceptable, then "slash," and finally what she really thought—or wanted people to assume she thought. Pat got lost somewhere way back.

When Pat got an envelope from the Bureau of Prisons, Ruby said, "Are they after you, too?" And when it turned out to be a form advising them that inmate Frank Foy had submitted Pat's name on his list of approved callers, Ruby said, "It will be nice to talk to him slash oh my God."

In the Touareg, on the way to Allenwood, Pat reached over and squeezed her daughter's knee as she always did when struck with a memory, and Ruby jabbed her back, hard, with her elbow, which was probably due to surprise. Route 78, of course, wasn't the best place to be jabbed, because here she was alone with Ruby—and hundreds of cars, trucks, and SUVs ready to kill them both after an instant of her inattention. Still, the intense physicality of her daughter's reaction reassured Pat that she was still a tomboy under all that fabulous tawdriness. Evidently Ruby felt she needed a different costume for her adventures now. "Do your friends dress like that, honey?" asked Pat.

"Like what?" said Ruby, one of her earpieces having shaken loose in the struggle.

"Oh, you know, like a prostitute."

"How colorful," said Ruby, straightening up with dignity. *"Slash disgusting."*

Up in the country, where poverty must lead to problems with wayward children, Pat had once noticed a youthfully dressed man give Ruby a measuring eye. It was annoying, because he was clearly of the helping professions, and he must have thought she was "at risk." Pat wanted very much to say that Ruby was most at risk from men like him, but she had to force all this information into one steely look.

The handsome, locally quarried stone pillars that marked the entryway to the prison camp loomed ahead. There were no gun turrets, no enveloping spirals of barbed wire. A month ago, when she'd been dropping Frank off, they'd snacked on black caviar, red grapes, and Bucheron cheese in the visitors' parking lot until an official in a blue suit rapped on the car window and said, "We were wondering what you were doing here." She had been quite nice, as Pat pointed out a dozen times, but the picnic took on a pathetic, tattered air, and Frank ended up reporting to the prison door fifteen minutes before it was absolutely necessary.

There had been no other cars in the parking lot that time. Now that it was visitors' day, there were many, and Pat noted uneasily that they were mostly cheap American sedans. Frank probably did stand out a little inside. A prison population, even here, was not going to be confined to accountants and bankers and disbarred lawyers, with a couple of doctors convicted of Medicare fraud thrown in for diversity. That would have been boring, anyway.

Pat took Ruby's hand as they walked up the bright white steps, and she was pleased when Ruby, instead of pulling away, squeezed her fingers so hard they hurt. Pat tried to remember a period of her life when she'd been as close-mouthed as her daughter had become lately, but she couldn't. Even when Pat's father had run off with the woman from the Chamber of Commerce, a subject that was actively discouraged in conversation, the family had found plenty of other things to talk about, maybe even more than usual. A rush of words was a good way to wash an event clean.

The guard who let them into the tiny glass foyer looked normal, too muscly maybe, but not at all sadistic. Pat was admittedly a bit nervous. Frank had told her to bring a hundred dollars in small bills for the vending machines, so she'd brought an assortment in a transparent cosmetic case, the only type of purse allowed in the visiting room. But the idea of gourmand Frank eating food from a vending machine was too ridiculous. (Jelly Bellys? Tootsie Rolls? A minuscule bag of oversalted, underflavored potato chips? Never.) So Pat had also put five hundreds in her bra, because you never knew what nefarious plots were afoot in prison and she thought that the mention of a hundred dollars might be code for "Bring me some real money."

The guard showed no inclination to search her. His lip did curl up at the corner when he talked, but you couldn't really call it a sneer. Fortunately Pat had never been a person who embarrassed easily. "Great. Perfect," she said several times in her sweeping soprano.

The people in the visitors' room looked normal, like any crowd at a bus station. Well, not quite normal. In every group was a man wearing khaki pants and a gray sweatshirt. Also, the proportions of the room were odd. Usually a room this size would have higher ceilings. Frank looked squashed when he appeared suddenly in the doorway, dressed like all the other inmates. The weight he'd gained before going to prison had disappeared. He was as skinny as he'd been in his twenties. In his forties he had earned a certain gravitas—not the killjoy sort, but the sort that comes naturally with age and comfortable living and unquestioned authority. That was gone now. His new leanness made him look older and frailer, and his eyes seemed to have sunk back a little in his head. As he moved toward his family, his cheap tennis shoes splayed out awkwardly. They might have been designed for something straighter and narrower than human feet.

As Pat embraced him, her face flushed, her pulse raced. The combination of strangeness and familiarity left her breathless. He didn't even look like himself. Yet she knew him through and through. She could reach in and touch his heart. It would be even easier now that he was smaller. Was that an age spot on his hand? Incredible.

As Frank tried to hug Ruby, who remained stiff and stricken, Pat looked over her shoulder to flash the guard at the desk a big smile. "What's he like?" she asked Frank in a low voice.

Frank shrugged. "He's okay," he said.

"You hear all these things about prison guards."

"Really, he's okay," he said. "Why don't you sit down."

"Happy Thanksgiving!" she said, perched on the molded plastic chair. She told Frank he was looking good, a little white lie. Because he had been defined by his decisive and sometimes overbearing energy, it was difficult to see him so restrained, so skinny, so watchful.

"So how's Winky?" he asked. Ruby had been given Winky as a puppy years before.

"Good," she said briefly.

Pat decided not to mention that Ruby's social studies teacher had called yesterday to find out why she was missing so much school.

"It's not bad here," said Frank. Then he attempted more jauntiness, maybe even irony: "Yesterday we had apples."

"How nice!" cried Pat. "I love apples! You know that the Forbidden Fruit was a fig, not an apple!"

"Sometimes I wish you were in here with me," said Frank.

"That's so sweet," said Pat.

"I don't know why you shouldn't be," said Frank, still smiling. "You're the one who's still reaping the rewards of my evil behavior."

"Oh, wow," said Pat, too startled to know what to say.

"*Daddy*—" said Ruby intensely.

"What, honey?"

When Ruby did not seem able to elaborate, Pat jumped in to say, looking down at the bright linen-white tiles, "I have never seen a floor glow the way this one does."

"An inmate buffs it every day," said Frank.

"Oh," said Pat.

It was better to ignore his flash of maliciousness about her incarceration. He had never before been anything worse than callous. Or obtuse. Oh, well, it was no wonder, considering all he'd been through. She smiled even harder. She wanted to reassure him with her own greater calm, the way she would one of the dogs. She knew she could pat him without being bitten. His weapons could not be fully unsheathed here, maybe they'd even shrunk with the weight he'd lost. Yet fear lurked behind this calm of hers, making it brittle. She was afraid for both of them—for Ruby, too—afraid that he might now possess a despair so great Pat would be incapable of divining the magic words to dispel it and he would say or do something that might never be undone.

Then he said, "It's wonderful to see you both," and of course he meant it—truly—anyone could see that. What could she have been thinking? But the visit was going to go on for *hours,* and she was exhausted already.

"Did you remember the cash?" he asked.

Pat lifted the see-through cosmetic case with its furled bills.

"Let's eat," he said with an uncharacteristically greedy gleam in his eye. Okay, he'd been greedy in the past. That, after all, was partly why he was in prison. He had never been greedy over petty matters, though. No matter how aggressive a driver Frank was, he wouldn't fight over a parking space. He would dismiss anyone who did, saying, "I guess he's too weak to walk a step or two."

But there was undisguised longing in his voice when he said, "We'll start with chicken wings." Evidently his request for cash for the vending machines had been completely straightforward.

Still, Pat had never heard of getting chicken wings in a vending machine. Self-consciously she looked around the room. A number of people did seem to be eating with great relish.

"Oh, I've been looking forward to this," said Frank. "You know some inmates never have visitors, so they never get to eat anything but prison food."

"Chicken wings," repeated Pat. "Do you want to be the one to get them?"

"I can't," said Frank, sitting on his hands. "It's against the rules."

So Pat gathered herself up and obediently strode off to one of the tall gray machines. There were the wings, in little plastic bags, slot after slot after slot of them, along with pizza and cheeseburgers and "beef steak," all for six dollars a piece. With the help of a chatty Ecuadorean woman in a white drawstring blouse, she microwaved one of the packages while looking over her shoulder at her family and once even archly waving. Ruby and Frank were not speaking to each other.

"Don't you want any?" asked Frank when she returned with only the one serving.

"Maybe later," she said.

He wasn't paying attention. He fell upon the chicken wings with little scrabbly motions of lips and fingers, which got shiny with grease; his age spot danced. Pat felt Ruby trying to catch her eye, but Pat couldn't let her do it; she was afraid of what might be written plainly across their faces.

"When Alice Paul was in prison, she organized a hunger strike," said Ruby.

Frank broke off sucking long enough to say, "Who?" His eyes flicked between his wife and his daughter, his face fell, and he abruptly dropped what was left of the wings into the packaging on his lap.

There was an embarrassed silence.

Then Pat said, "I wouldn't be any good at a hunger strike. And don't those wings look tasty! I think I'll have some, after all."

They were awful, of course, stringy and off in the way that chicken heated in a microwave always is, but there did not seem to be as much meat as sauce, which had a certain tang to it. Plus, of course, Pat hadn't eaten since breakfast. So she really wasn't insincere when she said, "My, yes, Ruby, you should try some," although she knew she may have *sounded* so, because of the way her voice swooped and soared.

Considering Frank had asked Pat to bring a hundred dollars,

he must have expected her to buy a lot of these tiny meals, at least a dozen. That would be four apiece. But he continued to ignore the chicken wings in his lap.

"You have to have a real Thanksgiving dinner," he said, as if to obliterate the wings' existence.

"That sounds good," said Pat. "But we're happy to be here with you."

"Stop near Camelback on your way home."

"That's an idea," she said.

"The inn there isn't bad," he said peevishly, as if his taste had been questioned. "They had rather good rémoulade if I remember. No! Don't go there. Drive down to Lancaster. There's a fabulous five-star restaurant among the Amish there. Remember? Go out and get your cellphone and see if you can still get reservations. I wish I could speak to them. I'm sure I could get you a table."

"I think I'll just get some more of these delicious wings," Pat chirped. Clearly she was going to have to do a very good job of pretending to like them, if she wanted Frank to pick up his again.

"Give me a moment, and I'll remember the name," he said.

"Are you sure you don't want any, Ruby?"

"*Daddy*—" she said, sounding strangled.

At the vending machine Pat wondered if she really had to get another package of those awful wings or if she could switch to another, no less unappetizing-looking food, like the "beef steak." Better to stick with the wings, she figured.

And it worked. Oh, he knew she was putting on a show, but so what? Shows work because performers and audience members all want them to. The audience cries out to be tricked. As Pat delved into her next package of wings with dogged cheerfulness, Frank finally went back to the last of his own and asked for pizza. Ruby frowned and again said, *"Daddy—"*

"Yes?" said Frank.

Whatever she'd been about to say she changed to "I don't know how you can eat that stuff," but neither Pat nor Frank paid much attention. The show had prevailed, so Ruby's words, however cutting, must have been indicative of her own misery rather than any acknowledged truth.

When Pat returned with the pizza, she said, "I caught a glimpse of Oliver the other day. Why, exactly, didn't you promote him?"

Frank's agitation returned. "Is he still angry at me? After I kept him out of that mess? My problem was, I wasn't a big enough criminal."

Pat could not see the logic behind the conjoining of those two ideas—the protection of Oliver with the insignificance of the crimes. Probably Frank thought his behavior was "wrong" in the way he'd know it was "wrong" to ski a trail that had been posted. It's the sort of thing you regret only if it fails. You can get down a dangerous trail—and then scoff at why it had been closed at all. You can continue to inflate your earnings—and then scoff at the rules that try to put a brake on a market that goes up as surely as a flood tide. You don't necessarily lose your way and put would-be rescuers in the hospital. You don't necessarily get caught and end up impoverishing your secretary.

"I ran into Ellen, too," said Pat.

"You know that she cried when I called her," said Frank.

Pat did not point out the many times Frank had already mentioned this. Instead she said, "Wouldn't it be nice to help her out in some way?" There was no point in telling him that she'd already sent a check; it would only upset him.

"Oh, yes," said Frank. "That's a great idea. Do something for Ellen. It wasn't her fault."

"Whose fault was it?" asked Ruby in a small voice.

"I don't know who was worse, Riley or Neil," said Frank. "In the two years before LinkAge went bankrupt, Riley Gibbs made seventy-eight million dollars. Neil Culp made thirty-nine million. And that isn't counting their unsecured loans. The shareholders lost a hundred and forty billion dollars. It was all rigged."

"One hundred and forty billion," Pat repeated slowly.

"I was a moron," said Frank. "They used me just the way they used everybody. The first quarter that LinkAge's numbers were bad, word came down from Gibbs: The Swat Team was to fly coach and stay in budget motels. Then he turned around and bought himself a horse farm in Hunterdon County. I thought Neil was so great, but he would do anything for Gibbs because whatever Gibbs got, Neil got half. I'm surprised he didn't get a half a horse farm."

"Why aren't they in jail?" asked Ruby.

"Too rich, I guess," said Frank. "Maybe if I'd worked harder and made more money, I'd have gotten off, too."

"Why didn't you do something about it before you got put in jail?" Ruby persisted.

"Maybe the government didn't have enough evidence," said Pat quickly. "It isn't always possible to change everything that's wrong."

"I don't see why," said Ruby, her eyes narrow and her lips tight.

"What shall we have next?" said Pat. "A cheeseburger?"

"Pizza for me," said Frank.

Pat came back with just the pizza, saying, "I changed my mind at the last minute."

Later, on their way out, as they stepped gingerly down the concrete steps into the wide-open world, Pat noticed tears streaming down Ruby's face. She tried to put an arm around her shoulders. But Ruby shrugged her off, saying, "Why were you such a pig in there? Maybe if you could stop stuffing your face for two minutes in a row, people like Neil Culp wouldn't get away with everything."

Pat had been rereading Lemuel Samuel's books for a while. She was surprised at how crude they seemed now; like early Technicolor, their effects were lurid and clumsy and heavy-handed. Bud Caddy actually cuts off a guy's foot in *The Fleabag Massacre* and leaves it lying in the road. But the roughness was the point. *Mallow* was the smoothest and most sentimental of the books, also the most lucrative. Pat had saved it for last, hoping to find clues about who she was. Instead she found the same joy present in all the books. You might mistake it for anger or righteousness or knight errantry. Bud Caddy often seemed to. But at the core of his every thought and action was a very American and very physical joy—in excess, in ferocity, in endurance. Halfway through *Mallow*, Pat decided she needed a drink. It was better that than look for a fight, which she would not have known how to do for fun, anyway.

Because she had thrown away all the half-full wine bottles, she decided to pick up a nice burgundy at the liquor store. She slipped on a pair of skintight black pants and a pair of sunglasses so narrow that they would have let in tons of light, had there been any on this gray day. Reconnoitering the stairway wasn't too hard, because there was a window at each landing, but she could hardly see as she picked her way across the shadowy kitchen.

"So what's with the shades?"

"My goodness!" cried Pat, her voice soaring.

At first she thought Ruby was referring to the shades on the kitchen windows, which had been drawn for some no doubt nefarious reason. She was sitting in the dark, possibly on some kind of drug that made the pupil take over the iris and thus be more sensitive to light. Hadn't there been a drug like that? Pat couldn't remember. If not, science and technology had probably come up with it in the last couple of decades.

"Pretty groovy slash embarrassing," said Ruby. This was the usual puzzle. She was already making fun of Pat in the choice of the word *groovy,* so how was *embarrassing* a twist? Ruby's disposition had not been improved by her father's absence.

"Yes," agreed Pat absently. "Why aren't you in school?"

"It was a half day. Testing slash torturing."

Pat wondered if this could possibly be true. "I'm sure you did very well," she said.

LaConte Liquors was not on the main commercial street of Hart Ridge, but in a less frequented shopping arcade nearby. On one side was an unpopular deli; on the other, a dry cleaners that still had aging sixties-style cardboard advertising in the window. In the window of LaConte Liquors, Christmas lights illuminated a little glowing Santa with an inflatable bottle of gin in his sleigh. Pat paused in front of it, ambushed by memories of happier times.

When she was growing up, the LaConte brothers were everywhere. LaConte & Company was the largest real estate office in town. The LaConte Funeral Home was prosperous, too, even though it didn't dominate its market in quite the same way. LaConte Liquors was the poor relation, covering the shabbiest section of the town's first tier. But Frank was friends with the son, Bobby, in high school, and when Bobby eventually took over the family business, Frank started buying all his liquor there. It was a store that Pat liked to shop in, too, because it sold grittier, more atmospheric stuff like forty-ouncers you wouldn't see in shops that specialized in fine wines. Not that Bobby passed up luxury items. He was the one who'd ordered Frank the cartons of reds and the carton of single malts. She took a deep breath and pushed open the door.

"Pat Foy," said Bobby, putting down an inventory sheet. "You're looking good. How have you been keeping yourself?"

Wine didn't seem quite enough then. Pat's eyes lit on some *poire,* and she decided to buy that, too.

"Couldn't be better," she said.

"You should come in more often and say hello."

"Oh, I've been so busy," she said. "You know."

"And how is Frank?"

"Fine," she said. She had been in and out of the store for years and had chatted with Bobby about their kids and their increasingly tenuous mutual acquaintances, eventually just recycling decades-old information. She did not feel she knew him. But she suspected that Frank did—or at least that both men considered themselves friends without ever having talked about much more than she and Bobby ever had. Men's friendships were so much simpler. Frank had never had any trouble getting Bobby on the phone in those two months after his sentencing—*despite the fact that Bobby LaConte had bought a lot of LGT stock.* Pat couldn't believe she had forgotten. Shortly after the LinkAge takeover he told her to tell Frank that he'd cashed in some and taken his family to Bermuda. With LinkAge employees Pat could entertain the illusion that everyone had profited and then suffered together. This was the first time she knowingly found herself with someone on the outside who'd lost money. Faced with Bobby LaConte's pleasantly jowly face, his thick ex-athlete's neck, and front hairs lying askew, like leftover wires, her normal exuberance faltered a little.

"Oh, dear," she said. Then she blurted out, "I'm sorry you lost money on the LinkAge stock."

"Don't worry about it," he said, twitching his meaty shoulders.

"How much was it?" she said. "Was it a lot?"

"Don't worry about it," he said again while ringing up her sale: The subject was closed.

"But Bobby," she cried, "I can't believe it! It's all so horrible! Please, please tell me how much you lost."

Bobby ran her platinum AmEx card through the machine, then examined it reverently as he said, "Pat, I never bought any stock. I didn't have the money. I told Frank I did because, well, I was a friend, and I would have if I could have. I mean, I really would have, it wasn't just talk. But then later I had an opportunity to buy this building, and obviously I couldn't pass that up, which thank God I didn't."

Pat was perplexed. "But didn't you say you went on vacation somewhere from the sale of some of your stock?"

"I don't know what I said." His tone was still pleasant. "But I didn't buy any stock."

"I guess that's good then," said Pat, wanting to believe him, but not daring to. "So you bought a little and then you sold it? Or what?"

"No, I never had any," he said. "Frank is a good customer, and we go way back. I always liked him."

"This doesn't make any sense," said Pat.

"Would you say hi to him for me?"

Pat nodded dumbly.

"Look at it this way," said Bobby LaConte. "I'm probably the only one in town who didn't buy stock."

Pat's voice dropped to her feet. "Really?" she said. "People all over town are broke?"

"Well, not broke." Bobby's face was pained. "My aunt lost some money. She got sort of upset. She's a widow, you see."

Oh. The very word squeezed Pat's swollen heart. Widows' peaks, widows' weeds, widows' walks. All bleak and lonely terms. Was Pat a "grass widow," or was that just if your husband took off of his own free will and wasn't hauled away in handcuffs?

"She lives here in town?" said Pat dully.

"No, no," said Bobby, as if this somehow made it all better. "In Darnley."

When Pat got into the car she felt like opening the *poire* right then and there. Then she thought longingly of her nice bed, with its periwinkle comforter, its heap of fruit-colored pillows, its pile of ready mysteries. But instead she took out her cellphone. She would at least try to get the address of Bobby's widowed aunt from information. Sure enough, when she offered an imaginary address in Darnley, the efficient voice at the other end of the line corrected her.

Pat wondered how you approached a woman who had suffered at the hands of the convicted felon you were married to. The aunt might not even let her in. Pat thought fondly of the maniacally escalating ruses from Ginny's story "The Red Door": flowers, a radio contest, a janitor's jumpsuit. Come to think of it, the purpose was as obscure. You never knew what Ginny's detective was up to, and Pat could not imagine what she was going to say to this aunt. What was she supposed to do—give her a check, as well? That would be too much.

She was surprised that she had not heard from Ellen Kloda yet. Ellen may have been embarrassed that she'd told her about the lost deposit. She still may not have made up her mind whether to accept the replacement. Or maybe she was disappointed that it wasn't more, closer to the total of what she'd lost. This last seemed the most unlikely. People tend to appreciate any amount of money that appears out of the blue. And Ellen did not seem to harbor any resentments—quite the contrary.

AnneMarie Mikulsky née LaConte lived in a town not far from Hart Ridge. Separating them was a curious stretch of warehouses, self-storage units, and "dealer services." Pat was not familiar with AnneMarie's street, but did not have much trouble finding it. It was one of the major thoroughfares running east-west—narrow and residential, but highly trafficked. The houses were set back unusually far, so Pat did not realize how big most of them were until she got stuck in traffic, horns honking randomly around her. The mature shrubbery also made it hard to tell where the houses began and ended. Paths to the front doors meandered around cypress and fir, giving the lawns an oddly woodland look, considering the glut of vehicles in front of them. Eventually she followed the lane of cars around the cause of the delay, a pint-size school bus, the type that private schools use, and the same type that Ruby had ridden to the academy before the Foys moved to Douglas Point.

That move had been slow in coming. Frank and Pat told the kids they didn't have time to look for a house when in fact they didn't yet have the money to finance Frank's grandiose vision. Young Ruby, impatient to be with her friends, slipped out of her bus one day long before her stop. A crisis ensued, with Pat tearing through phone conversations with the school secretary, the gym teacher who coordinated the buses, and the dean of students. It turned out that Ruby had gone house-hunting herself and picked out "the biggest one of all." When she pointed it out for her mother, Pat didn't have the heart to tell her that it was an apartment building, with dozens of tenants.

AnneMarie's house was a twenties Tudor with three gables, two chimneys, and a slate roof in various shades of pinky beige and gray. Long narrow casement windows echoed the decorative black trim on the door. All the evergreen shrubs were as perfectly shaped as fortune-tellers' crystal balls. To the right was a covered pool and a small pool house, an adorable but unsuccessful imitation of the Tudor. Six-foot-high grasses must mask it in the summer. Now you could see through the shrunken brown blades. Pat was no expert but the house was worth several million, anyway.

The Mikulskys must have been one of the wealthier branches on the complicated LaConte family tree. Pat doubted that AnneMarie could have been affected much by the slide of LinkAge stock, but of course looks were sometimes deceiving. Bobby had said she lived with her brother. They could be trapped in the heavily mortgaged family home, forced to cling to each other for economy's sake. Pat managed to park in front, although you would have thought several cars behind her had suddenly developed malfunctioning horns (stuck on). But no, the Mikulskys couldn't be hurting. In the driveway, pulled up beside the post-and-beam fence, was a red Porsche. Say what you like about the decline in quality of manufactured goods, it was fortunate they didn't make victims like they used to. Sympathy was wasted on people who'd lost money in the stock market if they'd made plenty, too. Maybe AnneMarie could give Pat some of hers.

Pat had enormous empathy. Her generosity and kindness were spontaneous and sincere. But her mind did not move in a straight line any more than a cow crops grass as a lawnmower does. The cow grazes a little here, a little there. As soon as she decided to drive home without getting out of the car, Pat forgot about the Mikulskys. She thought about 1) where to wire money for Frank's telephone account, 2) whether she should hire a personal assistant, which she'd occasionally done in the past, with varying results, 3) what vegetables she might cook with cheese, to trick Ruby into eating them, 4) where Ruby might be wandering off to these days, 5) why the flavor had gone out of life, 6) what had happened to Lemuel Samuel.

When she got home she Googled "Lemuel Samuel," and up popped an article in an online mystery zine entitled "Crime Writers Pick the Worst True Crimes." In it a dozen mystery novelists cited crimes ranging from the assassination of JFK to the Son of Sam murders. Lemuel Samuel couldn't decide between Enron and LinkAge.

Pat had read very little about LinkAge. Once Frank was arrested, she felt much more at home with stories like "Man
Drowns in Jell-O" and "You Are What You Watch: Your Person-
ality Revealed by Your Choice of Talk Show." Occasionally when
Pat turned on the TV, revealing further insights into her person-
ality, she'd see a clip of a perky newscaster looking straight and
hard into the camera and rattling off a few vague sentences
about one of the many companies that had been plagued with
accounting irregularities recently. These stories would often be
anchored with an incomprehensible statistic or two about the
loss to shareholders. When Pat came upon the article that mentioned Lemuel Samuel's condemnation of LinkAge, she printed
it out and then looked for others. In an interview with a local independent paper upstate, Lemuel referred to former CEO Riley
Gibbs as "another unindicted scumbag struggling by on hundreds of millions of dollars a year." A blog also quoted from him:
"No one is saying that Gibbs and Culp didn't pocket millions
from their company. What's bizarre is that we have to go to trial

to prove that it was wrong." Pat read articles online until late into the night.

At six she sat down to breakfast—coffee and a slice of cantaloupe. This followed her no-carbs-before-dinner rule, although she'd got so little sleep that maybe it still counted as after dinner. Ruby wasn't up yet, because it was Saturday, but Pat had set the table with ceremony. In the center was a fire orchid in a funky old cracker tin lined with sphagnum moss. A blue beaker held a soy substitute for cream. Her Wedgwood plate showed a blue lover strumming a blue mandolin at his mistress's blue feet.

Back at the computer off the kitchen, she did an address search for Lemuel, who fortunately had an extremely rare name. For the first time the leaps in perspectives offered by MapQuest made sense. To find a man like Lemuel Samuel you would of course start with the whole of North America and of course you'd eventually zero in on a single, mysteriously bending road amid a lot of blank space that could have been anything at all. What was hard to believe was that he lived less than an hour from the house in Lenox.

The phone rang, and when she answered, the prison announcement whirred to life with its usual *You are receiving a call from the United States federal prison system blah blah blah,* and then Frank's voice emerged as if from a tube, sounding even more agitated than during her last visit.

"I miss you so much. I hope you miss me, too. You couldn't possibly miss me as much as I miss you. I think about you all the time. I picture what you're doing. The hardest part of being here is being separated from you and the kids. Sometimes I think I can't go on, and then I think of you. I think of that great house I bought you. You forget how wonderful it is when you're in it. I can't believe I fell for the FBI's line of bullshit. Why did I trust anything they said? I turned myself in and out, and it made no difference at all. If only I'd been smarter. You don't see Neil in jail, unable to enjoy the wife he just bought and paid for. Do you think the kids miss me? I keep remembering that first time I saw you at the train station. You were so beautiful. Your hair was kind of fluffy from the heat. I can't get it out of my mind. It hurts to think about, but I don't want to stop. My roommate can't believe I have such a beautiful wife. I'm such an ordinary guy. Yeah. An ordinary guy caught in another dimension. There are some guys in here that you don't want to mess with, but mostly you'd never know these people were criminals. I don't think anyone will be able to tell when I get out. I try not to think about that, but it won't be too long before I can be with you again. Oh, how I love you."

Pat interjected remarks now and then, but this was Frank's call, and she was happy to go along for the ride. He never would have expressed such sentiments if he'd been home. The situation was heartbreaking, and as romantic as the Wedgwood, if you looked at it the right way. The forced separation, the unjust incarceration, the lovelorn cries. It was unfortunate that Frank's avowals sounded like so much whining and complaining. Pat decided it was time to go to the country.

Guests expected elaborate plantings up there, but Pat considered it the one place where she did not have to put on a show. She constantly moved single plants around to compare various combinations; there was never any sense of a harmonious whole. No matter what she did, though, Frank said it looked pretty. He really was a good person, even if he'd become more overbearing in the last few years. His job had made him believe that he could—in fact, that he should—throw his weight around. Certainly it was better than hanging back. Still, Pat did not miss the way he always seemed to smash the back door shut rather than simply close it.

The lightning that had struck the house in Lenox the year before had given it a piquancy it otherwise might have lacked. Every successful country house has a raffish air; that is its point. Cooking utensils are haphazard and largely impractical. Linens disappear. Random aesthetic impulses rule in the bookcases: A long forgotten bestseller about terror on the high seas molders beside a collection of funny stories about dogs.

Pat could feel herself happily unravel as soon as she pulled into the dirt driveway, tires crunching on all the little stones. "What are we going to do here?" said Ruby, and Pat said, "I'm going to see an old friend, and then you and I are going to do something fun tonight."

"Hooray," said Ruby lifelessly.

Rose had called Pat the other day and said that Ruby had IM'ed her to ask why no one had ever told her what a rotten place the world was. Pat had been very interested, of course, but she was not about to tell Ruby that Rose had betrayed her confidence. Rose had always been a bit of a tattletale, anyway.

"Oh, honey," said Pat. "We'll be all right. It's not like your father is a real criminal."

"Then why is he in jail?" asked Ruby.

"It's complicated," said Pat.

Pat was wearing her skinny sunglasses, jeans, a black cashmere sweater, and a brown barn jacket. Her landscaping work had kept her fit, if not exactly youthful. She pivoted out of the car, flexing her calves and thighs as if to prove this to herself. Her legs were strong, her shoulders square, her upper arms firm. At least Lemuel would recognize her. Once she'd left Ruby in the company of her laptop and she was on the road again, Pat felt free to imagine Lemuel Samuel's house but got nowhere. She did better with his yard, which would be neglected. She could take him out to lunch. She could meet him for a drink. They could see what happened.

The county road was pleasantly familiar. There was a gas station bordered with white painted stones, icy in the sharp air. The sign for the KwickCuts hairdresser had a scissors-shaped K. A garden store desperately offered half off blow-up Santas. But it was hard to find Lemuel's street, which was supposed to go off to the left after Elm and before Bridge. Once she'd driven back and forth a couple of times, she figured out the only road it could be, although it appeared to be a continuation of another one with a different name.

All of this difficulty seemed fitting as Pat had never seen Lemuel in any domestic setting. When they had known each other they'd met at her place or in bars. She was at an apartment of his only once, maybe twenty-five years ago, on Jane Street. It was a mess—every single dish was dirty—but no one worried about stuff like that back then, certainly not a rolling stone like Lemuel. He never entered a restaurant, unless you counted a pizzeria or a falafel stand. He bought all his clothes at an Army Navy store, even his underwear. He complained about "fern" bars, although he had probably never seen a fern in his life (and certainly never the fabulous staghorn fern).

His house was a small green ranch, with a couple of neglected thuja in the front, branches breaking under the weight of the snow, and some scrappy-looking pines invading from the woods beyond. The bottom branches were dead, which was supposed to happen because no light reached them, but here the trees were all by themselves out in the lawn, there was plenty of light, and the bottom branches were still dead. Almost any kind of landscaping would be an improvement.

A man in a red checked hunting jacket was shaving off the top layer of snow on the driveway with a shovel, evidently trying to prepare it for the more formidable snowblower splayed out in the road. He straightened up when Pat stopped and leaned his stacked hands, icon-like, against the squared-off handle of the shovel. His clean pink face looked open and guileless because it was wider than it was high. His hair sprang up from his forehead and then fell down on either side with a regularity that suggested either luck or a natural fastidiousness.

"I'm looking for Lemuel Samuel," called Pat from her car, window rolled down, letting in the heavenly smell of smoke from woodstoves. She *always* spoke to gardeners, no matter how foreign, and this one was cute.

He didn't answer right away, which was no surprise to Pat. She chattered on: "I'm a very old friend. I haven't seen him in ages. But we were very close. I wanted to talk to him about LinkAge, you know, the company that went bankrupt? I understand he was pretty angry."

"Are you from television?" he asked.

"Why, no," said Pat.

"I'm a neighbor," he said. "I live over there." He nodded at what could have been any of three or four more ranch houses farther along down the road.

"How convenient."

The neighbor blinked but recovered. "They put me on French TV once," he said.

"Really? About Lemuel?" She turned off the engine.

"They came to the house for more than an hour. I had to clear a space so they could set up their cameras. They had me move the cane chair under the deer head. They asked me a million questions. What sort of man is he? What sort of neighbor? What sort of town is this? And then all they showed was me saying that I hadn't read his book. They got a whole lot of people to say it and then showed us saying it one after another. Like we were a joke." As he made this statement, his expression did not change. He was still good-natured, matter-of-fact, ready to tell the story on himself, but unsure how to do so. "They got the mayor, too. They showed him sitting at his desk under his seal of office."

"That's awful!" cried Pat. "What did Lemuel do?"

The man shrugged. "He said they were trying to make us look like real Americans, only they didn't know how. He didn't care if I hadn't read his book. And then I did! I was going to tell him, but I didn't get the chance before his son found him."

Dread pricked the back of Pat's neck. "Found him?"

"I thought you were here because of that."

Pat shook her head.

"He fell down the basement stairs."

"Oh, no!" Pat's voice slid up and down the scale. "What happened? Is he okay?"

"He's in the hospital. He's been there a while. I figured I'd better clear the driveway just in case."

"You don't know what's wrong with him?"

"Not really," said the neighbor. "He just didn't wake up."

"Does his son live here with him?"

"Recently. But mainly he lives alone."

Her drive to the hospital was oddly like her trip to visit Frank when he'd broken his leg: empty roads, brittle surfaces, eerie light. This time Pat was at the wheel. You'd think that she'd have more of a sense of control, but she did not. She had a similar feeling of being suspended between two times. She realized now that it had been building for months. Would the new era begin today? Tomorrow? The next day? It was coming soon.

When Pat was directed to a room at the ICU, she thought at first that the nurse must have made a mistake. In the bed was a strange lump of wrecked flesh; you wouldn't even see someone so unhealthy begging for change on the streets. But as she was turning to go back to the nurses' station, she started to recognize traces of the earlier face: Lemuel's half smile was gone, of course, but the full lips were there, and the darkness around the eyes was the same, and a line on his cheek indicated where the crease had been. Pat sat heavily in the hospital chair near the bed.

The noise was incredible—whirring, beeping, buzzing, hissing. It couldn't all be normal. Through the glass window separating her from the rest of the ICU, she could see several people milling about, watching a wall of monitors, pushing at a huge stainless-steel machine on wheels, bending over to pick up ripped plastic bags. Two technicians conferred in urgently muffled tones. A sense of impending disaster was everywhere.

Pat peeked again at "Lemuel." Two tubes snaking out of his mouth were taped onto his bloated cheek. Another tube stuck out of his neck. Three wires sprang from pads on his chest. Two IVs were secured to a wrist board; the wrist was lashed to the stainless-steel piping that constituted the side of the bed. A final tube dropped from under the white woven hospital blanket to a heavy frosted-plastic sack in front of her. His urine.

The man was the size of two of the old Lemuels. He was as big and white and tightly encased as an overstuffed laundry bag.

His belly swelled under the blanket. You could tell he had no clothes on, but his ankles and legs, all huge, were tubed in stretchy black. A multitude of machines peered down at him.

In strode a young doctor writing on a clipboard. She was followed by a young man in an oversize pea coat.

"Doctor, please," said Pat. "Why is he making that sound?"

"What sound?" The doctor did not stop writing.

"That!" Pat pounced, then tried to imitate it.

"It's just moisture in the breathing tube. It's bound to happen when you've retained as much fluid as he has." The doctor turned over a few pages on her clipboard so forcibly they made a slashing noise.

Pat looked dubious. "What exactly is wrong with him?"

"Are you a family member?" More noisy ruffling as another page went over the bulging clip.

"I don't know," said Pat mournfully.

"I see," said the doctor, making long cutting marks across the paper. "Well, I hope you have some influence over him. He has congestive heart failure. And if he ever gets out of here, he's going to have to stop drinking."

"Oh, dear."

"And smoking."

Pat nodded.

The doctor looked up for the first time. "He has the body of an eighty-five-year-old man."

"I really wanted to talk to him," said Pat.

"I can't help you there," said the doctor. "He's going to be out for at least another week. He can't breathe on his own yet. Why don't you talk to his son." With her clipboard, she indicated the boy behind her.

He had a thin-lipped, wary mouth, which made him look as

if he was going to give nothing away. His fingers were hooked over the pockets of the pea coat.

"Are you looking for me?" he said in a polite, resolutely cool-guy drawl.

"Yes," said Pat, noting the eagerness behind the distrust. "Yes, I think I am."

IN THE
DARK
WOODS

The man's face was huge and moony, white, jowly. Rolls of fat accordioned as, sitting, he propelled his office chair with invisible feet into the well of a gray metal desk. His attitude, though, seemed neutral. Virginia decompressed by one turn of the dial but was brought up short by a curl of the man's lips. The fat made it impossible to tell what this movement meant. Was it a cough? A sneer? How odd that a person with such a face should be dealing with the public.

"Two dollars."

His mouth had barely moved, and Virginia doubted she could have heard right. She couldn't remember what minimum wage was now, but surely it wasn't as low as that.

"What did you say?" she asked. She knew she could not let him see her fear.

"Tuh duhs."

This time his words had been even more incoherent. His huge moony face had started to waver as well.

"I'm sorry," she said, gripping her legs to keep them still. She had to remember to keep her voice even. She had to be careful not to cry out. "I'm having trouble understanding you."

"Tuh duh."

If she concentrated, maybe she could lip-read.

"Tuhd."

"I can't . . . ," she began, but then he opened his mouth wide, and the words came out as plain as day: "You're not going to pretend . . ."

Although her sense of smell had failed, she could tell that the words were accompanied by an awful stench. No wonder he usually kept his lips shut when he spoke. "You're not going to pretend you're worth more" is what he said, and she knew that the stench had become fouler, as foul as rotting limbs, and that's what those were in his mouth, not teeth, but a fringe of rotting toes stuck in the gum line, each with a sharp curving nail and wiggling . . . jiggling . . . maggots. . . .

Virginia woke hot and sweaty, crusty all through her head, her heart pounding. "Oh, Jesus," she said aloud. Yes, it had been a dream, but she had escaped nothing by waking. She leapt out of bed as if she were on fire, grabbed her heap of black clothes, added a white shirt, and staggered out into the cold Maine morning. She was afraid she would be late again.

Virginia used to think that the whole point of a mystery novel was its solution. The criminal might be brought to justice, or might not. What mattered was that the truth resided somewhere. The detective knew it—and so did the reader. Now, however, the finality and stability of the end did not interest her. What Virginia sought was the transformation of facts. She didn't want order to prevail; she wanted a *different* order to prevail.

Logic is supposed to rule in crime novels. Clues pile up through the pages until they can be sorted out properly. But deep down all mysteries are contemptuous of evidence. This man's fingerprints are all over the murder weapon; he threatened the victim; he was seen in the vicinity at the time of the crime; he was the only one with the code, the key, the knowledge that the victim was home. *So of course he didn't do it.*

How wonderful it would be to live in a world where facts could be inverted. A suicide turns out to be murder. The actual love triangle involves the two less glamorous of the spouses. The victim is not the beloved mother, but a relative reported dead years ago—a relative no one knew, or cared about. And that man is not omnipotent; he is just a puppet. Watch his underling, who has a crafty streak. When Virginia learned of her ruin this past fall, she picked up *The Red Right Hand,* which explains away just about everything except for gravity.

The truth might be better than it appears; it might be worse; but at least it is different. At least it is not this unbearable present, this cruel betrayal, this lost hope, this dashed chance. A good mystery should turn under you so smoothly that you have to hold on for dear life.

Virginia was stunned. She'd been stunned for months. Her legs as they took her on her usual route past the first clearing uttered the whiff, whiff of worn black denim; her hands resettled themselves in the padded crevices of her pockets; her feet, well, her feet were cold, but they were there, reconnoitering the uneasy sand between asphalt and earth. These sensations seemed distant, though. It was her consciousness of being stunned that made her aware she was still alive. It was like a photographic negative of a feeling. It wasn't quite the same, perhaps, as a real feeling, but you could distinguish the outline, so it would do; it would do.

If only she had bought a new pair of boots.

It was ridiculous to think this way. She was probably never going to write again. She was impoverished. But oh, it would be so much easier to be poor wearing a sharp pair of black cowboy boots. You could even make a decent corpse.

Her own boots had split. The left one was perhaps as salvageable as ever, which wasn't much, but the right had a two-inch score in the outer seam. Virginia had worn them through much of the pleasant Maine summer, when it didn't really matter, but now the ball of her foot ached with the cold from the frozen ground.

Until her ruin, she had been planning to buy a new pair of Justins when they went on sale in January. Her stepmother, Pamela, always gave her a check for Christmas that would have been more than enough. The expense was of course inexcusable, the money should be saved for an emergency or at the very least used for a visit to the dentist, but the boots would probably last Virginia another nine years, if she kept them properly oiled, and who knew what would happen in the next decade; she'd probably be dead, and if she were dead, she wouldn't need teeth.

Virginia was used to doing without. Her freelance copywriting jobs, which had never paid much anyway, had become fewer and farther between in the last decade and a half. She'd sold only one story in years, and her two books, if you did the math, netted her about thirty-nine cents per hour, which looked weird on a census form. Her life as a result was very dramatic. A library fine could be a make-or-break matter.

For nearly a decade, however, she had always been able to count on the stock her stepmother had given her after her father died. It made sense that the proceeds of his careful middle-class life should go to his long-standing wife, Pamela, but in his will he had directed her to "make provision" for Virginia. The phrase prompted all sorts of questions. Had he despaired of her ever being able to support herself properly? Clearly he thought she should have a middle-class life. Despite her dedication to her art, she would have to have proper medical care. She would have to be able to get on a bus if a crisis demanded her presence elsewhere (i.e., the Berkshires, where Pamela lived). She would have to repair her eighteen-year-old Chevy if it broke down. But if this type of security was so important to him, then why didn't he leave her some money outright? She was afraid he had not trusted her with it—a feeling that Virginia could not help but think was justified by the outcome, even though it was Pamela who had bought the stock.

Virginia had thought her self-sacrifice was so canny. She'd cashed in some shares a few years ago, after a bout of pneumonia, but other than that she'd been firm and hadn't sold any more. She hadn't sold any even through this past summer, when her copywriting jobs had dried up altogether. She had been tempted, of course. Pamela had chosen the stock mainly because Pat's husband had worked at the company that issued it, and she'd always liked Pat, but the choice had been a good one; the stock had soared in value. Sometimes Virginia used to daydream about the things she could buy: the boots, of course, and a soft red rug, because the floor of her basement apartment was cold, and a sleek black sweater with a shawl collar that she'd seen on a tourist walking into the Dock. But while she was putting off the purchase of these pathetic luxuries, enormous and incomprehensible crimes were being committed, and the stock that was supposed to be her security turned into dust.

When Pamela had called Virginia about the LinkAge debacle, Virginia had not at first realized what she was talking about. Very little national news seemed to touch people in Damariscotta. LinkAge stock? What was that? She hadn't fully comprehended that Frank Foy's company, which was called LGT, had been bought out and so was known by another name. But it didn't matter what she knew; the company was bankrupt, anyway. And Frank himself was going to go to jail. For what, Virginia wasn't exactly sure.

She moved away from the side of the narrow road to avoid an oncoming car. Curious that this should be so automatic a gesture. But it was fitting that she find herself halfway into the woods, where the winter landscape was as still as death. The earth would be no colder than the asphalt, after all.

Why had she waited? *Why* hadn't she given into temptation as she'd envisioned doing? She imagined as she often did an improbable string of events that could have ended in the sale of her shares just-in-the-knick-of-time. ("Can you believe it!" she would have exclaimed to Pamela.) She hadn't spoken to Pat in years, but Pat could have called her out of the blue about something else, about, say, that crazy Lemuel Samuel, and said, "Oh, by the way, Frank's company isn't looking too hot." Or Virginia could have had an idea of her own: Buy video game stock! Video games were all that her landlord's kids ever talked about, and they didn't even own any. Or LGT could have swindled the local school board. She would have sold then. Definitely. No matter what the projected profit. She'd have put the money into bonds.

Shortly after she heard about her ruin, she'd driven from Damariscotta down to the shoe repair shop just north of Portland—just think of the money she'd wasted on gas—and the repairman, an Arab, had dropped the boots on his crowded and crabbed counter with such distaste and then had looked at her with such malevolence that she suspected a larger grievance.

He must have thought she was a Jew, trying to exterminate his people, or maybe he had some other delusion equally histrionic and shabby. Up until that moment she'd sympathized vaguely with the Palestinians and thought that since 9/11 Arabs in America were getting a raw deal. But there in the shop, if Mossad had been recruiting, she, an Irish Catholic girl, would have happily joined up and shot this hateful foreign man dead.

She was only sorry she had let him go so far as to quote a price to her—seventy-five dollars, which may have been real or not, but which he knew quite rightly she could not afford. Nor would anyone have taken up the offer; a bit more would buy a cheap new pair, and twice that sum would cover a well-crafted one with a little shrewd shopping. The encounter left her incapable of doing anything but reading the most ridiculously opaque of mysteries for days, helpless at the murderous rage that poverty had brought out in both of them.

Her anguish was hard to recapture, or even really remember, in her stunned state. But her incredulity was the same. How could *Virginia Howley,* who could read a nefarious scheme into a video rental contract, have fallen for this stock fraud? She had never given her credit card number over the phone, never used it online. She'd always been an inversion of Sherlock Holmes: From a spot on a sleeve she could spin a paranoid fantasy of monumental proportions. None of this had helped. Instead of using Pamela's Christmas check for boots, Virginia was using it to eat.

Her walk divided into three parts, just the way a good mystery did. It began with an expectant turn into the wide world, i.e., a departure from the basement apartment in the row of ranch houses where she'd lived for more than fifteen years. Next was the larger road, where she was walking now and where the winter terrain was as chaotic as her thoughts. Mud was frozen in in-decipherable contortions. Shattered skins of white ice covered empty little pits. Blocks of leftover snow lay here and there, im-pervious, fuzzy, and as oddly shaped as the Styrofoam braces used to pack electronics. The woods nearby could hold a body for days before it was discovered. Soon, however, the road would curve into the final part of her walk, the bridge from which she could see her previously hidden destination, the Dock.

The Dock was a nautically themed restaurant Virginia had first eaten at years ago, with a lawyer who owned a Christmas tree farm. They'd joked about the meaning of the word *dock*. He was well traveled—he'd hitchhiked all over the country as a young man—and although he was a native, he was friends with many newcomers, people from the Boston area for the most part. He had assumed at first that Virginia was like them. She supposed she should have been, but she wasn't. They were telecommuters, or they lived off trust funds, or they had some other arrangement through which money acquired elsewhere was used in Maine; it went a lot farther here. They had moved to Damariscotta to avoid work, which baffled Virginia, who was always hoping to burrow more deeply inside it. The lawyer, a ge-nial sort, never did understand that the telecommuters reflex-ively made distinctions that separated him from them. They liked him, yes, but what they liked was his slight Down East ac-cent, his casual references to catches, to boats, to local families. He was palatable as well as authentic. And the telecommuters were so well-meaning, you couldn't even complain about them; you'd feel like an idiot. Only the other day one fellow made a joke about having his beans "à la mode," and when Virginia didn't smile, his wife kindly explained to her that it was French

for "with ice cream." It was this sort of thing that made you want
to put a gun to your head. But anyone who blithely claimed that
such little slights were worse for the soul than worrying about
the rent never faced down the end of the month with dread.

The lawyer at first assumed that Virginia wanted to hear
about his Christmas tree farm. What else was there to come to
the area for, other than nature? But Virginia preferred to hear
about his engagingly raffish practice. Although it may not have
been particularly successful, he seemed to have made something vital and real out of it.

Problems arose when he expected her to join him in grilling a
piece of meat or watching a movie. He appeared quite natural in
the midst of these activities, but Virginia always felt as if she
were pretending to be someone else. It was nearly impossible to
agree on what film to watch. Virginia saw sinister overtones to
most comedies, which she wouldn't have minded, except that
the makers themselves didn't seem to recognize them. Dramas,
on the whole, were worse. Visual media by their very nature lied
about death, she claimed after sitting through a John Woo
movie.

"I guess it was pretty violent," said the Christmas tree farmer.

"I don't care about that," said Virginia. "What I care about is
the pretense that death isn't real. Look at it this way. Say you're
supposed to identify with one of the characters. Not the main
character, generally. But still, a key person. At least some of the
shots are from his point of view, and the emotional truth in a
couple of the scenes is his. In a sense, you become him. Briefly.
Now say this character dies. What you're essentially getting as a
viewer is the chance to see yourself after you're dead. The movie
implies that once you're dead you can become someone else, at

least insofar as you can come out of your body to look back at it. I'm not saying it's not a great fantasy. I wish it were true. But it's not. And it can make death seem all too attractive."

The Christmas tree farmer looked at her warily, as if he'd suddenly realized she was too crazy to talk to.

Did he think her theory was the result of an unhealthy obsession with death? Or did he think she thought he thought it did? A Möbius strip like this could wear you out in no time. It was the beginning of the end.

She still didn't like to think of the last time she saw him. It gave her the creeps. Afterward she became the true loner she was probably always supposed to be. Her unvarying black jeans, black zip-up sweatshirt, and black cowboy boots (now split) prompted a new checkout girl at the supermarket to ask once if she were in mourning. Virginia was tempted to say "yes"—and *mean* it—because she was mourning *her own self* but of course she said nothing.

Even before her ruin, her strict economies meant that she bought family-size packages for the savings and doggedly ate the same cut of chicken for a week. She knew that the discounted old vegetables were put out on Mondays at Hannaford and Thursdays at the health food store. She saved the juice from canned peas to make rice with. Oh, she managed to find further cuts she could make. She switched to lentils. She gave up coffee. She wrote down every penny she spent, even a quarter for a newspaper. Then she gave up the paper. Maybe she could move to a place without a kitchen? Raw food was supposed to be very good for you.

Her mind was spinning. Her thoughts were like paisley. It was as if she'd been hit on the head, and now she was seeing the stars. After all these years of struggle, it was over. She'd lost. In order to go out and grab life and throttle it and turn it upside down so that what she wanted would clatter free, she would have to transform the debacle itself, and she could not. She wrote about crime. She finally was the victim of a huge, head-line-grabbing one. You'd think that at least on paper she could find some alternate universe in which to fit it. But no, this bil-lion-dollar accounting crime was too big to flip over, too dull to dress up, too obvious to hide. Ruin had turned out to be com-pletely colorless, tedious, dull beyond compare.

She walked faster and faster as she crossed the bridge. The cold was creeping into her foot from the crack in her boot and it was blowing straight into her head through her black watch cap. She was surprised to see the youngest of the waitresses, Molly, standing coatless on the dock that gave the restaurant its name. She was a plump, pleasant girl who was as tough as fungus. Be-side her a tourist was leaning over the railing and pointing to the oyster "nursery" maintained there. The tourist wore a large L.L. Bean down parka, a fur cap, expensive jeans, and, despite the gray day, very dark narrow sunglasses. Her hair stuck out in styl-ish tousled wedges from either side of her hat. Her words wafted across the lazy silver meanders of the river: "It looks a lit-tle chilly to me, but then I'm not an oyster. I think it's really hard to identify with one, very different from identifying with a cat or a dog or even a fiercer mammal, but you probably wouldn't want to start identifying too much with an oyster, anyway, because how would you ever let one slip down your throat again? Empa-thy is all very well, but you can start out a vegetarian and end up afraid to walk outside for fear of stepping on an ant. And I do so love the tang of an oyster. Pemaquid, did you say yours was called?"

It was Pat Guiney, now Foy, Virginia's best friend from high school. Virginia stopped and stared. Her ex-husband had come to town a few years before, on his way up to Nova Scotia, and Virginia hadn't recognized him, despite the fact that he'd called and arranged to meet her in a café down the street, so she'd known he was going to be there when she walked in. The Boston Red Sox cap, coupled with the gray hair, had been a very good disguise. But Pat looked the same, only more vivid, as if she'd been styled for a magazine shoot rather than stuck in real life. Certainly no one in real life still talked at the high pitch she did, eagerly dancing from foot to foot. Virginia hadn't been back to New Jersey for years, since her father died and her step-mother moved up to the Berkshires. She hadn't seen Pat for longer. She couldn't even remember the last time she'd seen a picture of her. Yet here was Pat herself, resettling her fur hat on her head and calling, "Look at that! Do my eyes deceive me? No! It's Ginny, appearing like something out of a dream! What are you *doing* here?"

"I'm a waitress," said Virginia matter-of-factly.

Y ou never could fluster Pat—or maybe she was always as
flustered as she ever got. "Well it certainly agrees with
you!" she cried as Virginia found herself going into the restaurant with her. "What a wonderful place to work! And you're so
thin! I'd never have the willpower if I were around food all day.
Imagine being able to pick oysters whenever you wanted! I
thought I was lucky because I have fresh herbs on my kitchen
windowsill."

Virginia left to put her jacket in the back room, intending to
explain to Molly that she would sit for only a few minutes, but
Pat detained the younger waitress to compliment her gold hoop
earrings, which were in no way unusual except that they were a
bit bent: "I *love* them! Where did you get them? I must have a
pair." And when Virginia returned, fresh-faced Molly was actually in a conversation with her.

"How about I order lots and lots of things," said Pat. "To make
stealing your colleague here worth your while."

"Oh, it's not that busy," said Molly, waving her hand magnanimously. "Steal away."

Certainly an unfortunate choice of words.

Virginia was still standing, in her waitress position, order pad out. She felt slightly dizzy.

"Well!" said Pat brightly. "How are you?"

Virginia was stymied for a moment.

"That's a complicated question right now, isn't it?" said Pat. "For me, too. Do you recommend anything here? Each item looks better than the last."

It was all pretty ordinary. Pat was bound to be disappointed, used as she was to much more sophisticated places. "It's just regular food," said Virginia.

"Oysters! Regular!" said Pat happily. "Well, I know what I want. Scrambled eggs and oysters. Don't you see—it's breakfast and lunch at the same time. And I haven't had either."

When Molly rejoined them, she was wearing a black cardigan, maybe because she'd gotten chilled outside, or maybe not, because she had grown up in Maine, after all, where T-shirts came out at the first glimpse of snowmelt. Besides, she certainly didn't seem annoyed with Pat. Virginia had seen Molly freeze out tourists with politeness, and this was the opposite.

"I need coffee, too," said Pat. "I don't think I'll be able to go on without coffee. Is it good?"

"Yeah, it's pretty good," said Molly. "You think?" she said to Virginia, who frowned, but nodded.

"Wonderful! I can't wait! Ginny, you must have some, too. I can't be the only caffeinated person in this conversation."

Virginia, still standing, said that she wasn't hungry. It was the first thing that came into her head because it was such a total lie. Normally she would eat something for free in the kitchen,

but she couldn't expect to do that out here, and she had no capacity for the kind of calculations required before she ordered
food. Pat would probably pay, but right now Virginia could not
think out the implications of letting her do so. And Pat could
conceivably be ruined as well. Probably you should try to treat a
woman whose husband was sent to jail, anyway, although in this
case that was out of the question. Virginia had about seven dollars in her pocket, enough to cover the coffee Pat was ordering
for her, but not a whole lot more.

"I'm sure you'll be hungry by the time I finish talking," said
Pat. (Making Molly laugh! She couldn't have spent all her life in
Maine.)

When Virginia demurred again, Pat said, "I think we need
several appetizers then, to tide us over."

A couple whom Virginia knew vaguely came in, crossed in
front of them, and sat on the other side of the room, closer to
the pearly gray window. Pat had instinctively sat where it was
warmer, but this couple, if they were going to live in Damariscotta, had to wring every last bit of scenic pleasure from it.
They were fit, trim, dressed quietly in navy blue and beige, almost holding hands next to the nest formed by the salt and pep-
per shakers, sugar packet dispenser, and pimpled red candle
holder. Virginia had seen them in here before, eating with the "à
la mode" couple. They were the sort responsible for the success
of the Dock and for the hipness of the new tourist shops beyond
it. (The art gallery still closed for the winter, but the fancy children's clothing store remained open.) Their paper towels were
recycled and their eggs came from cage-free hens and their
clothes wicked away moisture from the skin. They would be
wondering who Pat was. Pat percolated as she sat there, everyone's eyes were drawn to her, and she did look absurdly well off.

Even Virginia could tell that the purse shaped like a doctor's bag had cost a fortune.

Handing Pat's order over to Molly, Virginia sat down at the table. "Are you on your way somewhere?" she asked.

"I'm on my way here," said Pat. "Ruby went on a school trip to Washington yesterday, and after dinner I fell straight to sleep. When I woke up, it was two-thirty. Eventually I just jumped in the car. Neil always claimed he could get to Maine in six hours, and I think I beat him."

An icy finger touched Virginia's heart. One of the most notorious of LinkAge's officers was named Neil. "Neil," she repeated, too disheartened to ask if this was the Neil that Pat was referring to. Absurdly, Virginia looked over at the telecommuters, to see if they'd heard.

"Someone Frank worked for," said Pat. "Neil Culp."

"You know Neil Culp."

Culp's appearance before a House investigating committee had been on CNN. Virginia would never forget his smug, meaty face. A congressman tried to ask him about a note he'd written to Riley Gibbs, which started, "I think they're onto us" and ended, "It's a crime." Culp refused to answer on the grounds that he might incriminate himself. Then he read a statement saying he'd testify and clear his good name as soon as his lawyers let him. In other words he had it both ways: He didn't have to answer questions, but he was allowed to speak to defend himself. She was astonished that Pat and her husband could have talked to him as if he were human.

Pat cocked and swiveled her head as she always had when she was upset, when she suspected criticism. Back in high school these bird-like movements of self-doubt would have been prompted by one of the popular girls policing Pat's behavior or maybe one of the wiseacre boys crashing heedlessly about. It would never have been caused by Virginia.

Pat pressed forward as valiantly as she always had, no matter what the company. In high school, she would have been claiming that Lemuel Samuel's books were better than any rock 'n' roll song ever written. Here at the Dock she was saying that Neil Culp used to be a neighbor in Hart Ridge.

Virginia's basement apartment was in a house owned by the local army recruiter who still found time to hunt most weekends despite the possibility of war in Iraq. He drove a jeep and had a rough, incurious hello for Virginia whenever he saw her. His wife told her where she could buy Christmas cards or winter gloves or rubber sandals off season at incredible discounts. Their two children stopped playing and parted silently whenever they saw Virginia approach or leave her separate entrance. These were the sort of neighbors that Virginia had—the sort you were supposed to protect. You could never allow them to discover some horror in their basement.

"Do you know Riley Gibbs, too?" she asked.

"Not really," said Pat. "I saw him across the room a couple of times."

There was a silence. In an earlier life Virginia could have at least imagined carrying on this conversation with aplomb. Now she did not even wish to do so.

"So, anyway," said Pat. "I left about three or so, and here I am." She opened her hands as if to show she was carrying no weapon.

"I see," said Virginia, eyeing the outstretched arms.

"I don't sleep a whole lot right now. I usually wake every hour or two. You know I always was sort of wakeful."

It was certainly true that Pat's eyes were as wide as empty plates.

"That's how I ended up memorizing all those plant lists," said Pat. "Very, very useful for a landscape designer. But it's harder for me to sit still now. I have a tendency to prowl. That's when I jumped in the car. I decided I simply had to talk to you."

"I was up at three," said Virginia suddenly. She'd been worrying about money, of course. It was odd that in the black hole of the night, for maybe an hour or two, she and Pat had been on parallel courses.

"I heard from Pamela that you owned some LinkAge stock," said Pat with a spacy smile. "I want to reimburse you for it."

Despair struck Virginia dumb.

"I can, really," said Pat. "We live on Douglas Point now, didn't you hear? Frank may not have made as much money as Neil, but he still made a lot." She was sitting up as bright as a squirrel.

Virginia shook her head.

"Frank feels uncomfortable having all this money, when his friends have been hurt," said Pat.

This notion of "being hurt" almost made Virginia cry. She tried to compose herself. "How is Frank?" she said.

"He's in jail," said Pat. "I visit him every two weeks."

Another silence. "Are you going to eat this roll?" asked Virginia at last.

Pat shook her head, shuddering slightly.

"It's pretty good." It had been supplied by the hippie bakery one town over. The top was floury, the inside was rich and heavy, and a hint of sugar syrup coated the bottom and sides. "I'll save that one for you, and have this other, if you don't mind," said Virginia, selecting a less tasty wheat roll, which at least had the virtue of biting back when you bit into it.

"It doesn't bother me that Frank is in jail," declared Pat. "Not one bit."

She really was a lunatic.

"Don't you need the money?" asked Pat.

Virginia frowned, her mind shutting with a snap. She couldn't take a handout, even from Pat.

"How much did you lose?" asked Pat.

"I don't want to talk about it," said Virginia.

Molly arrived with four plates of appetizers.

"My! How beautiful!" cried Pat. Then, right in front of Molly, she continued, "The judge told Frank he wouldn't ask for restitution because it was impossible to determine the victims. But it's not like you're the only person I'm reimbursing."

"Why don't you leave me alone?" cried Virginia, afraid that her face had crumpled. First she was ruined, and then her inability to deal with her ruin was revealed for all to see.

Pat looked stricken. "I've known Ginny for more than twenty-five years," she said to Molly. "And she is the only person who has always known exactly what I was talking about."

"Oh, Pat," said Virginia faintly. There were stuffed mushrooms, shrimp cocktail, endive salad, and a square foot of nachos.

"No, really," said Pat. "I mean it."

"She's a smart one," said Molly. An exit line.

"The food's great," said Pat.

Virginia nodded.

"Just as I expected."

Silence.

"Frank always insisted on leaving the shells on the tails of his shrimp to use as handles. He wouldn't eat them otherwise."

Virginia began to nibble on the roll.

"Have you read the new Lydia Bunting?"

Virginia shook her head.

"It's not bad," said Pat. "A little too much about the forensics."

"How much time does she have left?" asked Virginia. Bunting had declared in print several years ago that she would kill herself at the age of seventy-five, since the world had no use for old women.

"You don't really think she's going to do it, do you?" said Pat.

"Why not?"

"Well!" said Pat. "I don't know!" Something in her tone made Virginia glance up. She'd made Pat nervous. Just a little.

"You must come back with me," said Pat, anxiously.

Virginia stared.

"I have some people to see. People who lost money. I get the feeling I'm supposed to help them out. You know, with a small check."

"People like me?" asked Virginia quietly.

"Not like *you,* exactly," said Pat.

Virginia put her head in her hands. It was impossible to explain that losing money was bad, but not as bad as having been tricked—not as bad as having been so stupid she probably deserved it.

"Well, they're sort of like you," said Pat uncertainly. She evidently assumed that she could have both a big heart and a big appetite—to be, in effect, both generous and greedy. The rich thought they could buy anything. Or should be able to.

"Don't worry," said Pat. "Frank and I have a lot of money. Besides which, if worse comes to worse, the house is mine. I got it for my birthday, and I can do what I want with it."

"You got it for your birthday," Virginia repeated.

"Well . . . yes."

"Frank was protecting his assets," said Virginia.

Pat didn't seem to take this in. "Oh, Ginny," she said. "No one's around. My mother's in Florida, my brother's in Vancouver, and Frank's parents are both dead. . . ."

Could she be serious? Did she really need the company?

"Come with me," said Pat. "Please." She sounded as if she were still sixteen. Virginia felt her brain loosen and start to float.

In the Damariscotta library she'd discovered the mysteries of L. P. Davis, which were long out of print. Although not all of them worked, their ambition took Virginia's breath away. The main character in each thought he was someone else, and—here's the clincher—*he was right.* Moreover, he was right in a literal, not just a moral sense. The convolutions necessary to achieve this, the feints and sleights of hand, the serums and syringes, were wonderful to witness. But the audacity of the goal was even more delicious. Davis triumphed over the severest restriction on the self, i.e., its very singleness, and although dissolution was occasionally threatened, or courted, it was always avoided. Virginia found the high-wire act exhilarating. The allure of being another person while remaining herself dazzled her brain.

That is what Virginia thought about when she first considered going back to Hart Ridge with Pat. Slipping out of one life and into another possessed a horrible attraction. She could have tried to talk sense to Pat about handing out money, because, after all, the idea was nonsense. Any distribution, however insignificant, was bound to be unfair. It was impossible to tell who was really in need. Whenever anyone tried to give away money, it ended up in the wrong pockets. But why should Virginia try to argue any of this? She didn't have the strength.

She knew that Molly's father, who owned the restaurant, would be happy if she claimed a family emergency, sham or not. She'd been taken on at the Dock for the summer, when it was busy. Now it was overstaffed. Her two and a half days a week would disappear until the tourists came back in June. She was going to find herself with no work at all. It was as if she were being given the opportunity to walk off a cliff and remain suspended in midair. Let the eventual crash take care of itself.

Virginia finished all the appetizers except the nachos, she drank a second cup of coffee, she tried the eggs, she ate one of Pat's oysters. By the time the check arrived, she'd agreed to go pack a suitcase for New Jersey.

"Can I follow you in my car?" said Pat.

It would have been a little slow. "I walked here," said Virginia.

"How wonderful," said Pat. "You feel so good after you exercise."

Pat didn't stop talking as they shot south in her new VW Touareg, an SUV Virginia had never heard of. It seemed more like a club room, with deep brown leather seats and a skylight in the roof exposed by a sliding roof and a sound system that made you think the music was in your head.

"A cop stopped me for speeding on the way up, and really it was ridiculous," Pat was saying as she outraced a tractor trailer.

Virginia tried to catch a covert glimpse of the speedometer, then simply closed her eyes. She wanted to have a regular conversation, but she had found herself through the years increasingly incapable of holding one. She wasn't even sure people had them anymore. Or ever did.

"I should have been mad," said Pat, "but the cop was a woman, and she had on this type of round-toothed plastic headband that I've always wondered about. Do you know which one I mean? It clamps down and separates the strands of hair. It's almost scary. It looks as if it's cutting the hair, sort of ejecting it, like a pasta maker. So finally I interrupted her and asked whether it hurt. The trouble is, she had no idea what I was talking about. I don't think it's a great sign if cops can't feel pain."

Virginia kept her eyes closed, pretending to doze, and some of the pretense must have become real. She lost track of when they left Maine and how long they'd been traveling. She became aware of the road again only later, when a voice from the dashboard said, "Check your route, take your first legal U-turn." She was surprised at how big the cars had gotten and how dense the traffic. Maine had SUVs, of course, even the huge new ones that didn't look like passenger vehicles so much as armored trucks carrying sacks of cash. It was the telecommuters who drove them. But there weren't many, and because of the back-country you could say that they had some faint justification. None of the SUVs on these highways, however, had ever been driven off road. It was like being stuck on a conveyor belt in an SUV showroom.

"Are you all right?" asked Pat.

"Yes," said Virginia.

"You looked sort of, I don't know, pale in that nice restaurant of yours."

They zipped past a moving van. Maybe Virginia would simply die on the road.

"Frank sat on the subway once next to a person reading a mystery," said Pat, "while all over the car you could hear a woman telling a guy that she was going to cut him if he ever touched her again. Frank wanted to know why someone would ignore a real crime to read about a pretend one. He'd remind me of it every time I picked up a book."

"Maybe he wanted you to find him out," said Virginia. "I mean, you know, wanted you to ferret out his accounting . . . mmm, irregularities."

"That's so clever!" cried Pat. "I never would have thought of it. But Frank claims I knew all along."

A pause. "Did you?" asked Virginia.

Pat shrugged. "How was I supposed to know all that silly stuff was illegal?"

An interesting defense.

"You wouldn't believe who I saw. Lemuel Samuel. He said some really mean things about LinkAge, which I'm sure were true, so I went looking for him, but when I found him, he was in the hospital, near death. Oh, can you get that?" A thin tune trickled out of her doctor's bag, or rather, the beginning of a tune, repeated over and over. It was familiar, but Virginia could not place it.

The bag was bigger than it looked from the outside, and the four-note refrain repeated several times before Virginia identified the trim compact as a cellphone. She handed it to Pat, who opened it with a flick of the wrist.

"Why, yes, sweetheart, of course. Whatever you say. Are you having a good time?" Pat closed up the phone and handed it back. "Ruby. She's having a good time in Washington, thank God. I was a little worried. She's been having some trouble adjusting."

"Lemuel Samuel?" said Virginia. Pat must have toyed with the idea of taking up with him while her husband was in prison. "Is he dead?" How could she take it all in? It was too ridiculous! Just like Pat.

Suddenly a black car door was inches from the glass by Virginia's right shoulder, becoming her whole field of vision, like a "Kapow!" panel in a cartoon. An instant later Pat's car was in the left lane, and a black Lexus was sashaying off over the horizon. "Well!" said Pat in her pleasant soprano. "That was unexpected. We must have crossed the border into New Jersey."

Virginia had met her ex-husband, Alain, on the street in Providence. He was French-Canadian, and ostensibly the marriage was one of convenience, so he could get a green card. She had looked forward to the refuge of a paper marriage. She was surprised and disappointed when Alain took it as seriously as any of his many other hard-to-define plans and projects. Their relationship was half sham and half real, and the strands became harder and harder to disentangle.

Because Alain was older and had a lot of still older friends, he and Virginia started going to dinner parties together, a mind-numbing practice. Why file off in pairs to other people's apartments just to eat? It was hard enough to find one human being worth talking to, let alone two who were married to each other. The table settings, the boy-girl seating arrangements, and the stiff parade of courses were a grotesque parody of the upper-middle-class life found in a Golden Age mystery; movement seemed constricted to keep down the number of suspects. Virginia found it impossible to sit still. She was afraid that if she listened to one more interesting opinion or funny anecdote she would scream. Instead she jumped up. No one would question her; everyone would figure she was off to the bathroom, which was where she'd start. Then she would wander. Out to the back porch, maybe, or into the couple's bedroom, which they would have tried to make look normal.

A terrible and heavy black cloud could engulf her for weeks. After *Argosy* bought "The Red Door," the cloud refused to leave. She drank herself to sleep every night. In desperation she seized upon Alain's nervous evocation of "the dark woods" where he spent his enchanted childhood. She longed for countless black conifers, a wildness beyond fear, and a blanket of oblivion. Leaving her marriage behind, she got in her old Chevy Caprice, drove up the coast of Maine, and read in a pine-paneled motel room for days, living off grilled-cheese sandwiches she took out from a diner. It was amazing to think now of the money she'd wasted on prepared food. She read *The Cuckoo Line Affair* because the facts that had to be overturned for a happy ending were simple, and she could shut her mind down to a crack, which filtered out more powerful emotions. Around her, she sensed, the world was caught in a dizzying spiral, but by limiting her own vision, she could stay fairly steady.

All these years later, pausing in the center of Pat Foy's guest room, Virginia felt similarly unmoored. She wound her arms around her waist as her eyes swung here and there. The room was decorated in pale violet and cream. On one wall were nine framed noir paperback covers, all with brightly colored mats that picked up the lurid forties hues. On the wainscoting was a cunning collection of souvenir matches, pins, postcards, coasters, rubber stamps, and shot glasses. On the bedside table was an oversize encyclopedia of crime fiction. On the floor was a

Roman funeral urn and an early-sixties-era rug with huge orange dots.

In her twenties Virginia would have admired this décor. Now, though, she saw it through plainer New England hardscrabble eyes. It was a perfect example of the irony of plenty. Anyone can go slumming or indulge in reverse snobbery. Virginia did it all the time (although probably no one else realized it). But it took an immense amount of time and money to be this hip about icons of passion and intrigue.

She had no sense of the physical placement of the Foy home. Evening had fallen by the time Pat had driven up the short but surprisingly steep driveway. Confusing lights shone every which way from the garage and the path and the garden as well as the house, the sudden hulking presence of which was like an ocean liner moving out of the fog, its horn replaced by the full-ranged barking of Pat's dogs.

The layout of the house was also unclear. Virginia could not remember which way she'd come from the first floor, although she was just supposed to be depositing her "suitcase"—a black canvas tote bag that Pamela had gotten free with Estée Lauder cosmetics. It looked preposterous beside the Roman funeral urn. When she crept down an unfamiliar set of stairs, the dogs found her. They were still yipping and weaving and lifting themselves off their front legs. There were three of them, one big and black and short-haired, not very peppy, but his bumping and obstructing was the most annoying because of his sheer weight. The others were younger and friskier and louder, but kept their distance.

The noise attracted Pat's attention; she called from behind a closed door somewhere down the hall. Virginia opened a door to reveal a bathroom with a *Kiss Me Deadly* poster, soaps shaped like roses, and what looked like a jewel-encrusted drinking cup. It was the most heartlessly ironic drinking vessel Virginia had ever seen. Forget jelly glasses or mugs with cartoon characters. This brought the Borgias' poison cup to mind.

The next door opened onto a fully enclosed windowless space, where the walls were lined with shelves and bins. Here Pat stood on a painted wide-planked floor and turned whiskey bottles so she could read the labels. They were almost out of her reach. "Single malts," said Pat. "Frank loved them. Do any of them catch your eye? I know you used to drink Scotch." To the dogs, who had burst in behind Virginia, their claws clattering on the bare wood floor, she said, "Down, down."

Virginia suddenly realized they were in a storeroom, a *pantry,* that was bigger—much bigger—than her bedroom in Maine. She gazed around at the open shelves. One held just cereal. Two held pasta.

"Or do you want a martini?" asked Pat. "I've already started." She pointed to a glass on the ledge that separated the higher, narrower shelves from the larger cabinets below. "I'm exhausted. We'll eat, drink, and hop into bed." She sounded a little hysterical, actually.

Virginia tried to push the biggest dog away from her. "You drove both ways today," she said, conscious for the first time of how exceptional that was.

"Oh, well," said Pat, grabbing a bottle of Dalwhinnie. "You know me. Down, Foster! Down!"

The sight of so much Scotch made Virginia nervous, but she figured she might as well go ahead and have a drink. Although she hadn't had one since she'd ended up calling the Christmas tree farmer in the middle of the night, there was little chance of repeating herself.

"You know what I can't stand?" said Pat. "Prison break movies. Steel files and cracks in the cement and tiny pieces of string. Carefully hiding the dirt from the tunnel. All those close-ups! The housekeeping reminds me too much of my own life."

Much of the far wall in the living room was a Cinemascope-like black window in which a vast and curious collection of lights sparkled. After a moment Virginia picked out the familiar Manhattan skyline in the center. But it was dwarfed by endless points of light scattered into the inky darkness to the north and to the south.

Pat lowered herself into a huge green sofa, sighed, and said, "Ah, that's better. There's nothing like a drink."

"Yes," said Virginia, perching opposite her on a similarly over-size green couch. Pat had always used her enthusiasm as a shield, which Virginia respected. They'd never pried into each other's lives.

"And I love the idea of being a great philanthropist!" added Pat. "We're going to have terrific fun."

Virginia looked into her glass. She should be grateful to a philanthropist like Andrew Carnegie, who built thousands of libraries across the country, many of which carried her books. *But maybe he shouldn't have destroyed his steelworkers to make the money in the first place.* Sucking wealth upward and then letting it dribble back down was notoriously inefficient.

"I intend to have just as much fun at the age of seventy-five," said Pat. "That's why I don't believe Lydia Bunting will go through with it."

"I guess we'll see," said Virginia cautiously. She hadn't sat in a house having a drink with a girlfriend for so long that she couldn't remember how it was done. Where were you supposed to direct your eyes when you talked to her? If you kept looking straight at her, that was staring, and even if Virginia had been able to keep it up, which she probably couldn't, no one liked to be stared at; she surely didn't. But you shouldn't just gaze out the window, either, even if that's what you wanted to do, because then it looked like you weren't paying attention.

"Do you mind if I read this letter from Frank?" asked Pat. She ripped open an envelope Virginia hadn't noticed her carrying. Then she perked up. "Did you hear that?"

"No," said Virginia. At least now she had something to do with her eyes, i.e., look around the room—uselessly, because the source of any unfamiliar sound would not be found here. "It must be strange not to have Frank around," she said. This struck her as an appropriate remark.

"Yes," said Pat. "He doesn't like jail. It's made him sort of . . . peculiar."

"How so?"

Pat shrugged. "He writes letters all the time."

Half of Pat's drink was gone already, so Virginia took a few hurried sips of her own as Pat began to read. Drinking faster than Pat had obvious pitfalls, but drinking slower seemed to have drawbacks, too, though subtler ones. It could look purse-lipped and spinsterish. Virginia didn't want to appear to be too old for life. Nor did she want to appear to be *afraid* to drink, as if she had problems with alcohol.

"Listen to this." Pat began to read aloud. " 'Dominic and I identified so closely with Riley Gibbs and Neil Culp that we thought we were top dogs, too. It's pathetic. You'd never have a real pack of dogs like that, with every single dog deluded into thinking he's indistinguishable from the alpha male. Animals have more sense—' Will!" Pat jumped up.

Will was a young man—*very* young, actually, maybe twenty—who'd materialized in the doorway behind Virginia. Skinny as a wire hanger, he had some of the same buoyant tension. Virginia recognized that springy cockiness from her own youth. Surely people must have been young between then and now, but she couldn't think of any instances offhand.

"Ginny!" said Pat. "I don't believe I've mentioned Will to you yet!"

His sandy hair was long and thin and straight. His lips and eyelashes were oddly dark, his blue eyes oddly light under a pair of gold wire-rim glasses. He had a bony jaw, a long nose, and restless shoulders.

"Will is Lemuel's son," said Pat. "He's staying with us for a while. I don't know what I would have done without him. He's been a great friend to Ruby. He understands a lot of the stuff she's been going through. The pressure on kids these days is enormous."

This was Lemuel's son? He looked too . . . pale. And he was wearing an old sport coat. How extraordinary that Pat hadn't mentioned him before.

"Ginny was my best friend in high school," said Pat.

"I don't think I have a best friend," said Will with a brief frown.

"Pat must have told you how much we always admired your father's books," said Virginia.

It was hard to separate Will's wariness from his formality. "Yes," he said. His slow, clipped drawl barely involved his mouth. "I can't read them."

Virginia's own books elbowed briefly to the front of her brain and then receded. When you live alone, you can't exactly have a secret. Everything you do is a secret, in a sense, because no one else knows about it. But you're not trying to hide anything, either. The closest thing in her life to the conventionally covert was her writing career. The marketing directors in New York and Boston who'd hired her for her copywriting skills did not know that she'd published stories or, later, books. At first it was disappointing to realize how little the world cared, but later she realized she got a kick from treating her whole mystery-writing career as, say, an extramarital affair.

"Lemuel had a bad episode with his heart a couple of months ago," said Pat cheerily. "That's when Will and I met. He'd been living with his father for a while then. But Lemuel is better now, thank God. He's making money as a guest host on the "Ahoy, Murder" mystery cruise. And Will is staying with us. He took some time off before college to help with expenses."

Pat was beaming at her expectantly, so Virginia said to Will, "You're looking for a job?"

Will pushed his hands together, sucked in some air, frowned, and shook his head. Then he exhaled noisily and poured out some Pellegrino water from a bottle on an oddly placed tile-topped table.

Virginia wondered if he could have heard her.

"He's looking in the city," said Pat. "In the meantime, I've asked him to help out with Ruby. Isn't that wonderful?"

"It's Ruby who's wonderful," said Will promptly.

"That's so true," said Pat, lowering her voice. "How do you think she's doing?"

"I admire her a great deal," said Will. The conversation came to a temporary halt as he eased himself into the huge green couch next to Pat. His jeans were torn at one knee, and a tuft of threads hung from one side of the slit. The kneecap revealed was as intimate as bone.

"My number one priority in all this has always been Ruby," said Pat, beginning to wilt over the kneecap. "I'm sorry, I'm so tired, I've been driving all day, am I making any sense?"

"Always," said Will.

"She's the most fascinating child imaginable," said Pat. "Constantly thinking of some fabulous new deviltry. Oh, God, I'm tired!"

"Ruby is very idealistic," said Will, his tone reproving.

"Ruby follows Will around like a puppy dog," said Pat. "It's so adorable."

"I am her happy slave," said Will. He was wearing cowboy boots, maybe even the same ones Virginia had dreamed about.

"Where are you from?" asked Virginia suddenly.

"Upstate New York."

"Ginny lives in Maine," said Pat. "She's here to help me give money to people who had LinkAge stock."

"That's interesting," said Will, the very blandness of his words and tone implying reserves of meaning. "I didn't know you were giving away money."

"If our food doesn't come soon, I'm going to have to go to bed, anyway," said Pat. "Could you take care of it? You know where the money in the sideboard is."

Will nodded, but his mind was evidently stuck on the notion of charity. "I used to sponsor a kid in Nicaragua," he said. "I got a couple of letters from him. I couldn't understand them so I never wrote back. But I sent checks for a long time."

Virginia didn't believe him for a second. But Pat laid her hand on his forearm and let it linger there. "I should have known!" she said. Evidently she had transferred her affection for Lemuel to him.

A two-note door chime sounded, and she jumped up as if electrocuted. "Finally!" she cried.

She was gone in a flash. Virginia stood up to follow her, expecting Will to do the same. Instead he untangled his sapling limbs and warily approached the little table, shifting his weight from foot to foot for a moment before pouring himself more water amid a pop and a hiss.

"How old are you, Will?" asked Virginia.

"Twenty," he said stiffly.

When she didn't respond, he looked at her out of the corners of his eyes. "You're not very much like Pat," he said.

"No," said Virginia.

"What was it like when you were twenty?" he asked.

"I don't remember," she said.

"Oh," he said. "I didn't mean—"

Now they were both embarrassed. They seemed to carom off each other in their hurry to get out of the room.

15

When Virginia woke the next day, her thoughts as they surfaced were still so dark that she had to hit herself on the forehead with the heel of her hand to beat them back where they belonged. She couldn't believe she was in Pat Foy's house. The shift in the tectonic plates must have been enormous to have thrown the two of them together after all these years.

Often in English mysteries a murderer has to be discovered amid a variety of guests in a large country house. The addition of Will Samuel to the Foy household suggested a similar assortment here. But the crime was not one discrete element of this establishment; it was not hiding; it encompassed the whole building. And here was Virginia Howley smack inside, where her ruin had been hatched.

She was surprised to learn that she and Pat were going to visit a victim of Frank's fraud that day. Pat's plan had had a trumped-up air at the Dock. But they were on their way to Orange by noon. Frank's former secretary had asked Pat to check on another former employee, Simone Massey, who used to be head of LGT food services.

"I never dreamed you'd be working as a waitress," Pat said to Virginia as she fooled with the car window. "Was that because of LinkAge?"

"Sort of," said Virginia.

"Not that there's anything wrong with being a waitress," said Pat. "Look at *Shoot the Piano Player*."

"She dies at the end," said Virginia.

"Are you sure? I don't think so," said Pat, clearly lying. She closed up the window at last.

Orange was only a few miles from Hart Ridge, but was the kind of decrepit, unglamorous small city that only the grittier of the police procedurals ventured into. Originally a suburb of Newark, Orange was now just another dilapidated part of the greater metropolitan patchwork, sliced up and stitched back together by a crisscrossing mesh of major thoroughfares. Simone's street was in a pocket of two-story houses packed together behind chain-link fences. Gable-fronted, each house looked at first as if it were turned the wrong way. But all the glassed-in porches were clearly supposed to be facing forward, no matter how high and awkward they were, or how overfull with tables and chairs and odd plastic containers. Simone's house was one of the smallest, and it had not been painted any more recently than the others, but it possessed an exceptional alertness. Although the general desolation of winter had fallen upon it as it had upon the whole shabby street, nothing was broken at the Massey house, no step, no balustrade, no panel, no front light. The windows were clean. There was a welcome mat.

Simone Massey stood maybe four foot eight. She appeared young to have already retired. She was broad and thick and strong-looking. Her skin was caramel-colored. Her hair, still black, was short and flat. When she offered to take Pat's and Virginia's coats, Pat accepted and Virginia did not. She grew hot in her padded jacket, but this struck her as more appropriate than Pat's light and carefree appearance. Pat wore high-heeled black boots and a thick white ribbed turtleneck, and she carried a glossy black open-ended square of a purse with straps of a length Virginia had never seen before. The bag was meant to be carried over the shoulder, but snugly.

Virginia also declined Simone's offer of tea, but she began to suspect that this was a mistake as she watched the older woman retrieve cups and tea bags in a routinely homey manner, waiting for the kettle to boil. Hospitality for Simone was clearly the norm. She may not have seemed poor to herself, despite the difficult neighborhood and despite whatever LinkAge had done to her. The three women sat at an old-fashioned cabriole-legged table covered with a pure white eyelet cotton tablecloth—and a thick sheet of clear vinyl.

"I was sorry to hear about your husband's troubles," said Simone. "He was a very friendly man. Some people get so important they can't see past the ends of their noses, and Mister Foy wasn't like that. He always had a nice hello, how are you, how is your grandson."

Pat was pleased. And somewhere deep inside Virginia was, too. She was glad that Frank had been courteous to this decent and dignified woman. But maybe mere pleasantness of manner shouldn't excuse so much. It seemed unfair to the more socially awkward people who hadn't stolen a dime—Virginia, for instance.

"Frank can't bear to have his old colleagues suffer because of something he was part of," said Pat, spooning sugar into her tea. "And it seems that you lost an unusually large amount."

"I saved more than those whiz kids?" said Simone, surprised.

"Some of them," said Pat, smiling. "But I don't count them. They were part of the problem."

"I see," said Simone, stirring her tea. "You ever hear of Fripp College?"

Pat frowned in concentration, but shook her head.

"When I was younger I was not a saving type of person," said Simone. "My daughter felt neglected. That's probably why she got into drugs. I don't know where she is now, and I don't want to know." She ignored Pat's cries of sympathy. "Luster's father . . ." She dismissed him with a little dip of her hand. "Doesn't matter what happened to him. My grandson came to live with me, and I switched jobs so I could be there when he came home from school. I started out serving at LGT. Once you were finished with lunch your day was pretty much over. The cafeteria stays open later now, but back then it closed up at three. I was a lot better grandmother than I was a mother. Maybe I was better with boys. All I ever wanted was to make my grandson feel loved and secure. Sometimes even now that he's grown when he's sleeping I will go in and kiss his forehead."

"I know what you mean!" cried Pat. "I used to watch my daughters breathe when they were asleep."

"I don't need anything for myself," said Simone. "I have Social Security. I'm healthy. And if I get sick, well, I've already had my day. But Luster is very, very smart. When he first made the honor roll back in the fourth grade, I told him if he made it every year after that, I would send him to college. It wasn't easy, but he did it. The kids in the high school here fight all the time. It is not a good school. One Spanish boy teased him so dirty Luster finally had to hit him in the mouth. But he did it off school property."

Pat nodded as if this made all the difference in the world, and who knows, maybe it did.

"Luster has never given any trouble. He was in the National Honor Society last year. He was on the debating team, and one of his teachers, a white man, said he had never heard anyone who could speak so well. He said he was better than any politician on TV. He told him he could be a senator someday.

"Luster! Come here and talk to the ladies."

The boy on the stairs seemed especially tall because you saw his feet first and then a long unwinding of the rest of him. His feet were too big for the steps, too fast and irrepressible. Even on the thin blurred carpeting of the stairs the rapid scuffing sounded joyful. He was dressed like anyone—running shoes, jeans, sweatshirt. As soon as he entered the room and extended his hand, though, you could feel the flash of his charm. He was the baby. Beloved, he still sported tenderness. He smiled, and you believed in something again.

"Luster wanted to know why he had to go to such a bad high school, and I told him, life isn't fair."

As Simone spoke, Virginia was looking directly into Luster's face, and she could see the animation drain out of it.

"Isn't that true?" asked Simone.

"Yes, Mier," said the boy, automatically using what must have been a term of affection and respect, but his tone was inert.

"These ladies want to know about the 401(k)," she said.

Luster looked at the floor while Virginia murmured something vaguely negative, pressing her thumbnail deeply into her thigh.

"Mister Howard at the company, that is, the LGT personnel advisor, showed me how it was better to save through the 401(k) than at the bank because you didn't pay taxes on the money you put in. He bought company stock for me, which I was proud to have. I couldn't take any money out until I was sixty-five, but that was okay. I knew I wasn't going to want to touch it for ten years, not until Luster turned eighteen. All the time I got statements saying how much money was in there. At the end it was a whole lot. One day I put the paper on the refrigerator just to look at, but then I took it down because I didn't want to excite envy."

"Your grandson was planning to attend Fripp College?" asked Pat.

"No," said Simone, recoiling before politeness, or maybe a simple dogged hope, stopped her. "He was accepted to a real college."

"Oh," said Pat. She sensed that she'd gone wrong somewhere, but she'd never known much about schools.

"He was going to go to Villanova University."

"How nice," said Pat.

"It was a shock to me when the stock fell apart. At first I thought only the earnings in the 401(k) were gone. I was disappointed, because I had been counting on them for Luster's college. But I had saved plenty to put in the plan. And he was bound to get a scholarship. There was one given by a real estate man for three thousand dollars that his teacher recommended him for. And we could have taken out more loans. Then I learned that all the money was gone, not just the earnings, you know, the extra that it made, but everything—all the money that I had saved over the years. I wasn't even going to get a pension. College was out of the question. It was very hard for me, because I had promised him."

Simone seemed to be talking more to Luster at this point, although she wasn't looking at him or directing her attention
toward him in any way, and he must have already heard this explanation dozens of times. She had to have tried to add up her
zeroes in every different way possible, just as Virginia had, to
make sure that all there was in the end was another zero.

"Then he got some mail from Fripp College. There was a
photo in it of three nice-looking kids, one boy and two girls.
Black kids with nice neat clothes. The boy reminded me of Luster a little." Except maybe not the Luster sitting before them.
His face had contracted.

"I drove over there and spoke to the admissions officer, and
he explained about all the jobs graduates were eligible for. Good
jobs. In banking. And legal administration."

Virginia wondered what "legal administration" could refer to.
Nothing real, of course.

"So I sold the car and told Luster I had enough to send him
to Fripp. Now he tells me that the people there are the same
ones he was trying to escape from at Orange High, but I say, that
can't be true. Someone is paying for those courses. They have to
want to learn."

"The government pays," he said unexpectedly, his lip curling.

"And what's wrong with that?" cried Simone, suddenly old.
"Haven't I paid plenty to the government?"

But Luster had sunk back into silence, his chin dropping
toward his chest.

"Isn't it good to learn data processing?" she said.

"You can never learn too much!" said Pat with exaggerated enthusiasm. "I didn't realize this when I was young. I thought my
ninth-grade biology teacher was so boring I could scream. But
that's when I first heard about Darwin, and now I get such a kick

out of recommending the stately Darwin tulips to my meanest clients. My biology teacher loved talking about the survival of the fittest. I can still hear her saying it over and over in that squeaky voice of hers, 'survival of the fittest, survival of the fittest,' though she was so sick all the time that it was amazing she survived to the end of the year. Do you remember Mrs. Stutz, Ginny?"

Virginia was speechless. Did Pat have any idea of what she was saying?

"I guess your friend doesn't feel like talking," said Simone.

"That's okay," said Pat. "I've always talked enough for two."

Simone chuckled a little as Pat proffered a check. It was, grotesquely, one of those customized types that pop up as a sales pitch among other perfectly reasonable-looking checks. It was printed with the image of a skier on a slope.

"What's that?" asked Simone. Virginia, quite frankly, wondered the same.

"To help with your losses," said Pat.

Virginia's eyes were drawn to Luster. The struggle between his loyalty to his grandmother and his need to distance himself from her gullibility was terrible to see. Pat's babble must have sent him over the edge. He carefully lowered his head into his hands as if it were precious china and then spoke to no one in particular. "She has almost nothing left," he said slowly. "Why did she waste it on Fripp?"

Virginia tossed and turned that night. As usual, the shell of her, the outside part, the skin and muscle, was exhausted, but the inside part, her mind and nerves and will, were racing around and around on a single track. The check that Pat had given the Masseys could screw up Luster's chance of getting a full scholarship next year at Villanova. If they'd already applied for aid, and the college found out about the check, they might be accused of fraud. But if word got out in town, there would be problems sooner than that. The daughter could come back to get some of it. She might rob or terrorize them.

Virginia was used to not sleeping. Sometimes she thought of these nighttime hours as constituting a second, hidden life. It wasn't the moonlight, or the shadows, that truly characterized the night. It was the fluidity. She could not always distinguish among her wakeful cogitations, the quick flashes of her dreams, and the snatches of the mysteries she read in the interstices. She was reminded of the library on the third floor—a room right out of a whodunit. She would look for the new Lydia Bunting.

Earlier she'd had only a general impression of bookshelves. This time when she switched on the overhead lighting she felt the full force of the three walls of books. The upper shelves were accessible because of a library ladder on a hidden track. In the center of the room, wands of full-spectrum lighting were suspended above a cluster of leather club chairs and matching hassocks. The mysteries looked as if they were arranged aesthetically rather than alphabetically, with uniformly sized vintage paperbacks grouped together, as were the slim old hardbacks and the Detective Book Club threesomes.

Virginia tried to remind herself of the financing behind this bonanza, but it was hard not to feel a mix of awe and envy.

When she'd started to write, she'd wanted to do everything in an entirely new way. She reread Cornell Woolrich, for the horror, and Jorge Luis Borges, for the form to put it into. Her main problem, she decided, was what to do with the boilerplate of the more typical mystery. Most authors simply copied it, throwing in a few variations on their own. Others stripped it away, or ignored it, with mixed results. Virginia decided to zoom in for a close-up, and she ended up with "The Red Door," which was almost Dadaesque in its repetition. A man sought, over and over, to get in somewhere. He never gave up, just as men never give up trying to get inside women. "The Red Door" proved to be Virginia's entrance into the publishing world.

Her next story, "The First Funeral," zeroed in on the funeral of a postal clerk: The funeral was the only topic of conversation, and the motive for the murder turned out to be the funeral itself; the identity of the body was irrelevant. She also wrote about a killer's attempts to pass a Rorschach test, a duel between expert witnesses about maggots, and the angry confession of a private eye's "black widow" girlfriend. Virginia was elated when a small press offered her a contract for a collection. The press had previously published a book of morgue shots she actually owned, and she was happy to be associated with it.

She received two complimentary quotes for the book jacket. One came from a hot young story writer still in rabbinical school, the other from a no-longer bestselling author whose thrillers were set in carefully researched foreign lands. He referred to her "high-voltage" suspense. The best part of the book, though, was that it looked and felt real, with pages and a spine as well as a jacket. You could grab on to it, if you suddenly felt that you were in danger of falling backward through life.

For her next book, a novel, Virginia decided to reach deep into the innards of the boilerplate and pull it inside out so that all the flesh and blood and organs were protecting the skin. She called it *Hell Is a Mystery,* and the twist was that the detection itself caused the crime. The main characters were a pair of lesbian exterminators based on those who'd come to her apartment in Providence a few times. They careened through the book, laying rubber as they had in real life. But Virginia was not happy when she finished. The victims were lifeless even before they were actually killed. Her foreknowledge of their end suffused their very being. She went back to her stories and found them similarly static. When death marched in, it poisoned the past— before it happened. That was her greatest weakness as a writer, she decided. She could not grapple with death.

"So what's keeping you up?"

Virginia jumped.

Pat was at the door. "I heard someone up here and figured it was you," she said.

"Oh, I never sleep," said Virginia. But she explained her misgivings over what might happen to the Masseys.

"The things you think of," said Pat, shaking her head in disbelief.

"And who is this secretary of Frank's?" asked Virginia, worried afresh. "Why did she give you their name?"

"Well," said Pat. "Her name is Ellen Kloda. She told me she lost most of the deposit on a cabin, so I figured I'd replace it. But she didn't cash the check. Finally I called her and got her, unlike anyone else, and she said she couldn't take the money until I met with some other people who needed it more."

"It doesn't make any sense," said Virginia.

"Oh, nothing makes any sense," said Pat, starting to examine the spines on her books.

Virginia started to ask about the new Lydia Bunting, decided she was too tired, then rallied, and went ahead.

"I don't know why anyone would kill herself when there are so many murder mysteries left to read," said Pat. "I can always read about Nurse Pomeroy, no matter what state I'm in."

"You can't keep someone from killing herself by giving her mystery novels," said Virginia dryly.

"Why not?" said Pat. "Even if a mystery is really, really bad, I always stick it out because I want to learn who did it." She handed over the new Lydia Bunting, which was still in hardback. It had the usual innocuous cover: a plain white background, bold lettering, a disembodied hand with a red-stained knife. Then Pat fell heavily into one of the club chairs. "Not being able to sleep isn't so bad when you have company," she said. But she was blinking her eyes as she spoke, as if to blink away her fatigue. "Do you have, you know, a boyfriend or anything?"

Virginia shook her head dumbly and slumped into the chair opposite. Her current loneliness would make sense only in the grave.

"Sometimes all you need is company," said Pat earnestly. "It's funny that Will is Lemuel's son."

"Does he remind you of him?"

"I never thought about it," said Pat. "Lemuel wanted to get him away from certain 'bad influences' in the country. Isn't that sweet?"

"Maybe he meant himself," said Virginia. She thought she'd detected a desperation in Will Samuel that she sympathized with and had no desire to expose. Both of them were freeloaders, though probably not without good reason. Will's presence made her own feel less singular. Her plight became less pitiable, somehow, if Pat had plucked her out of Maine because that was the sort of thing Pat did.

"People like Lemuel don't get more virtuous when they get older," said Pat. "Just more exhausted."

"Not exactly ready for a roll in the hay," said Virginia.

"It might have killed him," said Pat.

"Maybe for him it would have been worth it."

Pat frowned, but Virginia closed her eyes. She was so tired herself that there were pictures on her inner lids, pictures of inert foliage. She felt herself floating away, and she imagined Pat floating away in tandem, each of them leading separate lives behind their eyelids.

During Virginia's brief romance with the Christmas tree farmer, he told one of the telecommuters, a young man from Boston, that he knew of an old woman who had a hand-sewn baby quilt for sale cheap. Without thinking, Virginia agreed to accompany them, regretting her decision only later, in the backseat of the car. It struck her that the men might be planning to exploit the woman's ignorance of her wares. Virginia's apprehensions grew when the car drew up in front of a shack that smelled even from the road. The Christmas tree farmer knocked on the door, and the other two followed him straight into the tiny front room as a doughy gray-faced woman was still struggling to her feet. She sank back, panting. In here the smell was nauseating, a combination of something like burnt sugar and a deep, deep rot. Beside the old woman's sprung armchair was a cradle empty except for a dirty, badly sewn, and irregularly shaped baby quilt. She pointed to it without speaking.

"Beautiful," said the Christmas tree farmer—a remark all the more astonishing because he didn't seem to realize that it wasn't remotely true. There were folds and bulges in the quilt where the pieces of fabric did not fit together.

The man from Boston was overwhelmed by the scene. He wiped his face with his hands, hard. "Yes, beautiful," he said. "My friends would appreciate it, I'm sure, but they are strict about federal guidelines. You know, they are first-time parents, very young and concerned parents. I'm not sure that this—"

"Just throw it in the washing machine," said the Christmas tree farmer. "It'll be fine." Except that the quilt couldn't have withstood a single wash.

The fat woman's sunken eyes and inexpressive mouth did not change. Virginia was afraid she was mute or even averbal. At least her state of mind seemed uncomplicated by hope of any sort.

"How much?" said the Christmas tree farmer. "Forty dollars, if I remember correctly?"

The woman moved her head in some ill-defined way.

"All right," said the man from Boston, taking two twenties from his wallet with bad grace. Then he plucked the quilt from the cradle and hurried out to the car.

"Nice to see you again," said the Christmas tree farmer to the old woman, whose face remained inanimate.

"I don't get it," he said to Virginia when he had closed the door, which was half plywood, behind them. "He didn't have to take it if he didn't want it."

Virginia said nothing. The stink had followed them to the car: It was in the baby quilt.

Virginia kept on saying nothing. She wouldn't have minded, really, if the Christmas tree farmer had been shaking the guy down, Robin Hood–style, but she didn't think he had been. Or maybe not consciously? The pity and repugnance she felt for the old woman filled her with disgust. She went home and wrote a story called "The Empty Cradle" about the woman, the sale of the quilt, and a missing baby. Evil hovered, diffuse, until the end, when it was pinned down to an unholy and surprising alliance. Virginia sold the story to *Black Cat* magazine and never saw the Christmas tree farmer again—never spoke to him, either, except for that one late-night call.

She could not have said exactly why. Certainly the results of the visit were, in sum, good. The man from Boston was out some cash, but he could afford it. It might even be argued that he deserved to forfeit the forty dollars because it was less than the difference between what he'd expected to pay and what he'd expected the fair market value of his purchase to be. Either way the benefit to the old woman was presumably greater than any loss he could have sustained. The Christmas tree farmer may have sensed some small problem, but he wasn't troubled by it. You couldn't say he tricked the man from Boston, because he had no consciousness of doing so. And Virginia had benefited the most of all, through her first sale of a story in several years.

The old woman remained a cipher. It was not clear whether she understood the true value of the quilt or the degradation of her circumstances. She may have endured their scrutiny simply in order to survive. She may no longer have been able to distinguish between humiliation and fraud.

17

P at and Virginia were sitting in a Teaneck bagel shop sipping coffee from Styrofoam cups when Karl Kupmann burst in. Even before he began on his excited tirade, Virginia had been overwhelmed with information and noise and choices. From a counter that stretched down the left side a handful of Hispanics dispensed two dozen different types of oddly puffy bagels and enough other foods of varying nationalities to fill three large chalkboards with cramped writing and to provide what seemed to be endless additional signage on the grill, on the microwaves, on the refrigerators, on the register, and even on the thick blond polyurethaned tables the women were sitting at, presumably after their decisions had been made. Televisions tuned to different financial stations were anchored high in opposite corners. They were on mute, but the two ribbons of words that crawled across the screen were more insistent than sound. Although their import escaped her, Virginia couldn't help reading them as soon as they jumped into her field of vision:

S&P . . . DOW . . . LKG . . . HOW TO GET IN ON THE BOOMING
LUXURY MARKET, TONIGHT AT 8 . . .

"I guess a lot of investors come here," Virginia had said.

"Oh?" said Pat, looking around at the customers. "What gives
you that impression?"

Virginia gestured at the TVs.

"They have this stuff on all over the place," said Pat. "I never
really thought about why." She made a face at the coffee. "Frank
called this morning and told me about every meal he's had in the
last three days. He complains when it's bad, because it's a waste
of money, and he complains when it's good, because that's a
waste of money, too."

Karl burst in at this point. He was a tall, stooped, ash-faced
man sporting a big gold watch exposed by a too-short shirt
sleeve. He looked a little trembly, and his bones jutted out in
unexpected places. He spoke with his chin out as if he were still
hurrying toward them. "I wish you could meet my wife, May," he
said. "But she's safer in the house."

He glanced at his watch, then glanced at it again as if he
hadn't taken in the time. He never stopped talking. He moved a
small A-framed cardboard sign, gingerly felt the bench for stick-
iness or moisture, and sat, all without pausing. He had met his
wife twenty-five years ago, when he was working for an American engineering firm in Hong Kong. She'd been born outside
Chicago, but her parents were from China. When she turned
eighteen, they sent her to Hong Kong to marry her own kind.
But what kind might that be? She did not speak Chinese. And
she was too quiet for many young American men, too deferen-
tial. Karl, more than twice her age, had never encountered anyone like her. "She was so beautiful, like a painting," he said

fervently. "She had a natural stillness. It made me calm and happy just to look at her. Her parents did not approve of the marriage, but she was American enough that they could not prevent it. She chose me because she thought I would always protect her. She used those very words when she accepted my proposal."

Virginia glanced at Pat to see if she had any better idea of what was going on. His wife was safer in the house?

"Don't you see?" he was saying. "We have two boys. They're men now. One is getting his Ph.D. in experimental psychology. The other is in business. I never had to worry about them. That was May's job. She made sure they worked hard and got ahead. She took care of them. She took care of all of us. You know what it can be like when you have a houseful of males. I guess it was hard sometimes. But she never complained. She was always content to be there for us. And now I can't be there for her. I've let her down."

The man's nervous volubility had prompted a similar response in Pat, whose head began to bob back and forth. Soon her words came tumbling down over his: "Don't be so hard on yourself. I'm serious. I tell Frank that all the time."

As Virginia raised her eyebrows at this sentiment, the other two kept talking at each other, louder and louder:

"I don't know what to do. I'm looking for work, but it's hard. Experience counts against you these days. It means you're hidebound. But I have to keep trying. And I can't let May know that at this point *I will do anything*."

"I know exactly what you mean," said Pat.

Karl blinked, then said, "If only I were younger. Then I'd have a fighting chance."

"I'm sure you still do."

"How was I supposed to know what was going on? Our division wasn't really profitable, but I figured everyone else's was. Sometimes at night I dream that I am drowning and I wake up gasping and choking for air."

"I wonder how anyone survives certain nightmares."

"It's very easy to interpret. I'm drowning—drowning financially. I'm desperate."

"That's why we're here! To give you a check! But first I promised you some coffee!"

"I don't know how I can thank you."

"I'm going to get the coffee!" Pat rushed off clutching her purse, this one covered with cherries.

Karl was left blinking uncertainly at Virginia. Although he'd blamed no one, his tone had been harsh, maybe out of fear of looking weak. He did not seem unusually weak physically; the height, the jutting bones made him appear brittle at most. But his features held an unmistakable softness. There was that defensive chin. And his mouth was blurry. His tall forehead, his arching eyebrows, his high cheeks, all served to accentuate the alarm in his eyes. He was probably dismissed all his life as a nice fellow and a real team player, although neither of these descriptions was necessarily true. Because of his looks, no one would ever look to him for inventive new ideas, or leadership, or strength of any sort.

He blanched. "May!" he breathed. "May, please!" He leapt up from the bench as if stung.

A very pale, small, beautifully dressed Asian woman was wavering silently just inside the door.

"I know these ladies from work," he tried. But there was only Virginia, in black clothes rusty with age, clearly not corporate material.

May was clad in slightly darker versions of the beiges and ochres in the room, and so looked as if she were not a person but a shadow of a person, cast upon the bagel shop wall.

"I know these ladies *through* work," he corrected himself desperately, not taking his eyes off his wife.

May appeared not to hear him. Her words, when they came, were gentle and held more wonder than reproof: "Who are you?"

"Virginia Howley. I'm from Maine."

"Are you buying our house?"

"No."

"Please, May. We're not selling the house."

May's eyes slowly shifted to her husband as if his childish importuning had finally penetrated. "I don't know why you keep things from me."

"I don't."

May simply looked at him.

"I don't anymore."

He watched Pat bring him his coffee.

"I just don't want you to worry," he said, although he was still looking at Pat.

"Are you a real estate agent?" May asked her.

"God, no. I would be a terrible real estate agent," said Pat. "I always say the first thing that comes into my head. I'm a landscaper."

"Sit down, sit down," said Karl. "You shouldn't have come. You'll tire yourself out."

"Are you . . . May?" Pat's voice soared to its very highest soprano notes as she settled herself perkily on the bench. "I'm Frank Foy's wife."

"Frank was in accounting at LinkAge," said Karl.

"Now he's in jail," said Pat brightly.

"I'm sure you remember him."

May shook her head.

"They want to help us," added Karl, looking at the Styrofoam cup Pat had placed before him as if he'd never seen anything like it before.

"Let me get you some," Pat said to May. "I'm afraid it's not very good, but at least it has caffeine."

"No!" cried Karl. Catching himself and lowering his voice as if he were confiding in them, he said, "May doesn't drink coffee."

"Frank feels terrible about what happened," said Pat. "And we want to try to make it up to you both. Speaking of landscaping, I can provide you with my services free of charge. You know the bog garden at LinkAge? I did that. LinkAge has let it go terribly. The reeds have taken over. But I could make you a nice perennial garden. All-season interest, that sort of thing. Right now I'm doing one in Rumson. Not that you probably want to hear about it."

May looked out the window.

"Well, I'm going to give you money, too," said Pat.

"I think money is a more immediate concern," said Karl.

"No one is ever interested in a free garden," sighed Pat.

NAS . . . RUS . . . INVESTORS CONFIDENT ONCE AGAIN . . . ran across the TV above her head. Pat had always been able to keep chattering in high school—no matter what state she was in or whom she was talking to. It was a real gift, although maddening, of course, to a person like Virginia, who was actually paying attention to all the different tensions in the room.

"Did you tell them you took out a second mortgage on the house?" May asked Karl quietly. "And did you tell them why?"

"May, please, it doesn't matter," said Karl.

This is when the tawdry secrets would be revealed, secrets that Virginia did not want to know. To preclude any confession, she said, "I lost money, too." The others turned to her in surprise. She was fleetingly afraid that the Kupmanns were wondering if they could sink to her level: rusty clothes, bad haircut, shabby purse.

May said, "When LinkAge declared bankruptcy, Karl lost his job, his savings, and his health insurance all on the same day." For the first time she let her bitterness show. "Then . . . then I got sick. I had two operations. Insurance covered some of the expenses, but not all, and now we pay more than two thousand dollars a month to continue it."

"It sounds worse than it is," said Karl. "We'll get by somehow."

"Then I had to have a treatment that wasn't covered, so we took out a home equity loan."

"How awful!" cried Pat. "What's wrong?"

May bowed her head. Yes, there was at least one secret, the nature of her illness, but she was not going to reveal it.

"May, please," said Karl.

"He's throwing away his future on a lost cause," said May.

"That's not true. The doctors say there's still lots we can do."

Pat had her checkbook out, and at this point Virginia wouldn't have been surprised if she'd simply emptied the account for them.

"You think I don't know what it means when the bank calls," said May.

"Take this," said Pat, filling out a check.

"Oh, thank you, thank you," Karl said brokenly. He was beyond his earlier desperation and beyond his subsequent sup-

pression of it. There seemed nothing left to suppress. Both Kupmanns stood up, drained, and walked wearily to the door.

"What do you think is wrong with her?" asked Pat. Earlier
she'd appeared to be her usual high-strung, speedy self. But her
exuberance had turned sour.

"Something awful," said Virginia.

Pat nodded.

CHAPTER

18

Virginia was puzzled by a van sitting in the middle of the street. Its engine was idling, so it hadn't broken down. She couldn't think of any other reason it might have stopped—there was no light, no driveway to turn into—so as Pat passed it in the Touareg, Virginia peered around her and caught sight of the driver resting his forearms on the horizontal steering wheel and eating a sandwich from a white paper bag. Virginia closed her eyes.

This time as Pat unlocked her door, the dogs were accompanied by music swelling from somewhere in the back of the house: strings, horns, war cries. "Will must be home," said Pat happily. She and Virginia followed the trotting, rippling dogs into a white room dominated by a huge TV as flat as a window. Will was indeed there, lying almost horizontally on the big black leather couch, head propped up so he could see, feet on a large square coffee table. At the same angle lay a girl wearing blue jeans and a plain gray athletic T-shirt as tight as a sausage casing.

"Ruby! Honey!" said Pat. "What are you doing back so soon? How was Washington? Did you pick her up, Will?"

"The last presentation was canceled because of the rain," said Ruby without taking her eyes off the screen, which, due to its size and place in the room, would not let you be. What Virginia saw from her strange angle near the door was great isolated shapes that seemed to jump from one part of the screen to another: a thick leather vest exposing biceps as rounded as a Poussin, laces crisscrossing arrogant calves, a row of Roman helmets bristling with spikes, a sword drawing a line of blood across pink flesh.

"This is your Aunt Ginny!" said Pat. "Can you believe it? Doesn't she look great? How was your trip? You definitely look older. People always mature when they travel. The dogs have missed you so. They've been disconsolate, you wouldn't have believed it, but of course they've behaved just as badly as ever. What do you make of Washington? It always struck me as one big slab of concrete."

In the midst of this Ruby said "Hi" with a brief glance in Virginia's direction. Her eyes were flat and black, but glossy, like stuffed animal eyes. Her cheeks bulged like a cherub's. Her lace-up suede boots, which wrinkled stylishly at the ankles, must have cost more than three hundred dollars. She wore a braided purple ponytail holder around her wrist.

"You should have called me," Pat finished up.

"Will gave me a ride."

"Will has his father's car here," Pat told Virginia with odd pride. "It's sitting in our driveway right now."

Lemuel Samuel's car? That would be no ordinary ride. Virginia felt a dreamy stab of memory—or desire. Late teens, an unexpected vehicle. What liberty.

The TV room's white walls, severe blinds, squared-off black furniture, and industrial gray carpeting set up expectations of a sterile environment. As Virginia moved farther inside, though, a sharp odor became even stronger. Unwashed socks, pheromones, old food, dog. The smell matched the glistening swagger on the screen.

"Will says . . ." Ruby was drowned out by some thundering hooves. "Will says that in Roman times you could do all sorts of things when you were thirteen. You could vote in the Senate and drive a chariot. I can't do anything because I can't drive."

"I'll take you anywhere you want to go," said Will, who was far less relaxed than his posture would initially lead you to believe. His arms made two tense V's behind his head. His dress shirt was too small for him, and the placket had raised up in three straining waves down his narrow chest.

Dozens of flaming arrows were released into the air.

"In Roman times you could go to war when you were thirteen, right, Will?" said Ruby.

A giant digital soldier staggered, pierced in his swelling breast. Another man, equally large, lost a monumental leg.

"You could do stuff when you were young, yeah," said Will.

Will's voice sounded stifled, as if it had got stuck somewhere before making it out into the world. This should have deflected attention, as intended, but it did not. The only real product of the most secret, inner part of a person is his voice. Secretions of other sorts may feel intimate and urgent, but they are not personal. Pat, who'd always been open and generous, had a voice that flowed freely. When Will spoke, you became more aware of the shadowy recesses from which his voice came, and you became more aware of the defensive posture that was protecting this voice: the tucked-in chin, the tilt of the taut, narrow shoulders, the gangly arms ready to spring into action.

"If it were Roman times," said Ruby, "I could get married."

Even at this distance, Virginia could feel Will's embarrassment. "I didn't say anything about that." His words, at the end, held a lick of the lash.

"Will," said Ruby, shocked. "Of course you did. Don't you remember?"

Pat was unfazed. "I thought we could rent *Mallow* tonight," she said. "In honor of Ginny. Wouldn't that be fun?"

As the camera panned silently over hundreds of hugely sprawling, mangled bodies, you could distinguish the odd hum made by the TV.

"Will hates his father's books," said Ruby.

"Really?" said Pat.

When the phone rang, Virginia followed her out of the room. From Pat's corner office in the kitchen you could hear the automated female voice of the caller ID begin its falling and then rising tones: "Call from in-mah-tah. Call from in-mah-tah."

"Who's that?" asked Virginia.

"Inmate," said Pat, springing for the handset.

"Yes, Frank, yes, it's all set," said Pat. "Yes, tomorrow." Then she started saying "Mmm, mmm, mmm" in a way that made Virginia realize Pat wanted to talk but couldn't because she wasn't alone.

Virginia felt as if a heavy net had fallen on her from above. Where should she retreat to? The situation was becoming clear. Pat's designs on Lemuel had been thwarted, so now she was unconsciously fostering a substitute relationship between her daughter and his son, despite the difference in their ages.

It was still early, but Virginia decided to pour herself some single malt in the living room. She wouldn't need ice with it, after all. As she sipped, she looked out over her old town. Maybe she would have been better off growing up in a time like this when order and civility seemed to have disappeared. Her childhood misery certainly had not been alleviated by Hart Ridge's carefully graduated houses, its lawns with crisply edged borders, its hours punctuated by train whistles.

Even now she couldn't find a place for herself. From her freelance work she knew that jacket copy for mysteries had its own code:

"A delightful puzzle, yet so much more than a mystery, with an unusual depth of characterization" meant that the book was a straightforward whodunit. Characters revealed their keen intelligence through the liberal quoting of poetry the author did not have to know himself because of course he could look it up. All of Lydia Bunting was of this type.

"Not a puzzle, but an exploration of the underside of society" meant that any grade school student could guess the murderer and instead of suspense you got lots of pornographic videos, drug dealers speaking a far-fetched vernacular, and exploited child prostitutes in need of rescue from men in sleazy suits. Lemuel Samuel's *Fleabag Massacre* was a good example.

"A far-reaching novel that does not sacrifice the satisfactions of the genre" meant who knew what the hell was going on, but it wasn't pursuit or deduction in the usual sense. Not many of these were published, and fewer were bought. That was what appeared on the dust jacket of Virginia's first book. She seemed doomed to this inscrutable noncategory.

"So," said Pat, "here you are. Don't you think Will is wonderful with Ruby?"

"Oh, dear," said Virginia.

Pat sat down and secured a bottle of wine between her knees. "So what horrible thing is going to happen to the Kupmanns?" she asked.

"They could spend the whole amount on quack remedies," said Virginia. "They're so desperate they could be prey to any huckster that comes along."

"Wow," said Pat. She started to thread a corkscrew through the top. "Wouldn't that be terrible."

Her apparent naïveté sent Virginia's mind spinning. How much money had Pat's checks been for? Had Frank's secretary made specific suggestions? Could Pat afford this? She'd never had a very firm grasp of financial matters.

"How well do you know this Ellen Kloda?" asked Virginia.

"Pretty well," said Pat. "She's not the most exciting person in the world."

"But what is she like? I mean, was she really angry about her loss?"

"No more than anyone, I guess."

Virginia tried a different tack. "Are we seeing anyone tomorrow?"

Pat sighed. She popped out the cork. She poured a glass of wine. Finally she said, "I'm going to Rumson."

"Rumson? Why?"

Pat glanced at Virginia uneasily. Her smile was in place, but her head swiveled from side to side. "Long before Frank was arrested, I agreed to do a garden for Neil Culp's wife, Yolande," she said. "It was a weird arrangement, I suppose. I designed a garden for her, and in return Frank got a big bonus from Link-Age. In effect the project has already been paid for. But it fell through when Neil abandoned Frank. Yolande left a message telling me not to come. Now suddenly she is pestering me to start up work again. It makes you think."

"Wait a minute," said Virginia. "You're going to go see the Culps?"

"I told you that Frank has gotten sort of strange," said Pat. "Well, he's completely obsessed with Neil."

For a moment the house around them had no sound, no smell, no temperature. Virginia drained her Scotch.

"He insists I go down there. I think he expects me to stare at them balefully and make all sorts of accusations," said Pat. "You know how unhinged I'm supposed to be."

Of course she wasn't serious, but then, with Pat, you could never be sure.

"Why?"

"Maybe I could trick them into confessing," said Pat. "Wear a wire."

"Everyone already knows they did it," said Virginia.

"Frank thinks something's going to happen if I actually see the Culps," said Pat. "Like on TV, when the good people get to yell at the bad people at the end of the show. Or get to shoot them. He's convinced that if I go down to Rumson, I'll see Neil as well as Yolande. That's the first questionable assumption. The second questionable assumption is that there will be some big change in the world or in Neil's situation or maybe even Frank's as a result. I don't see it, but I agreed to go down and talk to Yolande. It's the least I can do."

Virginia just shook her head.

"Look," said Pat. "I can't pass up the chance. Why did Yolande call me out of nowhere? Just to get the free garden? She can't be that cheap. Well, she could, I guess, but that would be interesting, too. She's going to have to say something to me when I'm there. Will she pretend that her husband is some poor innocent? Will she pretend that he didn't double-cross Frank? Will she pretend that Frank didn't then help the feds with the LinkAge books? It's not like I expect an apology. That really would be a shock. More?"

Pat replenished Virginia's glass.

"It's going to be fascinating," she said. "Neil is a wizard. And an escape artist, too, I guess. I can't even imagine what he's pulled. The stock market, the telecommunications industry, the whole business world, they're all shady. It's a known fact. But so what? Are we supposed to go off to a South Sea island? It wouldn't be any better there."

"I don't know," said Virginia slowly. She eased herself into one of the huge green couches and lay her head against its back. "Sometimes I toy with the idea of escape. There was an American in New Zealand who staged at least two fake deaths, both of them drownings. He was 'rescued' the first time. He was gone for years after the second. Eventually he was caught and sent to prison for insurance fraud. When he got out, he disappeared once more."

"This is a real person?" said Pat.

"Yes," said Virginia. "He was never found again."

"Why did he do that?" Pat was disapproving.

"For money," said Virginia. "But was that all? Sometimes at night I try to imagine where he is now."

"He's dead," said Pat with alarm.

"Probably," said Virginia. "Not necessarily."

Not many people knew that Virginia's mother had killed herself. Pamela, who was pretty cheery for a stepmother, used to say that with the new antidepressants she would have been fine. Virginia was supposed to take comfort in this observation, but it made no sense to her. It seemed to imply that her mother's experience was less than real. Sometimes things were too much to bear—and that was the sane response. Sometimes you had to ask how to go on, or even whether to.

The sky was a bright empty blue pasted with a few fat white clouds. From a stalled feeder street Virginia could see the sun glittering off a moving carpet of cars on Route 287. Ahead of them was a camouflage Hummer pulling a flatbed of saplings. Pat said she thought the next entrance would be better, so she drove off into a labyrinth of brilliantly light-filled working-class streets. At the next entrance the traffic was indeed more fluid, and it remained so for at least ten minutes, until the lane on the far right backed up behind a dense line of cars exiting onto the Garden State. In exasperation Pat swerved into the faster moving lane and then edged back in about a half mile down. Soon she got tired of that, too, moved back out to the center lane, sped nearly to the exit, and shouldered her way in again. She had jumped dozens and dozens of cars.

From the sidelines of the shore drive came a piquant, seedy mix of offers—shellfish, auto parts, tattoos, wicker furniture, artificial limbs. Crossing the bridge into Rumson you immediately felt the difference. The town was set on a bold coastal bluff between the mouths of two rivers, so it had water on three sides, all prime real estate. The roads were hung with branches and edged in cut stone. The houses were immense. They were surrounded by smallish, slightly cramped, stagey-looking versions of gates, horse paddocks, and duck ponds.

"Do you know how much it costs to plant a full-grown tree?" Pat asked dreamily.

Rumson was an enclave of wealth. A few of the grander establishments were originally summer residences that dated back to the eighteenth century. But you could detect a dissoluteness even here. This was no Pound-Ridge-by-the-Sea. Sudden, frequent variations in fence style, in grass length, in paving material made it appear as rough as it was prosperous. Many renovations were going on, even a tree house was being given a second story, and because the painters and (Virginia was sure) *landscapers* were not allowed indoors, Port-A-Sans stood sentinel everywhere. The ramshackle air suggested that what was being grafted onto these huge houses was something shifty and commercial—clam bars, or maybe tattoo parlors from the shore nearby. The other, untouched homes looked like locked-door rehabs or maybe full-blown loony bins.

The Culp estate, which was set far off from the road, behind an acre of trees, certainly had the right proportions for a rest home: two and a half stories high, and four times wider than it was tall. It was red brick, with variegated gables, a porte cochere at one end, and a pleasing series of high mullioned windows, recessed window frames, and pedimented French doors. Running along the entire length was a terrace with a low balustraded stone wall, just the sort of terrace the killer snuck down in *Murder with Mirrors,* hoodwinking everyone but Miss Jane Marple. The estate in the book had housed juvenile delinquents.

Back at Hart Ridge, Virginia had thought it her duty to come. Now she was not sure why. To witness? To denounce? Her heart raced. She couldn't think of what to say. Numbers as clean and bright and bland as LinkAge's could not have been true to life, but early investors had made money; she hadn't objected when the stock price rose. Even if the final layer of buyers was destined to suffer in this pyramid scheme, that was a risk everyone took—everyone except Gibbs and Culp, but they were supplying the opportunity. When a crime was this big and glaring, it didn't look like a crime anymore. It looked like business. When a crime wasn't sinister or underhanded or ashamed, it was virtue that felt compelled to skulk and hide.

Pat said, "I can't wait to get my hands on this property!"

Yolande Culp was standing in the porte cochere when Pat pulled up. As a figure of evil, she was a disappointment. She was very thin, not much more substantial than her spiked boots, and she did not look strong enough to cause any direct damage. She was more the sort of person who wore footwear that had poisoned the leather maker and clothes that had blinded the seamstress and gems that had killed off half the miners in a cave-in.

Pat's window slid down. "Where do you want me to park?" she asked, her former enthusiasm turning brittle.

Yolande's eyes flicked briefly over the car. "Right there's fine." She was uninterested, but tense. She had a surprisingly peevish face, dominated by big, black, heavily mascaraed eyes and a cute feathering of blond hair.

"The back is really the front," she said through the open car window.

"You mean that the house faces the river?" said Pat. "I know." She had her hand on the handle but couldn't open the car door because Yolande was blocking it.

"I want you to do a lot out in front where everyone can see."

"I guess it is kind of exposed," said Pat. From where Virginia sat, the lawn seemed to jump into the choppy river.

"And I want you to start right away."

"I'll just draw up some plans for your approval."

"Whatever," said Yolande. "But get some guys in here right away to start digging beds or something. And all those plants there. Get rid of them. Just rip them up."

"Really," said Pat, her face impassive. "The ground is still pretty hard."

"I'll be back out later," said Yolande, and disappeared.

Pat slid the window closed and said, "What a weirdo."

Virginia bent over, snorting with laughter.

As they walked the grounds, whipped by the wind, Pat carried a surveyor's map folded up on a clipboard, to which she added notations. The Culp property was long and narrow, and most of it lay between the house and the road. The area between the house and the river was covered with a thick, expensive-looking, greenish-blue lawn. It was bordered on two sides by trees and on the third by a section of river so close to the sea that it felt like an inlet. The downstream pressure of the river and the tidal sweep of the ocean kept the water churning.

"What are you going to do to this place?" asked Virginia, hooding her eyes with one hand to keep her hair away.

Pat smiled. "I will agree to every cheesy thing Yolande suggests, and it will still be gorgeous." The fierce offshore wind, the blinding sun, the violent changes in temperature—Pat was obviously relishing it all.

Virginia broke away to contemplate the jagged, heart-stopping drop to the purply-brown water. The sight suggested dominion over the ocean, quite a step up from the dominion over a small town that the upper reaches of Hart Ridge enjoyed. The wind whipped her rusty black clothes around her limbs and threatened to toss her over. She felt the same shiver of attraction to the dark river that she had to the dark woods.

What she needed was *two* endings, the way *Scorpion Reef* wound up. Oblivion was the obvious ending, the unavoidable one, but the novel managed to posit an equally persuasive, equally palpable parallel course. It was the perfect fantasy. Only a mystery writer would wrench events into such preposterous shapes simply to double up the finale. She wondered how far forward she would have to leap in order to clear the vicious-looking rocks below and make it out into oblivion. She'd never succeed. She'd have to be able to fly a little—not full out, like a real bird, but at least a short hop, like a dodo. Even that was beyond her, she thought with a pang. She thought longingly of the moment that the sea swallows Maggie LeFevre of *The Silent Siren,* and she is both dead and not dead.

When Virginia loosened her gaze from the river and turned to join Pat, she caught sight of Neil Culp looking at them from a second-story window. Instinctively Virginia kept her movements fluid and her eyes down. She dared not stare. But she would have recognized that smug, jowly face anywhere. Pat was several yards away, standing above a dome-shaped shrub, writing on her clipboard. Virginia ambled up to her without a break in her stride. Keeping her voice low and her eyes innocently unfocused, she said, "Don't look now, but Neil Culp is watching us."

"What?"

Virginia rolled her eyes upward, miming a request to look up with similar discretion. "Second floor, center right."

"Neil!" said Pat. "I wonder what he's up to."

"Nothing good," said Virginia.

Pat openly craned her neck at the windows but no one was there now. "They're all such crooks," she said airily. "But Neil Culp will get off because he's who everyone wants to be. No one will touch him."

For the first time Virginia was really irked by Pat. Virginia would not have been Neil to save the world. It was as if Pat, a little monster, was transfixed by the glamour of a giant monster while it was eating her: his wonderful sharp teeth, his incredible jaw span, his outsize appetite.

When Yolande appeared on the terrace chewing gum, Pat cheerily asked her how she'd been.

"Okay," said Yolande. "I miss Snowbelle."

"Your cat?" said Pat. "What do you mean? What happened?"

"Nothing," said Yolande, chewing faster. "She's at the vet's."

"But everything is okay?" Pat could not make sense of this.

"Of course," said Yolande. "She's having a microchip put in."

"Really," said Pat.

Her puzzlement was obviously annoying and embarrassing to Yolande, who said, "It's not that strange. It's like LoJack."

"The things they think of," said Pat. "So what's Neil up to these days?"

Yolande hesitated in her gum chewing for a minute, as if she couldn't believe what she was hearing. Then she said, "Nothing. How's Frank?"

"Great," said Pat. "He's met such interesting people. Not at all the sort you'd expect."

"Do you get to talk to him a lot?"

"Sure," said Pat.

"I guess your conversations are recorded, right?" said Yolande.

"Yes, we're quite the celebrities." Pat had tugged the wedges of hair back off her head. Ostensibly she was trying to keep them out of her face, but she also gave the impression that the subject was driving her to tear out her hair.

"I lost twenty-five thousand dollars in LinkAge," said Virginia. In trying to keep her voice steady, she'd clamped down on anger or blame.

A look of surprise crossed Yolande's face, as if she'd been addressed by one of the help, and maybe she actually did think Virginia was Pat's assistant.

"Neil and I lost twenty-five million," said Yolande. Her tone was on the surface neutral as well, but it sang like a high-tension wire with individual strands of evasiveness, whiny regret, and suppressed fear.

"Oh, well," said Pat brightly. "You can still have a beautiful garden. There's a famous one nearby. It was put in by Vito Genovese in the thirties. You know, Vito Genovese the gangster. It's open to the public now, and it's huge. He had an incredible replica of Mount Vesuvius made. It's gone, though." Here her voice dropped like a stone. *"Can you imagine? A replica of Mount Vesuvius?"* This was pure irony. Her voice started another slow rise. "But he had an eye for rare plants, and a whole bunch of them survived. There's lily ponds and rock gardens and an azalea walk. He got a lot done, considering he owned the property for only two years. He had to flee to Europe because he was about to be arrested."

Leave it to Pat. By the time she'd ended on this high note, Yolande's face was fully transformed. She'd stepped back, so her features were in shadow, but you could make out the mottled flush in her cheeks and the curl in her upper lip. "That's ridiculous," she said, turning on her heel. Then added fiercely, over her shoulder, "Tell Frank about the garden. You have to. Tell him how much it means to me."

Darkness was gathering by the time Pat and Virginia returned from Rumson. They pushed through the dogs and
found Ruby sitting in the gloom of the kitchen, drinking pink
vitaminwater and eating potato-like chips so uniform that they
stacked neatly in a tube. She let out a cross "Hey!" when her
mother flipped on the overhead lights.

"Don't you look pretty," said Pat.

"I need fifty dollars," said Ruby. "Maybe a little more."

"What for?" asked Pat, dumping her tote bag on the built-in
breakfast nook.

"Stuff."

"Well," said Pat with cheerful doubt. "I just gave you a bunch
of money last week. I don't see why I should give you more without a clue as to what you're going to spend it on."

Ruby scowled. "It's important," she said. "It's for Dad."

"Oh, honey, you want to buy him something?" said Pat. "He
won't be able to keep it in his cell, but you can give it to him
later. Get the cash out of the sideboard."

"There's nothing there."

"Nonsense," said Pat, opening up a cabinet stacked with wicker baskets. "I put in a few hundred just last week."

"You never know where anything is," said Ruby.

Could that much money really just disappear? Or was Virginia to assume that either Ruby—or Will—took it? Virginia didn't know what to think. The scale of the Foy household was dizzying. When did people get the idea that this was the norm?

"I don't know how I'm going to pay Chef Pete," said Pat. Chef Pete was a prima donna who cooked one dish a night, and you never knew what it was going to be until you called. As far as Virginia could tell, Pat was on the phone to him every night.

"And where is my ice bucket?" Pat added.

"It's in plain sight on the counter," said Ruby with disgust, "right where you left it." Her potato-like chips had shattered oddly, into a fine dust that coated the floor, the table, and her red-striped boatneck jersey.

"Do you know where Will is?" Virginia asked Ruby mildly.

"No," said Ruby. "Why should I know where he is?"

"I was just wondering."

"Who wants to take the ice into the living room?" said Pat.

"There is so much ritual associated with the consumption of alcohol," said Virginia, picking up the brushed-steel bucket.

Ruby followed her out of the room, trailing her hand around the door frame and across the wall. "Why did you ask me about Will?" she said.

"I don't know," said Virginia, placing the bucket on the little tile-topped table behind one of the couches. "I was wondering. I like him."

"So does Mom," said Ruby, her black button eyes steady.

To see the driveway below, Virginia had to move to within a few inches of the panoramic window. "His car is gone," she said.

"That's his father's," said Ruby. "Will would never own such an old car."

Someone had taken good care of that missing Mustang, but Ruby was right, it was old. Virginia felt a stab of pity for the car and for Will or whoever had lavished it with such hopeful attention.

"Why do you always wear black clothes?"

"Because black is very safe," said Virginia. "I used to think that the only problem was with green. You mix greens, and the results can be toxic. Then I realized that the same is true for blue, only worse. Lots of blues will bleed each other out so much that they get left for dead."

Ruby swayed and then scampered out of the room. Virginia followed her more slowly to the door of the kitchen, where she heard Ruby say in her piercing little-girl voice, "But there's something wrong with her. She's really scary."

Virginia did not wait for Pat's reply. She retreated back into the living room and stood right up next to the window. Still no car. Then she crossed to the little table and poured herself a couple of inches of Scotch. She sat with a dull thump on the huge green couch and looked first at one end, and then at the other. She seemed to be measuring its absurd length with her eyes. She lifted her glass of Scotch to the light as if to gauge its contents.

People didn't used to think there was something wrong with you if you didn't have lots of money, but nowadays it was your own fault—and you should have seen someone about it ages ago. Frank Foy had glad-handed his way to the top of this new parallel world, but it was an uninteresting one, where moral questions did not exist and all that mattered was risk and style. Virginia poured herself another drink.

Back in the forties and fifties any regular reader was thought capable of identifying with the poor and the desperate. A noir hero was not expected to be able to buy himself a splendid life. No one assumed that if he could not, it was his fault. His yearning was a given, its object (girl, cash, or serenity) less important than how far he was from achieving it. It was the agony, not the crime, that made the work real.

Virginia checked the window again—no car.

Chef Pete's dinner was on the table by the time Will appeared amid a great yelping and yipping and howling of dogs, who wouldn't leave him alone. His shirt was disheveled, and Virginia couldn't help noting that his narrow but evenly triangular chest was like that of a varnished wood figure used in a scientific model. His skin had a similar glow.

"Hey, Will, you handsome devil," said Pat, sticking a fork into a piece of chicken. "Where have you been?"

"Mom!" cried Ruby.

Will dropped his eyes. "I had to go . . . to the store," he said. Virginia idly wondered what bad influences Lemuel had wanted to get him away from.

"God, these dogs," said Pat. "Down, Winky."

Will slouched by the table, his hands in his pockets. Because of his downward gaze, he appeared to be studying the crimson cloth napkins and the centerpiece of glass balls, red pears, and pussy willows.

"Wait while I put this guy in the basement," said Pat. She dragged one of the dogs across the bright light wood, his black backside on the floor, his hind legs splayed, his toenails scrambling. Virginia could not see how his behavior had been any worse than at any other time, but she took advantage of the break to get herself another Scotch from the living room. Everyone else was seated when she returned.

Now Will's hooded eyes were fixed on Ruby. His shoulder was tilted to one side, and his shirt was askew as if it were about to fall off a hanger. Was Virginia the only person who noticed all this?

"I cannot believe it's chicken alla diavola tonight," said Pat. "Such a treat."

Whatever Will was up to, he ate heartily. Young people consume anything put in front of them as if it's their right—or their duty. Ruby, too, looked capable of consuming Pat without blinking.

"While you eat," said Pat, looking around and beaming, "I'm going to read you a wonderful letter I just got from Frank." She was wearing reading glasses. Reading glasses! Pat Guiney! They were bright pink, peaked in a punkish cat's-eye design.

"My dad is in jail," said Ruby to Virginia. "But he's not really a criminal." Virginia looked away. "His boss took advantage of him. Now my dad is in jail, and his boss is still free. And very rich."

"This is my favorite part," said Pat. "He's just been talking about how he wishes he could go back and do things differently." She began to read: " 'But I can't go back, except in my head, which I do every night. My cell is my new LinkAge time machine. I go back and rework my mistakes and then I go forward to be reunited with all of you.' Isn't that wonderful?"

While Pat read, Will picked up his steak knife and studied himself in its blade. Then he shot Virginia a sharp blue glance that plucked a single startling cord inside her.

"I want to hear more," said Ruby.

" 'Before I went to jail,' " read Pat, " 'I was very concerned that I not be afraid. I was afraid to be afraid, if you know what I mean. I didn't realize that I already was. I'd been afraid for years. That's why I ran so hard at the end of each quarter. I'm not saying it was all bad. The work could be exhilarating. It was hard to come up with a new raft of numbers at the last moment. The adrenaline would start pumping. You had to think hard and fast for days. But adrenaline is fear. Skiers say they own their fear. That doesn't change what it is. When you're afraid, all you can see is the immediate problem. You see these numbers, this quarter. I was running like a rat on a treadmill, and I didn't know it. Who was I afraid of? Neil? Riley? When you go to Rumson, be careful of . . .' " She trailed off.

"What do you mean?" said Ruby, narrowing her black button eyes. "Are you going to Rumson?"

"Well, yes," said Pat, laying aside the letter. She took off her glasses and folded them up as delicately as a praying mantis folds its legs. "Virginia and I went today."

"Why?" said Ruby.

Pat gave an exaggerated shrug. "I'm doing a garden for Yolande," she said.

"That's disgusting," said Ruby.

"The Culps are planning to leave the country," Virginia said suddenly.

"What?" said Pat.

"That's why they made such a show of how excited they were about the garden," said Virginia slowly. "They want everyone to think they're staying. But they're afraid Neil is going to be arrested. Didn't you see how freaked out the wife was when you told her about the old gangster fleeing to Europe?"

"That's hilarious!" cried Pat. "Ginny, you are so clever."

"What are you going to do about it?" asked Ruby.

Pat laughed. "What could I do? Tell? Who would I tell? My husband's in jail. But I might ask for expenses in advance."

"I hate you," said Ruby.

"People around here seem very unhappy," Will said slowly. "You'd think they'd be happy because of all the money they have, but they're not."

Virginia loved it when a high-level plot was revealed at the end of a mystery. A paranoid solution justified any feeling of discontent. But there was no real cover-up here. Riley Gibbs and Neil Culp, as the iconic directors of the LinkAge fraud, had got the biggest cut of the spoils. But many, many people had profited while it was still churning along. If Jesse James had used the LinkAge method, he would have paid off everyone who worked at the banks he robbed and then convinced the depositors who lost their money that as long as they didn't change the system they too had a chance at being a Jesse James someday. *There will always be losers, just make sure you're not one of them.* He probably would have been made an advisor to the president.

Hundreds of Gibbs and Culp collaborators lurked at lending institutions, investment banks, consulting firms, and financial newsletters. Thousands more didn't exactly know about the accounting crimes, but didn't want to know, either. Being with Pat had given Virginia a better idea of how pervasive the corruption was. What "authorities" would Pat (or Virginia) inform of Neil's possible intentions? They already knew everything, and they had done nothing. It's like when everyone speeds; you can't stop all the cars on the road.

Ruby had stormed off, followed by Pat. As Virginia pretended to concentrate on the dark and winy heft of the chicken, Will stood up, examined portions of Frank's letter from afar, then glanced around and pocketed it.

Virginia escaped to her room, *which had been subtly rearranged since she'd left it that morning.* No, no, she had to get hold of herself. Pat had a cleaning lady. Or someone like that. The dogs began to howl again.

Former LinkAge salesman Phillip Hipkins had "dropped from sight," according to Ellen Kloda, but there was an address Pat might try. Virginia, bunched up in the front of the Touareg, meditated on the phrasing. Had she "dropped from sight" when she left Maine? She was trying to avoid touching a carefully folded white paper bag on the floor mat. She told herself that it was just a bag, but someone else's discards were gross, no matter how nicely folded.

Pat and Virginia drove to Wayne, less than half an hour away. The houses in the area were half stone-face and half aluminum siding, new enough to be flimsily constructed and old enough to show it. The address they sought was down a short street. A young woman with a red bandanna wound around her head sat on the front steps and smoked a cigarette.

"What luck!" cried Pat, pulling up to the curb.

When the young woman realized they were getting out of the car, she stood, started to throw away the cigarette, then changed her mind, checked on the remaining length, and took another hungry drag.

"We're looking for Phillip Hipkins," said Pat, her voice going through its usual high-noted curlicues.

"He's not here." The woman was in her twenties; the shoulder-length hair under her bandanna was thin and blond; and her face was scrappy-looking, despite its even features.

"But he does live here?" pressed Pat.

"For more than three months." It was not a fact she was happy about.

"My husband used to work with him."

"Oh." The young woman relaxed, lost interest, scraped the end of the cigarette on the cement step. "He's already down there."

"Down where?"

"With the rest of them. Out on Forty-six." When Pat just looked at her, she added, "Isn't your husband at the lunch?"

"Frank is actually in jail," said Pat, and for the first time she looked a little embarrassed.

"Jesus," said the young woman. "And I thought my father was bad. What did he do?"

"He was one of the LinkAge accountants who, you know . . ."

She took this in slowly. Then she said, "I've got to get back to my kids."

"We're here about a reimbursement check," said Pat, not showing the best judgment, if his own daughter had reservations about him.

"I really do have to get back to the kids." The young woman eyed her front door.

"I lost everything, too," said Virginia.

"And she's my best friend," said Pat.

"Oh, all right."

Her name was Myra, and her two toddlers were sitting in front of the TV in the living room, watching a talking yellow sponge. Their attention was not diverted by the presence of two strangers. "Come into the kitchen where we can talk," said Myra, picking her way through a scattering of guns: army green, navy blue, and battleship gray. "Boys," she added by way of explanation.

"What a nice house!" exclaimed Pat. "I love the picture." A framed child's drawing of some sort of animal was the only decoration.

"So who's your husband?" asked Myra as she moved dirty plates off the dinette set.

"Frank Foy."

Myra shook her head. "Never heard of him. He's one of those big bug criminals? A mastermind?" She ran an appraising eye over Pat's leather car coat. "I thought they all got away with it."

"Frank wasn't big enough to get away with it," said Pat. "If you know what I mean."

"No," said Myra, "I don't."

"He got caught up in this thing, and now he feels awful about it. So many people have suffered. I got your father's name from Ellen Kloda. Do you know Ellen?"

"No."

"A wonderful woman. Frank's only true friend at the company."

"That company destroyed my father," said Myra. "He lost his job, his savings, his pension, his wife, and his house all in about six months. He had nowhere else to go, so he came here. He walks around like he got kicked in the stomach. My husband says I've got to tell him to leave, but right now I just can't, even though it's turned out to be a disaster."

"I'm sorry," said Pat.

"I don't mind for me so much," said Myra. "And my husband isn't around a lot. But I mind for my kids. My father is angry all the time, and I don't like the kids to see him like that. It riles them up. It riles everybody up."

"I know," said Virginia sheepishly. "I threw a glass."

"Really?" said Pat with interest.

"The only thing that calms him down is his lunch with the Marks," said Myra.

"That sounds nice," said Pat. "Who, exactly?"

"The Marks," Myra repeated. "I don't think all of them are really named Mark. My father isn't, obviously. But the two guys who organized it were Mark Upshaw and Mark Land, and a few of the first people they asked to join them were called Mark. Because of the double meaning. It's sort of a joke."

"Oh," said Pat.

"They meet at BreeZee's," said Myra. "But I would be careful if I were you. They're pretty pissed off."

When Pat and Virginia got back into the car, it occurred to Virginia that she should ask whether they were going to go out to this lunch, but it didn't seem to matter enough. She frowned out the side window.

Route 46 was a strip lined with franchises. Their entrances, which were as frequent as every hundred yards or so, continuously sucked in and belched out more cars. BreeZee's was on the right side of the highway, which was handy, because there didn't seem to be any way to get over to the left. In an SUV waiting to exit, a teenage driver had one hand on the steering wheel and the other in her mouth. She was staring wide-eyed—and biting her nails.

"I guess there'll be a lot of guys like Hipkins here," said Pat.

"I guess so."

"I think I'm nervous," said Pat. "But I know I'm going to survive, and that's what matters, right? Right, Virginia?"

Virginia did not answer. What was Pat talking about survival for? It was maddening.

The parking lot was huge, broken up by baffling concrete markers, and painted with irrationally placed arrows and lines. They were evidently supposed to regulate traffic flow but it was hard to tell exactly how. BreeZee's was marooned in the middle: a pink stucco façade that turned a blind eye to the world. Thick tabletops, high-backed banquettes, and oversize menus suggested that it would be the ample portions, not the taste, that would justify the inflated prices.

A couple of long tables had been pushed together by the far wall, and three men sat together amid the picked-over disorder of maybe a dozen completed meals. Pat strode on back, the flaps of her leather coat stiff and her matching taffy-colored clutch firmly placed under one arm. "I can't believe I caught you!" she said.

Two of the men looked up with puzzled annoyance. The third, the one whose curly gray hair had missed its last couple of cuts, said, grinning, "Sit down. Tell us what you're selling, and we'll each take two." He was wound as tight as a watch.

Pat did take a chair, a couple of seats away from him. Virginia remained standing, reluctant to inconvenience the waiters and aware of a keener disturbance in the air, some kind of crawling nervousness.

"I'm looking for Phillip Hipkins," said Pat.

"Now why would a woman like you be looking for Phil Hipkins?" The flirtatiousness was heavy-handed, hard to listen to.

"Hipkins? Which one was he?" The other two men consulted each other.

"It's complicated," said Pat. "I'm Frank Foy's wife."

"The lowly accountant who corrupted an entire Fortune 500 company? How interesting." This was from the flirt. His tone had soured.

Pat laughed. She could always talk. She just sailed right through. She didn't have to understand what was going on in a room. "He's awfully sorry. Is your name Mark?"

The man shook his head. "Ted. This is Mark Upshaw." He pointed to the skinny fellow. "And Mark Land." He indicated the light-skinned black.

"We were all rich once," said Upshaw. "Hard as it is to believe. We would come in to work and check the stock price. Then we'd check it again at lunch."

"It was never real for me," said Ted. "It was real for other people, I could tell. But it was never real for me."

"I've got to go . . . ," said Land, turning to leave.

Ted drew a breath. "I could feel the end," he said. "But no one knew exactly how it was going to go down." Everyone was listening to him. The Marks, Virginia, even the waiters. "Enron had already disappeared, leaving behind nothing but a puff of smoke. At LinkAge we all thought, Jesus, the smoke over there used to be a billion-dollar company. I don't mind giving a nice spin to some facts. I'm a salesman, that's my job. But it's tough when you don't have any idea what the facts are. The bonuses that year were really chintzy. Word came down that lunches were going to have to come in at under twenty dollars. In Manhattan! Can you believe it? They were cutting costs right out of our wallets. And you could read on the Yahoo! message board what kind of Christmas the top brass had. They got millions and millions of dollars' worth of bonuses."

Like Frank's, thought Virginia. *For the garden.*

"It was a real challenge," said Ted. "After the arrests we expected to go bankrupt at any minute. Toward the end we'd go out for a few hours at lunch, just as if we were Riley Gibbs and his cronies, and we'd take a friend or two and get really shit-faced. But we'd always get the chits upstairs by the end of the day. We'd parcel them out in different ways. One guy actually wrote in the space for customer or contact 'George W. Bush.' The girls downstairs knew what we were doing and tried to push the expenses through right away so we wouldn't get stuck with them. Everyone started putting stuff in their briefcases. You know, the stuff that accumulates over the years like photos and mugs, but also pens, paper, enough to equip a dozen Shakespeares."

"Oh," said Pat. Virginia thought she was going to jump out of her skin.

"You remember Neil Culp's retirement party?"

"Sure," said Pat.

"I don't mean I *went,*" said Ted. "I wasn't *invited.* But everyone knew all about it. It's not like they tried to keep it a secret so no one's feelings would get hurt. Just the opposite."

"It was really boring."

"I wouldn't know," said Ted. "But Johnny Spaulding did go, and somehow he got hold of all these big cutouts of Culp."

"There were these huge photos scattered around at the party," Pat explained to Virginia.

"They weren't just photos," Ted argued. "They were freestanding cardboard cutouts, about three-quarters size."

"The High Risk boys started dancing with one of them really late," said Pat. "The band was gone by then, though, so it looked pretty dumb."

"There was a band?" asked Mark Land.

"Yeah," said Pat. "It wasn't very good."

"After the arrests," said Ted, "the cutouts started appearing all over the building. If you went up to the cafeteria for coffee in the morning, there he'd be, Neil Culp, with a mouth balloon saying, 'Let them eat cake.' Or you'd go to the men's room and Culp would be saying, 'You'll find the accounts in the third stall from the left.' That kind of thing. Eventually someone from upstairs would show up, but meanwhile everyone would have seen it. And who knows, management might not have even minded, figuring Culp was taking some of the heat off them."

Two waiters started to ostentatiously remove glasses and silverware. Ted began to talk faster. "I was going up the elevator one night to pick up my wallet—I'd forgotten it earlier—when I ran into Johnny Spaulding with a big suit bag. One of the cutout's feet was kind of sticking out, so I said, 'Don't forget your shoe there.' Don't forget your shoe! It was great. We were the only ones in the building, because no one was working late by then. Spaulding didn't care if I knew.

"You may not believe it, but I cheered when the stock price fell under five dollars. And I wasn't the only one. You could hear the cheers all over the building. It was a relief after all those months. We hated that company so much we didn't care what happened to us."

Then, without warning, Ted jumped up and bolted out the door.

"My goodness," said Pat.

"What do you expect?" said Mark Upshaw, his hostility unmasked. "When people get hit hard, either they punch back, or they turn on themselves. You're lucky he didn't wring your pretty neck."

"Pat—" said Virginia.

"What did you want to see Phil Hipkins about?" said Mark Land quickly.

"I just heard he had some problems."

"I guess," said Upshaw. "But at least he didn't have a total meltdown, like Ted."

"We can't all be Johnny Spauldings," said Land. "Spaulding's incredible. He lost bundles on LinkAge, but he's made a lot of it back in wind farms. I saw him on TV just the other day talking about renewable energy. He's put together his own farm with over a hundred turbines. Returns can top twenty percent. That's where I'd put my money if I had a nickel."

"I'm glad there are still some happy endings," said Pat.

"Yeah," said Upshaw. "Wind farms are an incredible tax dodge."

"Really," said Pat.

22

Desperation in today's thrillers is often expressed through shopping. It is supposed to be every reader's fantasy. A threat will force a regular person into frantic extravagance. He or she must spend more and more money until finally delivering a package across the street costs four thousand dollars cash. A character fleeing a bad guy will purchase plane ticket after wig after used car after listening device after digital camera after arctic boots. *Your Honor, I did buy an entirely new wardrobe on this credit card I found. But I had to—to save my life.*

Pat and Virginia were in the first-class section of an airplane on a runway in Newark. Pat had bought the tickets as soon as they'd returned from BreeZee's, just like that, online. Whether this was a sign of desperation, Virginia did not know. The impulsive extravagance was similar. Pat was going to turn around this problem with her husband if it killed her. Her smile was as bright as a hubcap.

"What do you think," she said. "Do we have enough magazines?" She was not asking a question; she was relishing their

sheer plenty. She had a thick stack, with as many spring-
time flowers as celebrities on the covers. (Or at least Virginia
assumed they were celebrities; she didn't recognize any of
them.)

"It's too bad we're not on an international flight," Pat continued. "You could have gotten a bottle of Scotch at one of the
duty-free shops. You wouldn't believe the deal Frank got on
some twenty-four-year-old Macallan last year."

"Yeah?"

"It was only two hundred dollars, or maybe it was half off two
hundred; I forget exactly."

The two women were on their way to Oswego County in upstate New York, where they had reservations for a suite in a pic-
turesque old hotel. Tomorrow Johnny Spaulding was going to
show them a prospective wind farm site near Lake Ontario. Pat
had postponed her search for Phil Hipkins and made the ap-
pointment with Spaulding in order to invest some money for
LinkAge's victims. "It's the ideal solution," she said.

Virginia had no idea if it would work. Certainly if anyone
could pull it off, it was Pat. She thought back to the Marks and
idly wondered what Ted had done to distinguish himself among
his unhappy lunch crowd. Refuse to leave his bed? Have visions? Drink vodka for breakfast? None of it sounded like much,
put so baldly. Yet somehow he had separated himself out. Everyone had suffered, but it was Ted who'd had a "meltdown," like
an ice-cream cone in the heat. Maybe this counted as a "nervous breakdown," a term that had a quaint appeal. Virginia wondered what she could do to qualify; she seemed to be stuck
putting one foot in front of the other forever.

"Look!" cried Pat. "That's a good sign. Basket of gold." The
curled-up left side of the gardening magazine was trying to un-

furl as she excitedly tapped a (very short) fingernail against a photo of a dozen dense yellow floral mounds whose shape echoed the light-colored rocks they were interspersed with.

"Basket of gold," said Virginia, unexpectedly tickled. "Basket of *gold*. How about planting it in the Culp garden?"

"I can think of all sorts of plants for that one," said Pat. "How about Japanese blood grass? Love-lies-bleeding. Bleeding hearts. All sorts of satisfyingly bloody names."

The engine began its airy roar.

Virginia hadn't been on a plane in years. The Christmas after her father died, she and her stepmother flew to Costa Rica and stayed in a hut that was part of a resort. Everything about the flight emphasized the suspension of your life. All airports were alike, as were all airplane seats, all airplane hues, all overhead luggage compartments, all seat-back trays, all window glass, all asphalt, all signalers with their futuristic jumpsuits and their arcane hand gestures. She'd been prepared by television for the long, apparently intermingling lines of would-be passengers snaking back from conveyor belts, and for having to take off her shoes while her carry-on was being X-rayed. This simply meant that the process was longer, the interruption of her life more insistent. The tacky uniformity remained.

In one book, a mystery masquerading as science fiction, future humans snatch people from planes about to crash and bring them forward to their own time, leaving behind simulated body parts in their place. Virginia wondered about that moment when you think you're going to die and instead you're propelled into the future. It would probably be hard to tell the difference between death and time travel. Your mind would likely disintegrate no matter what strides had been made by then in understanding how the brain worked.

"Thank God for Will," murmured Pat. "He's the one who made this trip possible."

Ruby had been pleased when Pat had announced their departure. "I guess we'll find something to do," she'd said in a put-upon voice that wouldn't have fooled a two-year-old. It fooled Pat, of course, or maybe she was simply used to it. Ruby could have flaunted that secretive smile with impunity for years. Pat might have even got a kick out of it.

Pat did enjoy so very many things. Her taste, in truth, was a bit slack. She was not as discriminating as Virginia and so probably did not appreciate how superior Will was to any other young person who might have happened by. There was great charm in his aloofness, his vulnerability, his slight shiftiness. Although he may already have been cruel—or suffered cruelty—he was still fresh. You had to guess at his past as well as his future.

"I like Will," said Virginia. "But do you think he's the right chaperone for a thirteen-year-old girl?"

"Why not?" said Pat, lifting her brows. She extracted some lip balm from her purse, which was silk-screened with the face of a glamorous forties blonde and the words "If I Have One Life to Live, Let Me Live It as a Lie."

"Do you really have enough money to invest in wind farms?" asked Virginia.

"Sure," said Pat, offering her the lip balm.

"For a while I thought Ellen might be trying to ruin you."

"Ellen?" crowed Pat. "Wait till you see her. But I suppose there's no reason not to tell you." When Pat had asked her why she hadn't cashed the check, Ellen had said she didn't deserve it. Apparently she felt guilty about sending out the memo with the real figures. Pat tried to reassure her. No one blamed her, not even Frank. But finally Ellen confessed that she hadn't sent out the memo by accident. She'd done it on purpose. "It was just after 9/11, when everyone wanted to go out and save the world. She thought it was the right thing to do. She didn't know it would destroy everyone's savings."

Virginia laughed. "So she set out to destroy the company."

"I think it would have happened anyway. Eventually."

"Still . . . ," said Virginia.

"Yeah," said Pat.

Virginia leaned back against the headrest, her brain sated.

"It's not something I would tell Frank, of course," said Pat.

"How incredible, to think of what one person can do," said Virginia.

"You're looking a lot better than you did up in Maine," said Pat.

Virginia's thoughts jumped briefly to the man in New Zealand who kept faking his own death. His name was Milton Harris. You could see him in a lot of different ways. The crude view would be that he kept pretending to die so that his insurance would pay off and that the pretense eventually caught up with him and he really did die. But what if his goal was not money. Surely there were less risky ways of making it, even illegally. What if he was getting what he wanted every time he played at death? What if he longed for that middle land, that death-in-life and life-in-death? Maybe there was nothing wrong with reaching out and touching death. Maybe you were supposed to wonder how it tasted.

For the first time, though, Virginia felt that she was on the outside, rather than the inside, of this question. No matter how insistently it demanded an answer, no matter how entangled she might be, no matter how dire her situation, she was distinguishable from the question itself.

"I'm not going to kill myself," she said.

There was a silence.

"I never said you would!" cried Pat.

But Virginia peeked and saw that *Pat Guiney* (or rather *Foy*) had turned red.

"I probably wouldn't have even if you hadn't whisked me away from Maine," said Virginia.

"Oh," said Pat. She dropped the magazine, but strapped in side by side as they were, all she could do was grab Virginia's shoulder. "I knew you were thinking of it!" she said fervently. "And thank God you didn't go through with it! What would I have done?"

"I don't know," said Virginia. "But I liked being whisked."

Pat became voluble. "Johnny Spaulding is a great-looking guy," she said. "He was in the Hart Ridge paper when he lost his money in LinkAge. Not that I saw the picture back then, but it's online now. And there was a more recent picture of him in front of a row of wind machines. They're so weird, you wouldn't believe it, not at all like in *Foreign Correspondent*. They have blades like scissors."

"Some would call it poetic justice if he swindled you out of all of your money," said Virginia.

"No, no," cried Pat, upsetting what was left of her wine in her enthusiasm. "Don't you see? Johnny Spaulding changed the whole character of what happened. He's going to do well for himself, for his investors, and for the environment. We have to help him and do right by ourselves as well. Besides, I think you should marry him."

That was really what she said.

Because the plane was small (and had not been snatched by time travelers), it stopped in the middle of an expanse of asphalt rather than at a gate. They were going to be the first people off the plane. Pat started poking at her cellphone. "Five messages," she said to Virginia brightly. "I wonder how many that is per minute."

Overhead compartments sprung open as the passengers twisted underneath them, groping upward. Virginia hoisted her Estée Lauder tote bag to her shoulder.

"What?" Pat's startled sob was terrible to hear, and everywhere eyes turned toward her with alarm. She fell heavily into her seat and burst into tears. "It's Ruby," she said. "She's in trouble. She's at the police station."

"Ruby?" said Virginia, shaking her head in disbelief. "But what happened to Will?"

BY
THE RIVER

The house loomed above several cars, including a Touareg, a model Will had never seen before. Even without his Mustang GT convertible (well, his father's, really), the number of cars meant that they'd have to be arranged and rearranged for access. Inside the house was a lot of the usual crime paraphernalia, only fancy. Even the girl blended in at first—not a campy "girl" spread across an old Lemuel Samuel cover, but a real girl, a little girl, with sleek black hair and bright black eyes. She said, "Are you the babysitter?"

They were in the kitchen. Pat Foy had disappeared in a swirl of words, and he was standing there, looking absently at a glass-fronted cabinet filled with stainless-steel canisters and mounted knives. He said, "Do I look like a babysitter?"

Ruby was her name. She examined him with an air of defiance. She was not tall, yet she appeared to look at him straight on. "No," she said at last.

"I'm a trapper," he said.

She nodded. She was wearing skintight jeans and a snug little navy blue T-shirt. She knew he lived near her "country" house; maybe that was why "trapper" had popped into his head. But he didn't think it was a big lie; he had everything a trapper needed. Really. He was shrewd, intuitive, independent, strong-stomached.

He was supposed to look for work here. That had been the plan concocted in his father's hospital room a few days after he'd come out of his coma. Lemuel was cranked up in his bed, frowning; Pat was in tandem, rocking from foot to foot, and Will sat in his usual foldout chair, the one the young nurse had found for him to sleep in the first night. He was not enthusiastic—nor was his father—but anything would be better than this three-sided hospital room. Will felt like he'd burst and scatter pieces of himself across the walls. Besides, finding work couldn't be too hard. Lots of guys his age secured jobs every day, and New Jersey appeared to have plenty of people, plenty of buildings, and plenty of money lying around. Jobs must be everywhere, like rubber gloves, just waiting for him to slip into.

But already the plan seemed less likely, and he'd dropped his father off at Newark Airport only a couple of hours ago, just in time for his flight to Miami, the embarkation point for his mystery cruise. It was hard for Will to conceive of any job he might do here. The airport, for instance, was full of individuals in their official capacities: ticket takers, baggage carriers, security (lots of security), cashiers, flight attendants, pilots, limousine drivers, fast-food workers. Not one of these positions was suitable. Some, like pilot, required unfathomable training; others, like cashier, required unattainable personal qualities, as all cash registers seemed to be run by dark-haired women with accents. He did not see injustice or even inconvenience in this state of affairs, however. He did not expect to be hired for a job he could not picture himself doing.

When Pat bustled back into the kitchen, she said to Ruby, "Isn't he nice? I told you you'd fall in love with him."

Will frowned.

But Ruby's gaze, which had been fixed on him, swung implacably to her mother. "Where's my peach yogurt?" she said. "You don't expect me to eat blueberry, do you?"

It was hard to figure out whose statement was weirder, mother's or daughter's. Will liked Pat fine, but he'd noticed right off that although she was the sort of woman you'd theoretically want to watch over you—and in fact she'd whipped Lemuel's hospital into shape—every time she'd talk, she'd leave you as jumpy as a cat. Sometimes her laugh would tickle something at the back of his head, and he'd end up laughing, too, until he realized he was laughing at nothing and he looked like a moron. Or other times she'd set her hand lightly on his arm, and his skin would start to pop. If only he could forget that she was Mallow. Or at least used to be Mallow.

Ruby's self-involvement was easier to deal with. When her gaze swung back to him, he thought, *She expects me to root for her.* He was flattered. The seven years separating them made him into a sort of superkid, whose allegiance was worth seeking. What's more, he admired her dogged hope. *She wants me to be on her side so much that I am.*

After reading through the want ads the next day, pages and pages of classifieds with not one actual job offering that Will could discern, he began to suspect that here in New Jersey you had to be a person like Pat Foy, who already had money (stolen, apparently), or be her dependent, like Ruby, or her employee, like . . . Will. When she handed him a wad of bills from the side-board at the end of the week, he was grateful. "Some trapper," said Ruby from the doorway, fixing him with her unblinking black eyes.

You'd think that this would drive a wedge between them, but it did not. Will recognized Ruby's dissatisfaction. The two might not have a lot in common in the obvious sense. When Will saw an ad, he was painfully aware that this little girl had the money to buy whatever was pictured. Ads therefore made him think in a certain way about Ruby and in a certain way about himself, because for him the ads would always remain just ads. It was complicated, and a real live person at the end of all those ads and feelings about ads made it more so. This probably meant that Will ended up thinking more about her than about some-one he'd known his whole life. You'd never wonder if a person you'd known your whole life was on your side, because what would it matter? You'd know the sort of things he was going to say to you when you ran into him at the town plaza. Other stuff didn't come into it.

Will wasn't sure what he was expected to do at Douglas Point other than hang around and go for the occasional drive. The more specific and tiresome jobs were already filled. A dog walker showed up twice a day. Tuesday and Friday mornings three cleaning ladies arrived in a white van. At various times during the week different men would pick up scattered twigs or old leaves and then disappear. Will's presence seemed to be enough, as if he were substituting temporarily for a member of the family. Ruby was in school till four. Then she went on one of the computers to IM her friends. Later she'd ask him what he thought of easy things like TV shows, types of food, or vacation spots he knew only by name.

Will's problems with her began one evening in February while they watched a program called *Heist or Hoax*. The TV screen was pretty amazing, high-definition plasma, about forty-two inches—although that's not as big as it sounds, because it's measured on the diagonal. Will found himself watching a lot of shows like *Heist or Hoax* that he wouldn't have normally because of the quality of the picture. The TV itself might have been as thin as a sandwich, but the world it contained was so three-dimensional he would have liked to walk into it.

The set was mounted high on the wall, probably by an ambitious immigrant, not by a lazy discontent like his new stepfather, who installed cable boxes but who was always going on fruitlessly about leasing an electronics or hardware franchise. "This county is wide open!" he would say, then start naming the various chains that had interested him lately. Will's mother couldn't have known that he—*Will*—would soon become unwelcome in their home, but she should have guessed. Still, she'd struggled for so long it was hard to hold it against her. And Will had fantasized about living with his father for years.

Will and Ruby were alone when they watched *Heist or Hoax* because Pat had driven off to visit Ruby's father in prison. Instead of accompanying her, Ruby had made him a card from a digital photo of her dog Winky, which looked professional to Will, since Pat's color printer made copies with no visible lines.

Heist or Hoax was a reality show in which a dozen contestants were told that one of them was going to try to burglarize the estate they were staying at. In a twist known only to the audience, every guest thought he (or she) was the one playing the criminal.

"Jeez, it's like really stupid, isn't it?" said Ruby, with her usual mix of strong opinion and need for reassurance.

"That's for sure," said Will. They were laid out on the black leather couch with the dogs, the Lab's hot, fragile muzzle resting on Will's thigh.

"It's supposed to be in the Palisades," said Ruby, "but I don't believe it for a minute. It looks like Florida or someplace. See those palm trees? There aren't any palm trees in New Jersey."

Will looked at her quizzically, then had a faint recollection of a "Palisades" nearby. "I think it's supposed to be the *Pacific* Palisades," he said. "It's in California."

Ruby flushed and muttered, "It's still stupid."

"East or west," said Will gallantly, "they're a bunch of amateurs."

"Yeah," said Ruby, giving him an interested, sideways, newly measuring glance.

At that moment one of the contestants hid some high-profile jewelry in a jar of peanuts. What to do with the extra nuts? Stuff them in your mouth, of course.

During the next commercial break Ruby said, "I guess you know about jewel heists and all that."

Will shrugged. "Whoever set this up couldn't rob his own grandmother," he said, although his single brush with the law had been the year before, when he'd brought a can of Mace to school to defend himself and had been suspended for carrying a weapon.

"The two of us could really do something," said Ruby. "About Neil Culp, I mean."

"Mmm," said Will, beginning to stroke the dog's black head, figuring he'd let the whole subject float on by.

"We could break into his house," said Ruby in a low voice. "We could take Snowbelle! That's his cat. I'm sure she'd rather live with me."

Will's hand paused in midair. "Who exactly is this guy?" he

asked sharply.

"Oh, you know," said Ruby, backtracking, startled by his reaction. "He's a big criminal." She lowered her voice still more, as if Pat would have paid any attention even if she'd been around. "It's all his fault that my father is in jail."

As soon as the show was over, she made Will take her to a diner where certain kids from her school hung out. "They're afraid of me already," she explained, "because of my father. But they'll *really* be afraid of me once they see you."

A lot of the things Will had done recently had ended wrong side up, and it was hard to tell beforehand which ones would. It would be easier if, say, doing forbidden stuff always turned out badly. But there was no clear pattern. Sometimes it was the punishment that was the fun.

Not that Lemuel spent much time telling Will what to do. The closest he'd ever come to suggesting a rule was the previous summer, when Will had first come to live with him. They were watching baseball in the living room. Lemuel had his feet up on a wooden crate in which one of his fans had shipped him an ancient car horn in commemoration of some endless drive in *Road Kill*. Now it was covered with randomly folded newspapers. Lemuel said, "You didn't let your mother down, did you?"

Will did not take his eyes off the TV.

"Because the only thing you have to remember is, never abandon a woman in need."

It was enough to make you gag, this nonsense straight out of one of the Bud Caddy novels. What did Lemuel think he'd done when he left his family (i.e., Will and his mother)? And how could Will have let down his mother with his stepfather standing in the way? Lemuel had been drinking all night; his once neatly trimmed beard had become more and more erratic, as if straw had started to poke out of a scarecrow; he was lucky to be upright. Still, he seemed to have guessed at certain of Will's secret lapses or evasions. For a long moment all that kept Will tethered was an image of the stadium on the television. He knew that sometimes you could do the wrong thing—the truly awful, sickening thing—when you thought you'd settled on the right.

But then Lemuel said, "I don't care if you drink beer here as long as you don't drink it all up," and the creepiness passed, and soon the two of them were just sitting around watching baseball again. Will even fetched his father another can of beer, although he declined one for himself.

Will could tell that Ruby did not think her father was innocent, exactly. But that evidently did not make him guilty. And it was obvious that this man Culp must be worse. "He tricked my dad," said Ruby before dinner one cold dark evening. "He tricked him and he took all the money and now he lives like a king while my dad is in jail."

Ruby was picking at her white paper napkin as if it were skin.

"When he takes my dad's place," she said, "we can all go to Six Flags. They have a ride there that twists you upside down."

Pat bustled in. When she'd showed up at intensive care, Will had thought she was in the wrong room. She was too glossy-looking to belong in the country, and although she was old, she looked nothing like the old women in the Berkshires—women, that is, who taught school, who shopped at the supermarket, or who came out of his friends' houses late at night to berate them for missing their curfews. The lives of those women were over. You could tell that Pat was still centered in the whirlwind of hers. "What could the dogs have gotten into?" she asked, with that slightly clumsy energy of hers. "They are not at all well."

"Neil Culp must have poisoned them," said Ruby.

"Well, I don't think that's very likely," said Pat, diverted by this entertaining new possibility. "But I wouldn't put it past him."

"When we get my dad out," said Ruby, "my horse can greet him by whinnying and licking his hand."

Will looked back sharply and swiftly at Pat, but she'd noticed nothing out of the ordinary about Ruby's phrasing. Instead she asked, "What horse is that, honey?" You couldn't claim that her voice held any particular surprise, since she always sounded like that—as if she'd just gone over a big bump in the road.

"You told me I could have a horse this year if I still wanted one as much as I did last year," said Ruby.

"Really?" said Pat. "Wasn't that two years ago?"

"Then I've wanted a horse for *two whole years*. I should probably get two of them."

"But, honey, I'm afraid that's impossible," said Pat an octave higher.

Will could see her mind starting to spin like a hamster wheel, filling up with words, but Ruby forestalled them with a "Pl-e-e-e-ease." She drew it out like gum; the initial resistance was followed by a weak string that finally snapped. "It's only right," she said, her flat black eyes fixed on her mother.

Will was used to this tone of voice now. Ruby wanted a horse the way she wanted justice. She was *greedy* for justice. She *demanded* a horse. You couldn't distinguish between the cravings.

Let Pat deal with her wheedling, thought Will; then he

wouldn't have to. But Pat was slippery. In a transparent attempt to avoid further entreaties, she suggested that Will take Ruby to the Red Barn for ice cream after dinner. Actually what she said was "I have an idea! Ice cream in February! Wouldn't that be marvelous! It's really better in the winter months, because that's when you need the extra animal fat in your diet. I've found that often received wisdom is just plain wrong, and something else is going on entirely. Did you know that chocolate makes you feel loved?"

Will didn't mind. He took the Touareg because it had the best heater, and he left it going full blast as they idled in front of the barn-red building with the crossed white boards.

"She shouldn't tell me she's going to get me a horse if she isn't going to," said Ruby, her pink tongue smoothing an arc around the ball of ice cream.

Will, who was more of a biter, consumed a chunk of his cone as he resettled his left arm around the steering wheel. "Mmm," he said.

"It's not right."

"This is good ice cream," said Will.

"Yeah," she said, showing a gleam of little pointy teeth like an animal's. "I got into that weird stuff but then I realized there was nothing like an ice-cream cone."

"Weird stuff?" said Will cautiously. "What weird stuff?"

"Not—" she said, coloring. "I mean here!" she practically shouted. "Stuff that isn't ice cream! Like fizzes! And soft serves! Mistos!"

If she was going to get freaked out so easily, she shouldn't wear a shirt that was barely held together on top by a leather shoelace, especially considering it was about twenty degrees out. Oh, he knew she had a crush on him; Pat hadn't been far wrong. You'd think that this would give him some leverage with her, though, and it didn't seem to.

"I wonder if we could get both of them," said Ruby. "Neil Culp *and* Riley Gibbs." Her pronunciation of the two names reminded Will of the way his mother had spoken the names of the lawyers when she finally divorced Lemuel. They became the whole outside world.

"I thought you wanted a horse," said Will.

Ruby narrowed her keen black eyes. "I outgrew horses long ago," she said scornfully. "I only want what's right."

Will basked in the heat whirring from the dashboard. Maybe greed always infused a crusade; maybe action was necessarily propelled by narcissism. Maybe both impulses stemmed from the same deep wiry root. Maybe that was the way it was supposed to be.

Will didn't read any of his father's books until long after the divorce. Once he had, certain scenes kept popping into his head: Bud Caddy hiding a runaway under his bed, Bud Caddy forced to shoot his friend through the heart, Bud Caddy's taillights disappearing over a hill. Soon the bed, friend, and taillights all seemed to belong to Lemuel. They became the key elements of his other life, the one he'd come from and then slipped back into when he left the family. Sometimes Will envied this other life, sometimes he hated it, but it had always been as real to him as the side of the room he didn't happen to be facing at the time—until he actually moved in with Lemuel and saw him watching TV in his undershirt.

Wouldn't it be funny if this other sort of life, which was hard and glorious and free, did not belong to Lemuel, but Will. He pushed the exposed ice cream into the cone with his tongue.

25

"Follow me," whispered Ruby.

She obviously didn't recognize this as the title of Lemuel's first book, which was good. But Will had been overtaken by doubt since the cold night they'd gone for ice cream, and her words set his teeth on edge. He covered by affecting an even greater lassitude than usual. "Where now?" he said lazily, his eyes half closed.

He was sprawled on the futon in the sunroom, which normally wasn't used much. Will didn't know why—maybe because it was on the third floor, at the end of the hall, away from everything; maybe because of the disconcerting skylight set into the roof; maybe because the thick-leafed plants looked vaguely like man-eaters. But since Pat's friend Virginia had appeared early in the week, Ruby had tended to drift in here to get away from her.

"Wait till you see this," said Ruby from the doorway, beckoning.

Will hoped she would produce nothing more than an uninteresting drug or even a faddy and expensive drug substitute, like clove cigarettes. (What a middle schooler in Hart Ridge would have access to, he had no idea.) But he feared she'd taken a new step in her revenge against Culp.

"You won't believe it," said Ruby. Outside the library, she carefully placed her finger on her lips, snuck a peek round the door frame, and then pointed with the top couple of joints of this same index finger. Will had to look twice to see what Ruby was trying to call attention to. Virginia was sitting in one of the club chairs reading. She was also poking herself hard in the thigh with the sharp end of a pen. Out in the hall, Ruby began to imitate her, again with the finger. Will turned on his heels.

The dislike between the two of them was kind of gross, really. It was true that Virginia sometimes looked as if she were going to break in half right in front of your eyes, but Will knew she wouldn't, and it was Virginia's plainspoken dourness that he respected. You had to make room in this life for scary stuff, which wasn't going anywhere; it was here to stay.

Oddly Pat could be as spooky around Virginia as her daughter was. Pat handled her old friend more carefully than you would a normal person. So that night, when Virginia rose to do the dishes and Pat did not try to stop her or tiptoe around the subject in any way, he knew that something was up.

"I have something to tell you," said Pat. She was practically jumping out of her chair, eyes bright, hands clasped with restless excitement. "Virginia and I are going to check out a wind farm tomorrow." She glanced from Ruby to Will, evidently searching for a corresponding enthusiasm. "You're going to thank us someday. It's about time we harnessed the energy of the wind. I was thinking I would set up a fund for the LinkAge victims with the profits! Can you believe it? Me? Who would have thought? It's all here, in stuff I got off the Internet. I always print everything out. I hate reading a screen. I just can't get used to it. Do you have your own computer, Will? You should. That's the only way to really learn how to use one. You have to fool around with it a lot. I have some of the cutest photos of wind farms. I hate to tell you what they remind me of. I may sound a bit raunchy. And such a crop of them!"

Ruby narrowed her eyes. "How long will you be gone?" she asked.

"It's in upstate New York," said Pat, "so we're going to fly up tomorrow night to get an early start the next day. But we'll be back before you know it."

Ruby gave Will a significant look and said, "What time to-morrow?"

Will frowned. He knew he should not be as irritated as he was. It was a sign of nerves. He started to yawn, but remembered that his father had told him that yawning was also a sign of nerves. His mouth snapped shut. Then he was reminded of something else his father said: Keeping your hands in your pockets was an indication that you had something to hide. Will immediately took out his hands and crossed them over his chest. He started up the stairs that way. He was not sure that he intended Ruby to follow him, but she did. At the second floor, he started to follow her.

Once the attic door was shut behind them, Ruby prevented him from pulling the chain on the single naked bulb. She did not turn on the flashlight that lay in front of her. Instead they relied on the stripes that an outside floodlight cast through a side vent. They sat cross-legged on raw plywood at the top of the unfinished stairs. There was an odd sour underscent.

"We've got to move tomorrow," she said, "while my mom is away . . ."

The words, borrowed from some movie, were self-important, irksome.

". . . if we want to hit the Culps before they flee the country." Worse.

She was sitting amid all the equipment they had accumulated over the last couple of weeks. In addition to the flashlight, there were several printouts of a satellite photo from Google Earth, two pairs of black leather sneakers without a centimeter of white; two pairs of black leather gloves, two black turtlenecks, two pairs of black pants—leggings for Ruby, sweats for Will—and a pair of black pantyhose that Ruby had cut in two. Will had willingly helped with the logistics of the purchases, but the apparently endless supply of cash Ruby got from Pat made their efforts seem unreal. Ruby was a *child;* she was *playing.*

"What, exactly, do you want to do with this stuff?" he asked.

"Get Neil Culp," said Ruby.

"Right," said Will. "But how?"

"I thought *you* were supposed to know what to do!" She, too, was querulous, as she always was when thwarted. "Can you cut a pane of glass?"

Will frowned, glancing unconsciously at the door at the bottom of the stairs. Although they could both see that it was still closed, they were keeping their voices low. He began to roll up his shirtsleeves.

"Just a small hole," said Ruby, "so you can reach around and let me in one of the Culps' windows. Or maybe you can cut a bigger one, so I could crawl in and then I could let you in the cellar door."

Will was discomfited by the far-fetched scenario. "We might be able to just walk in," he said.

"Why?"

"Most burglaries are inside jobs, you know."

Ruby nodded, impressed with this expert knowledge.

"But then what would we do?" said Will reasonably. "You couldn't get into their computer."

Ruby shook her head. "Neil Culp and Riley Gibbs didn't use a computer," she said. "They passed notes."

Passed notes? As if they were in math class? "You're kidding," said Will.

"My father said that Riley couldn't even use a computer. Unlike my father, who could do anything. He was a whiz. There's a plaque in his office that says so."

Will was barely listening. Until this moment he had been unable to remember exactly what had first excited him about Ruby's plan. Now, once again, he was startled by an atom of happiness. Here was something that might be worth doing. Many, many things were not worth doing; whole weeks could pass that offered nothing more than the emptiest of possibilities, like his unrealizable hopes about a job. But Culp's boss couldn't use a computer! Whatever space he'd been taking up in Will's brain suddenly dwindled. Will was familiar with this incapacity. Lemuel couldn't use a computer, either. Will was no haxor or whatever those computer nerds called themselves nowadays, but he didn't know how Lemuel had survived without him. The man couldn't handle a download. And look at Pat's excitement about the simplest search on the Internet.

"Well?" said Ruby.

Will had a brief vision of throwing her to the ground as bullets whistled overhead. "Let's see one of those printouts," he said.

Ruby, who had been to the Culps' estate once with her parents, pointed to one of the satellite photos. The polish on her little round circle of a fingernail was flaking. Along the river was a series of very long, narrow lots which made no sense until you realized the layout maximized access to the riverfront. Each of the houses dangled at the end of a long driveway as straight as a string.

The lots were covered with trees, so Will did not expect to have any trouble approaching the Culp estate. He could park on the road, sneak up the driveway, and then creep around through the thick trees. He had always been comfortable in the woods, and his night vision was good. He might not move as noiselessly as an early Indian—a legendary figure he had his doubts about, anyway; there were too many brittle crackling leaves in the world, too many tiny, snapping branches—but it was easy for him to picture slipping through darkness. He still had Frank Foy's letter folded in his back pocket. Although he had not showed it to Ruby, it might be useful. In it Foy reminded Pat of the placement of the single alarm at the Culp mansion. Evidently he'd expected *her* to confront Culp.

"It's outrageous, what they've gotten away with," said Ruby. "We're going to make them sorry."

Will wanted to laugh. She sounded awfully self-righteous, considering that her father was in jail and she was planning to break into an estate on the Jersey shore.

26

Late the next afternoon, after Pat and Virginia had left for the airport, Will found it hard to believe that he and Ruby would go through with their plan. For one thing, Ruby had disappeared. But soon she was back downstairs again, dressed in black, her hair braided and wrapped around her head. So Will changed into his new clothes, too. Then he went looking for something to cut out the weird tag at his waist and ended up making himself a sandwich with the pork left over from the night before, scraping off most of Chef Pete's sauce.

"We'll take the Mustang," he said, watching Ruby pick at the skin on her thumb. Pat wouldn't mind if he drove the Touareg, wouldn't even have noticed most likely. But Will's Mustang—okay, Lemuel's—could feel like a shooting cork.

"I don't think anybody will be mad at us," said Ruby. She would not stop picking at her thumb.

"We don't have to go," said Will.

"Yes, we do," she said. "We'll be heroes. All the victims will thank us."

"Could be."

She was picking that skin raw.

"Maybe you should eat something."

Ruby grabbed a bag of popcorn with rare obedience. "Virginia always makes me feel as if I'm about to commit a crime."

"Well?" said Will. "Aren't you?"

Ruby looked shocked for a moment, then giggled. "I guess so," she said.

The phone rang, and the caller ID spit out a fizzy sound.

Ruby giggled again.

Will looked at the handset and saw a string of consonants, followed by "Corp."

"Yeah, it's me," said the voice, which belonged to . . . Lemuel! "The flight takes a couple of hours, and we left Miami . . . When did we leave?" He was talking in a courtly fashion to someone next to him. "So when do we land? Of course I want another. I told you, you won't be able to keep up with me."

Will broke in. "Okay, okay," he said. "When and where?"

By the time he got off, Ruby's face had closed like a fist.

"I've got to pick him up first," said Will. "Otherwise there's no telling what he'll do. We'll be visiting him in jail."

"My father is already in jail," said Ruby, her voice little and hard.

By the time Will parked at the airport, his father had already pulled his luggage off the carousel and sat on it, legs spread wide. He didn't look too bad, considering, but he was wearing suspenders over a waffled long underwear shirt like some old coot brandishing a shotgun in a southern gothic. "Will, my boy!" he bellowed. "I barely survived! My knees are too big for those seats!" Just the sort of nonsense he always came up with. Knees couldn't be too big. They were probably the only part of you that couldn't.

"What made you come back so soon?" Will asked, exasperated. Lemuel wasn't due till next week.

"It was great for a while," he said. "But I got bored."

"You can't leave a boat at sea because you get bored," said Will.

"Why not?" said Lemuel, standing up and kicking his suitcase. "Who says?"

"How did you get to land? Swim?"

"Ha!" said Lemuel. "I'm no fish." As he spoke, he nonchalantly but covertly allowed Will a glimpse of the Swiss army knife cradled in the palm of one hand. He then raised his eyebrows and gave a secret nod, as if to suggest that he'd had it with him on the plane—maybe even on the boat—which was of course impossible, though where he might have picked it up, Will had no idea.

"Come on," he said. "Ruby's waiting."

When Will had spotted his father in a heap at the bottom of the basement stairs, he felt as if he'd never actually seen him before. That's because Lemuel, when he wasn't in a coma, was always coming at you or ducking away from you or somehow involving you so much that you were more aware of your reactions than his.

Will picked up Lemuel's suitcase, which was heavy and wheel-less, with a handle on the top. This close, Will could smell the alcohol. Even before Lemuel had ended up at the bottom of the stairs, he hardly ever got noticeably drunk, just sodden and slow. His skin was spongy; his face, red.

He got into the back of the car meekly enough, although he

did yell, "My knees! My knees!" Then he asked, "Are we going to take this little lady home with us?"

Lemuel always tried to act the gentleman around kids and females, and Ruby was both. But Will wished he would just shut up.

"No one is taking anyone anywhere," said Will. Which was the absolute truth, because where *was* he supposed to take his father? Back upstate, as he seemed to expect? Then how was Will going to get to Rumson? He found himself heading west, toward Hart Ridge, as if the other two impulses were canceling each other out.

"Your mother was one class act," said Lemuel. "So I never knew what she was up to."

"Where are we going?" hissed Ruby, squirming in her seat.

"I vote for some sustenance," said Lemuel.

Will pounced. "That's a great idea. A nice place by the water."

"We'll get some seafood. Maybe a beer," said Lemuel blandly.

"Sure, sure," said Will. He'd find some restaurant on the shore to park his father in for a while. He looked for an exit. He could take the turnpike south.

"Look. Perth Amboy," said Lemuel, reading a sign. "I was once in a great bar in Perth Amboy. I stopped for directions and ended up staying the evening. I think they served food, too."

There were four signs, three arrows. What on earth did they point to? Fortunately the Mustang responded so quickly it could have been alive. Will merged left in the nick of time.

"Yeah, that was an awfully good bar," said Lemuel. "I wonder if it's still there."

He sounded more speculative than manipulative. Will had never seen him descend into any kind of savagery, no matter how drunk he was. *And that was because Lemuel had always al-*

ready got what he wanted. Will could not believe it when he caught sight of his father drinking straight from a bottle of rum in the backseat. "What are you doing?" said Will.

"It's all right. It's duty free. My choice was that or perfume. Of course if I'd known I was going to be seeing the little lady here . . ."

Lemuel seemed to have expanded to take up the entire back. He must have been buckled into the middle seat belt—or maybe he wasn't wearing a belt at all. Will didn't want to know.

"We're not going to stop at Perth Amboy," said Will shortly. "We're going to Hart Ridge by way of the Jersey shore."

"By way of the Jersey shore?" His father's voice boomed. "What kind of way is that? Oh, you are your father's son."

Traffic was heavy, worse than any Will had ever seen, and he had a flash of insight into the SUV/rolling living rooms: They might be handy if you were barely moving.

"Before the cruise, I never paid enough attention to rum," said Lemuel. "I'm glad I got a chance to rectify the situation."

He was smacking his lips.

"I never could follow that goddamn mystery on the cruise. There were clues and deathbed utterances and oversize plastic weapons lying around everywhere. A lot of short underpaid foreigners were running around, babbling like idiots. Half the time they'd be cleaning your stateroom, and the other half they'd be saying something like 'The pretty songbird was seen with the captain on the night in question.' I was supposed to memorize a bunch of nonsense, too. I remember something about a casino and a button that looked like a chip or vice versa. They were always trying to get those poor suckers into the casinos.

"I never could keep any of my lines straight. So they soon gave up and loaded me down with matches. Nice ones, too, considering they were supposed to be clues. I still have some. I'll give you one. I'd wander around, go from bar to bar, and if anyone spoke to me, I'd hand over a matchbook. Sometimes I'd stand in the middle of the main deck and demand rum at the top of my voice. Those mystery nuts loved it. They'd crowd around, and I'd give them all matches. I never did have to pay for a drink. Other times, I'd waylay a guy at night and force him to take a few extra books. A couple from New England complained that nothing made any sense but I don't know what they expected. We were all just floating in a floating chamber of vice."

Ruby was squirming so much she was making the seat squeak.

"I thought you said you got bored," said Will.

"I was exaggerating," said Lemuel. "Is that what it's called? Yeah, exaggerating. I haven't slept in days. I've got to get a little shuteye."

Then he passed out.

27

My friend Sydney was on TV for raising hundreds of dollars selling cookies and lemonade after 9/11," said Ruby. "That's good."

"But you know what? All those cookies were bought by her mom for like a hundred dollars apiece."

They were crossing the bridge into Rumson. Ruby's breathing was shallow, and she kept checking to make sure she hadn't forgotten her gloves (supposedly important because of fingerprints, though there was no way he was going to let her near the house). At a rest stop Will had checked to make sure his father was really out. Now Ruby was filling in the silence he'd left, and she was certainly equal to the task. Will had never before met anyone so determined, so grandiose, so anxious.

"Do you think we'll be on TV?" she said.

"I hope not."

"Why not?"

"You don't want anyone to know about this."

When Will had first moved in with Lemuel, he'd hoped to get

some mileage out of being related to him. But because his old friends weren't around, there was no one to get mileage *for*. Too bad, because Lemuel had let him take the Mustang the first morning. The top was down. It was a clear July day. When Will came to a deep, slow slope, he left the car in second, pulled himself up onto the headrest, and began to steer with his toes. To be above roof level was to soar, unconstrained by wall or windshield, connected only by the curious sensation of cool plastic wheel tucked against the instep of one foot, and between the first few toes of the other. The air hummed. He raised his hands into the sky as if he could touch the dark leafy greenery around him. He felt as if he could. He felt as if he could do anything.

That sense of buoyant power came back to him as Ruby said, "I think someone should make a movie about us. I wonder if you ever get to play yourself."

There was no moon that night. The lights of the town provided only the dimmest illumination, which was probably good. Will had to leave the car at the side of the road a ways down from the Culp driveway. There was no point in advertising their presence. He cut the engine, put his finger to his lips. What he was listening for, he couldn't have said. The engine ticked as the crickets resumed. Ruby refused to stay put. Will started to argue with her and considered driving off, but he finally figured she might be safer with him. He took a last look at Lemuel and told her she could come as long as she stayed out of sight at the edge of the woods. "Don't say a word," he said.

It was so dark, though, that he had to tell her to be careful once they got to the driveway.

"How come you can talk, and I can't," she said.

The Foy house back in Hart Ridge was so big—and so close to the driveway and the road—that it looked as if it could fall over and crush you. Here the Culp estate, which was lit up in vertical bands like an alien spaceship, looked as if it would always be far in the distance, no matter how much you traveled toward it. Will slowly inched along, partly because he didn't want to be heard and partly because it would be easy to stray off the asphalt; they could trip or fall or run smack into a branch or tree. But they were doing okay. This quiet creeping around was exhilarating. He shivered in the cool, damp air.

"Stay here," whispered Will, heading around to the front of the house, where the river lay in wait. He would be okay as long as he stayed close to the building. That way he couldn't fall in. The grass was spiky with a mix of old and new shoots, but its pile was deep and soft; no one could hear him. He followed the edge of the lawn, fearing that the ground would give way beneath him at any moment, because of Pat's landscapers. Who knew what holes they had dug or what equipment they'd left out. But he reached the other side of the house without incident only to sense the vast, troubling emptiness beyond. He could hear some hungry lapping. That would be the tide, reaching into the river, stirring it up.

He crept to the window beside the French doors, careful to stay to one side, away from the light. Inside he could see a huge, white, airy living room. Leaning haphazardly against the walls were several wavery pastel paintings as big as panel trucks. Stacked opposite them were similarly sized sheets of plywood: shipping material.

The next room was half a dozen windows farther down. In it was an old man, bald, sitting in a brown leather recliner that was tipped back about halfway so that he could watch a huge box of a television. Neil Culp. He was wearing a burgundy wool robe over a pair of gray slacks and matching burgundy slippers.

The room was large and somehow recessive, notably lacking in bad-guy equipment. There was no levitating swivel chair, no capped pipe for noxious gas, no secret panel behind which lurked Culp's zombie minions. This room was very much just a room—like a department store display you'd walked by dozens of times and never could remember.

Will looked again at the man, who did not have lizard skin, fly eyes, or slit nostrils. Not close. But he wasn't constructed of simple shapes like squares or circles, either. He was riddled with pointy curves. His slope-shouldered body was dome-like. His fingers were slightly convex. The edge of his sash was puckered. The flaps of his robe hung down in pointy V's. His slacks were slightly belled. His slippers were the leather sort that crossed at the arch.

The table lamp next to the old man shed so much light on his face that his features were whited out. There seemed to be a slight uptick in the right side of his upper lip—a sort of sneer—but it was hard to be sure. His nose was waxy. And his eyes—they were closed. *He was asleep.*

A blow to Will's head sent him forward; he was on his knees. For a moment the invisible river seemed to have vomited up some violently sharp rocks through the damp night air. But no, there was a boot, definitely a boot, and a river had no need for boots. Another kick jerked his head up as it sent his body sideways. Then his elbow exploded in electrical sparks. His chest was pierced, and a thin grunt was released. Was this a fight? He had seen no one. He heard a grim voice: "You little shit."

Later he opened his eyes and saw a hank of dark, dense, dead grass. His cheek was pressed against a couple of cold stones. He heard footsteps retreating, a string of curses. Then, a chilly, lonely silence. Shouts and shrieks existed, but they were trapped within him. He lifted his eyes to the edge of the woods and thought dreamily, those trees are going to fall on me.

Instead an image rose before him. It was Pat Foy, fluttering and chattering, or maybe the sound was the sweet high sort a brain in pain emitted as a natural narcotic. The sound organized itself into a wail. It was a siren, he realized foggily, and this person was not Pat, but Ruby; hers was the face that was taking shape in the near darkness. As she bent over him, he could smell tropical fruit.

"What are you doing?" she cried, her flat black eyes gleaming with fierce panicked excitement. "I've already been in the house. I got it. He wrote it down. *It's a crime.*"

The sirens were suddenly close upon them. Will pulled himself to his knees, then staggered and fell forward again as Ruby screamed.

The police car paused in front of a row of floodlit Victorian houses decked out in convivial towers and porches. Then it turned into the small parking lot for the station, which was across the street. In contrast to its neighbors it looked modest and domestic. This is the sort of home you get, Will told himself bitterly. Isn't it nice? You're *lucky* to find a home at a police station.

The next thing he knew, he was slumped in a gray chair next to a gray desk, one of many in the unpartitioned room. His hands were cuffed in front, his shirt was bloody, his black pants were torn. He was having trouble catching his breath. Ruby was huddled over by the window. She was not cuffed, but she looked all knotted up.

"What's your name?"

The cop questioning Will was not the one who'd put the handcuffs on him; he'd done the driving. He had a soft, pained, creaky voice. Despite the uniform, he did not look like a policeman. He was young and dark-haired, clearly strong, the sort who, if you didn't watch, might pick you up and set you aside, as if you were an inconvenient traffic cone.

"Is Ruby . . . okay?" said Will. He managed to raise his voice enough to say "Ruby!" then coughed weakly. The cop did not lift his eyes from the paper in front of him.

Will should have been terrified. There was plenty of reason to be: the cuffs, the cops, the guns, the nightsticks. But he seemed to have crossed the line into a realm of suffering where none of that mattered anymore.

"You better. Call. Her mother," said Will. He knew that rich people did not stay in police stations long. He was just hoping that this magic would extend to him. "Her name is. Pat Foy. Get the number. From Ruby. They live in Hart Ridge. In a big house. Really big. Believe me." He was panting, and he smelled like the creepy air freshener in the police car that had transported him and Ruby here.

"Where are *your* parents?"

Will's mind took a quick zigzag. "My father. Is on. A cruise," he lied.

This did not have the effect he had hoped. The cop merely nodded. His face was too white, as if he'd grown up in a basement. His ears were the smallest Will had ever seen. When the cop lifted his eyes from his paperwork, Will could see the pity in them. Will's chest grew cold. He had always thought of himself as one sort of person, but the cop seemed to have recognized him as a different type altogether.

"A mystery cruise," Will elaborated, trying to conceal his breathlessness, that sign of nerves.

Ruby still hadn't moved. Her upper arms were pressed to her sides, and her forearms were crossed at a weird angle. Will wondered if she'd been injured, but didn't think there'd been time.

Her braids were coming loose. Elbows of hair stuck out here and there, and one hank in the back had pulled entirely free. It made her look as if she'd been in a fight—wounded, maybe, but also tough and hard.

He tried again: "Ruby." This time he'd found enough breath to catch her attention.

"I've still got it," she mouthed, without relaxing her odd slanted posture. Will realized then that she was protecting the paper she'd found at the Culps' house.

"Got what?" said her cop sharply. She was older than Will's cop, and sturdier somehow, despite being female. Her face was covered with freckles. On her the uniform looked like a park ranger's. She should have been out searching for lost children, not persecuting them.

Where was Pat Foy, with all her energy, her sense of entitlement, her weirdness?

Instead a girl appeared. For a brief moment Will in his confusion thought that she was the nurse from Lemuel's hospital, the youngest one, who'd been on the night shift and who'd found him the foldout chair. She'd also told him there was a cafeteria on the third floor without implying he was too much of an idiot to know that hospitals had cafeterias. (Which he was.) This girl had the same exhausted confidence, and her bangs fluffed out over her eyes the same way, as if she'd blown on them from her bottom lip, and her hair was trapped in the same clip in the back. For a moment Will wondered if the world was full of competent young women ready to parachute in during crises.

"What's going on here?" asked the girl. "Ruby! Are you all right?" She looked small among all the desks. She was wearing a white jacket that sort of fluttered out at the hip and made you want to rest your hand there. "I hope you realize she's only thirteen years old." Her tone was severe. She herself must have been Will's age, but that wasn't stopping her. She had a natural imperiousness.

"Rose," said Ruby with wonder.

"That's Rose? Foy?" asked Will.

"I thought you were good friends of theirs." Will's cop was disgusted. His creaky voice thinned to nothing. He had to clear his throat to say, "You're such good friends you don't know what they look like."

"Okay," said the female cop to Ruby. "What exactly have you got there?"

Ruby's arms tightened.

"You can't just go around breaking into people's houses," said the cop. "I don't know what's wrong with you kids. Don't you have enough stuff already?"

"I'm sure this is all a misunderstanding," said Rose. "The Culps are friends of my mom and dad's."

"Maybe you can tell me how you knew they'd been at the Culps'."

Gotcha, implied her tone, but Rose was unmoved. She said, "Ruby text-messaged me."

"I understand you took something from Mr. Culp," said the cop.

"I didn't," said Ruby.

"Mr. Culp doesn't know what it is, but he says he won't press charges if you give it back."

"No, no," said Ruby. "I didn't take anything I shouldn't have."

"Why don't you just give it back," said the cop impatiently, sounding for the first time like a real person. "It doesn't make any difference to me," she said. "But it sure looks like he's offering you a good deal. Then we can forget the whole thing."

"Have you called Mom?" asked Rose.

"I don't suppose you know what your sister has been up to," said the cop.

"Not exactly."

"She could wind up behind bars."

"Can I talk to her alone?"

"Are you twenty-one?"

Rose stared at her, then decided on evasion. "What does that matter?"

The cop stood up. "You're going to have to hand it over one way or another," she said to Ruby, who shrank back into her seat.

"No! No!" she cried. "It's evidence!"

"My father. Is in! The car!" said Will brokenly. "The Mustang. Down the road."

The cop sitting across from Will started shaking his head again, displaying his tiny ears, but Ruby's cop was not distracted. She barked, "Tell Conner to get over there." And, to Ruby, harshly, she said, "Okay, what did you take?"

"You don't have to give anything back to the Culps, do you?" Rose asked the cop.

"We don't have to do anything."

"Neil did it!" said Ruby to Rose excitedly. "Neil did everything, I mean. I can prove it. He's the one who should be in jail. We can get Daddy out."

"What did you find?" asked Rose.

Ruby's eyes flicked to the right and to the left.

"A piece of paper?"

The flicking of the eyes again. But this time, Ruby nodded.

"That's why you went to the Culps'?"

Another nod.

"What an amazing girl you are. Is it . . . a letter?"

"With highlights," said Ruby.

"Highlights?"

"You know, like with a yellow marker."

"Yellow. Marker," breathed Will.

Even the cops were interested, puzzled.

"Our Dad worked for Neil Culp at LinkAge," explained Rose. "I suppose you know what a mess that is."

"Culp did work for LinkAge," said Ruby's cop to Will's. "What's your dad's name?"

"Frank," said Rose, her mouth closing around the name.

"He's in jail!" said Ruby.

"Why doesn't that surprise me," said the cop.

Will had never hurt so much in his life.

"Look," said Rose, her eyes traveling around the room for help. "We're all witnesses. I am." She scratched at the air in Will's direction. "He is."

"That's Will," said Ruby.

"Will? You mean Will Samuel?" said Rose. She immediately shook her head as if to dislodge the information, there being no room for it. "If it's evidence, you're going to have to show the police anyway. Show me first, and then I'll give it to them." She looked up at the female cop. "Okay?"

The cop shrugged and nodded. The room grew hushed: Everyone was very still so as not to interfere with the transfer. Ruby slowly straightened up, felt around under her arm, and just as slowly drew out a single piece of copy paper, unevenly creased.

Rose carefully unfolded it and smoothed it out. " 'They're on to us,' " she read. She looked up at her sister with inscrutable intensity. "Is this what you mean?" Her voice was disbelieving, unlovely. The note had flopped back, and she curled it slightly to stiffen it. " 'Clean up your e-mails,' " she read. " 'It's a crime.' "

"That sounds kind of familiar," said Ruby's cop.

"Yeah," said Rose. "It was on the news."

"What?" said Ruby.

"Everybody's already seen this memo. It was quoted in the hearings, and it made headlines."

"Everybody?"

Rose nodded. "The SEC, the U.S. attorney's office. Everybody has always known about this."

The others in the room stared at the paper, silent.

Will was filled with great disappointment. This was it. He had not done what he was supposed to, although he could not remember what that consisted of. Maybe there was no point, no point to anything at all.

There was a crackle nearby, and a rasp. "That was Conner," Will's cop announced. "There's a Mustang parked near the Culp place. But no one's in it."

"I. Can't. Breathe," said Will, sliding toward the floor.

The nurse attendant, an oversize woman in oversize purple scrubs, pulled aside the curtain on the ER cubicle where Will lay on his side. "Put this on," she said over the clatter of the rings on the metal rod. She tried to hand him a folded hospital gown. "Someone will be right with you."

"Ah-h-h, no," said Rose, who was perched on the edge of the green chair beside him.

The attendant gave her a hearty smile. "Your girlfriend is a little shy," she said. "Come on, girl, let's both leave, and he can change in peace. We can join this po-lice here."

They both glanced at Will's escort, who was leaning dispiritedly against the wall.

"It's a possible punctured lung," said Rose. "He has to be brought to X-ray immediately."

Will was still lying down, the folded gown clutched to his chest.

"Calm down," said the nurse attendant to him. "Take slow, even breaths. Okay, what happened?"

"Complainant's bodyguard was forced to subdue him," barked the cop.

"He kicked me," said Will. "And kicked me."

"I'm a first-year med student," Rose lied as she pried the gown from his fingers.

His heart leapt straight to his head. "Rose," he said, his voice thin and dreamy.

"I'll be right back," said Rose.

"Ruby. Always. Gets. Her. Way. Too," he said, closing his eyes.

The next day Will awoke hazily to see Ruby standing over by the window of his hospital room. Because she was looking out, he could see only her back framed against the soft morning light, but he recognized her tightly combative posture. Then his eyes closed. When he woke again, the phone was ringing. It was Rose.

"I know you're not supposed to talk," she said, "but I wanted to know how you were." She proceeded to have both sides of the conversation, stopping only to confirm the happy ending of the story she was relating. His left lung had collapsed because his chest cavity was filled with air, she explained. The pressure had started to affect his right lung. An intern inserted a chest tube and suctioned him out. The lung filled for the first time in hours.

Rose was trying hard to be cool about her role, but the story itself still carried her away. Will was quick to adopt this outside view of his experience. It was not that he didn't remember the events of the evening before. But he'd gotten a peek at the abyss a person could tumble into. Any alternative was attractive, and Rose offered a powerful one. If she got to be the white knight, he remained solidly worthy of rescue. He had not led Ruby astray in his ignorance.

"Is Ruby okay?" he asked, his chest aching.

"Sure," said Rose. Still voluble from her triumph, she told him that Ruby had simply walked into the Rumson house and grabbed some papers off Neil Culp's desk. The document that excited her was confidential because it came from Culp's attorney, but it was nothing more than a copy of the now infamous note, with a promise that an outline of possible interpretations would be forthcoming. In any investigation, the "smoking guns" are copied endlessly and referred to in many of the other documents. As long as Ruby had found anything from the case—as opposed to, say, household bills—she was not likely to come away without inflammatory material.

The light at the window seemed to dim, then darken. It was only now that he fully understood the insignificance of Ruby's memo. He'd always thought that she was, at least in part, playing make-believe. But it turned out that he had been just as childish. And he'd had a real audience—cops, criminals, victims. What could be worse? There was no clue to unearth, no evidence to secure, no mission to pursue. *There was no mystery.*

From where he lay, head elevated to ease his breathing, he could see through the window a gloomy green bough nodding, as if in agreement. He watched all of its different types of nods after getting off the phone. When another nurse attendant came in to take his temperature and blood pressure, he asked her what happened to the girl who'd been there that morning.

"No children allowed on this floor," declared the attendant.

"She's not a child, exactly," said Will.

"No one at all allowed in the morning," she said.

That would never have stopped Ruby, thought Will, turning away.

"Look," said the attendant. "Here are some visitors."

Pat and Lemuel were at the door.

"Will, my boy," said his father. "Are you all right?"

"Mom and Dad will make everything better," said the attendant.

When an embarrassed silence fell, Will realized that Pat and Lemuel had been uncomfortable even before the attendant had spoken. They had walked in uncomfortably. Partly that was because of the difference in size. Lemuel was big and swollen-looking, teetering a little in his ruined cowboy boots, and Pat was quite a bit shorter, with clothes that fit like a candy wrapper. But there was also a sort of shrugged-off intimacy between them. They were so pointedly not together.

"What happened to you?" said Will.

"To me?" said Lemuel.

"You weren't in the car."

"I went looking for you," said Lemuel. "And I found a pay phone at a fancy grill a couple of miles away. The next thing I knew, I was waking up at a place called the Hide-Away."

"That's a motel," said Pat. "Not too bad, either."

"I spent the night alone, of course," said Lemuel gruffly.

"Oh!" said Pat. "Well, I had to get the kids back to Hart Ridge."

Will contemplated the two of them with a stone face. "What happened to Ruby?" he asked.

"She's grounded," said Pat, still hanging back. "For at least a dozen years. Which means no visitors."

Will blinked. Visitors? Could she possibly be referring to

him? He refused to believe it. Yet a shutter seemed to close at the back of her eyes.

"Hart Ridge may be a little lonely," she said, sneaking a spooky smile at him. "It turns out that Virginia has to disappear to write a book about disappearing. But she's still out there."

"Out there?" Will repeated blankly. "Out where?"

"She's on her way to New Zealand," said Pat.

"You remember Lydia Bunting?" roared Lemuel. He was leaning against the bathroom door.

"Of course!" said Pat, perking up.

"She was on the cruise."

"Wonderful!" Pat's voice soared. "I thought she was supposed to kill herself!"

"If so," said Lemuel, "she must have changed her mind in time. She was just married, and she stowed her husband in her cabin somehow. I guess they thought they could get a free honeymoon. He kept pretending not to speak English. Or maybe he really couldn't, I forget. But it was a big ruckus."

Will found this sudden joviality incredibly irritating. "You're not supposed to be drinking," he said.

"But I've given up so much already," said Lemuel.

"Like what?"

Lemuel thought for a moment. "Crank," he said. "Betting on football games. Running around with women."

"The doctors told me you're trying to kill yourself," said Will.

"Come on," said Lemuel. "I'm trying to have a good time. Though it might come to the same thing in the end."

"I hate all these phrases like *dead to me, might as well be dead,* and *a living death,*" said Pat, her half circle of a smile unfaltering. "I don't care whether you see a person or not. It all counts as life."

What this meant, Will did not know, but Lemuel seemed to accept it.

"Virginia Howley didn't kill herself," said Pat.

"I guess the world is full of people who haven't killed themselves yet," said Lemuel.

Pat looked around the hospital room, then cried, "I nearly forgot! Look what I got for you!" She finally approached Will's bed and handed him an iPod, still in its origami-like folded white box. "Isn't it adorable?"

Will turned it over as if to read the back. The iPod, he realized, was a goodbye present. His stay in New Jersey was over.

"I still don't know what you were doing at the Culps'," said Lemuel.

Will did not look up. He didn't have the heart to answer.

When Pat responded at last, she sounded like a windup doll: "The kids thought they'd look for . . . oh, you know, evidence at the CFO's estate. Neil's bodyguard attacked Will, which he didn't even get in trouble for because supposedly Will was trespassing. I *tried* to tell the cops that I'd sent the kids down for an edger I left behind—"

"I'll kill that Neil Culp," said Lemuel.

"Oh, Jesus," said Will. At least the nurse was long gone.

"What were you thinking?" said Lemuel.

"Uh . . . We thought we'd help," said Will in a low voice.

"Who? Who were you trying to help?" Lemuel turned on Pat. "Was it that criminal husband of yours? Hasn't anyone figured out yet that it was wrong of all those assholes to take hundreds of millions of dollars from his company? Or is that still up in the air?"

"He's not exactly . . . ," said Pat. "It's hard to know what that means . . . There are degrees . . ." She drew herself up, saying— and it was about time—"I suppose he is a criminal."

"You did just what Bud Caddy would have done," said Lemuel to his son.

"I wasn't Bud Caddy," said Will. "Ruby was."

"You're older, you're the boy, you take responsibility."

Will should have known that Lemuel would get everything wrong. His ideas of chivalry were so simple, so remote from what had happened. Will was not trying to avoid responsibility. He was giving out credit. Only Ruby was young enough to retain any dignity after the Boy Scout aspect of the evening in Rumson. Will was left scrabbling around in his own brain.

"How were the wind farms?" he asked Pat. It was not exactly a friendly question, though his tone was pleasant enough.

"We never got to see them," she said. "You can't do everything."

CHAPTER

Some gas stations have walled-in lots. Maybe the law re-
quires them to put up the ivy, the concrete barriers, the
high woven-wood fences if they have neighbors. But most stations, especially in western Massachusetts, are out in the open
for "high visibility" and "easy access," terms that cannot mask
the bleak vulnerability of the sites. These stations are not half
repair shop but half convenience store and so are more likely to
hire girls. And everyone knows that gas stations and convenience stores are the most dangerous places to work.

These were the thoughts that passed through Will's mind as
he waited to pay for his gas one late afternoon in October. A
teenage girl with a pierced brow was trying to do something to
the cash register—ring up the sale or key in the right code or figure out the exact change. Will wasn't really paying attention.
She was doing her best to look unfazed about her difficulty, but
for some reason that made her discomfort all the more obvious,
and he did not want to be a witness to it. Instead he turned to
watch an overhead TV tuned to CNN and realized he was look-

ing into a familiar face. It was Neil Culp, flashing a smile beside Riley Gibbs. White type appeared over their torsos: a FEDERAL JUDGE DECLARED A MISTRIAL IN THE CASE AGAINST LINKAGE BIGWIGS RILEY GIBBS AND NEIL CULP TODAY. THE SURPRISE MOVE COMES AFTER DEFENSE ATTORNEYS CONDUCTED A BLISTERING WEEKLONG CROSS-EXAMINATION OF STAR GOVERNMENT WITNESS FRANK FOY. . . . Then Frank appeared walking alone up the endless steps to a courthouse, as skinny as a pogo stick, his stride jittery.

"He joined AA in prison." These words were spoken aloud, by a real-life Lemuel, suddenly large and solid inside the jangly glass door to the gas station. "Now he goes to court every day and drives around New Jersey all night drinking coffee at four ninety-nine a pop. Even though they're broke. They lost the civil trial, and the only thing they have left is the house."

"You talked to Pat?" said Will. He had left Lemuel in the car, by the pump.

"The trial has been in the news for a while. I gave her a call."

Will kept his eyes on the screen, still trying to make sense of what he saw. A photo of a page of the *Daily News* appeared. It showed a drawing of a juror standing in front of the jury box. IN HIS RULING THE JUDGE SUGGESTED THE POSSIBILITY THAT JUROR NUMBER EIGHT, A RETIRED BUSINESSWOMAN, HAD MADE REASSURING HAND SIGNALS TO THE DEFENDANTS DURING FOY'S TESTIMONY. A SPOKESMAN FOR THE FEDERAL PROSECUTOR'S OFFICE SAYS THAT THE CASE WILL BE RETRIED AT A LATER DATE.

"Incredible," said Lemuel.

Will silently accepted the change for the gas.

His father turned to walk heavily back outside, swinging his heft like an old buffalo. "Gibbs and Culp claimed that the LinkAge board signed off on all their shenanigans," he said. "And the auditors okayed the accounts. So there was no crime. There's nothing they could be guilty of. Incredible."

He held on to the roof to ease his ponderous bulk into the front seat. He was not one for personal chitchat. It didn't go with his idea of manliness. But now he chuckled and said, "You and Pat's girl took on the whole lot of them."

Will did not start the car. Instead he grasped the steering wheel with both hands. "She screamed," he said.

"Nothing wrong with screaming," said Lemuel, misconstruing the situation as usual. "The way things are going, you gotta scream."

But Ruby's scream wasn't that sort, thought Will. It wasn't strategy. It was fear.

"I don't know why everyone isn't screaming all the time," said Lemuel. "The problem is, no one is even opening their mouth nowadays except to stick in a bottle of water like a big suckling baby."

Will turned the key.

"The prosecution introduced evidence that the Culps were going to flee the country," said Lemuel. "Was that your doing?"

"Oh," said Will slowly, considering. "Yeah, they were going to go to Ireland. So maybe we did help."

"Isn't that something," said Lemuel.

On the short drive home, Will wondered where Ruby was. At this hour, she'd probably be in school, devising another plot to save her family, maybe restore their wealth. Then he daydreamed about Rose. There was no telling what she might be up to.

Acknowledgments

With belated but heartfelt thanks to Roy Blount, Michael Frayn, Jamaica Kincaid, and Cathleen Schine. Also with thanks to horticultural experts Joyce Robins and Michele Eichler; to Ursula Abrahams; to Ursula Tomlinson, R.N., P.N.P.; to Alison Carey; to Craig Seligman; and to Josette Zielenski, Bobby Meeks, and Craig Apker of Allenwood Federal Correctional Complex.

About the Author

JACQUELINE CAREY lives with her family in New Jersey. Her previous novels include *Good Gossip*, part of which appeared in *The New Yorker*, and *The Crossley Baby*, which garnered her a Guggenheim Fellowship. She used to write a mystery column for Salon.com.